RCISE

by

KATE BENEDICT

CHIMERA

Punishment Exercise first published in 1999 by
Chimera Publishing Ltd
PO Box 152
Waterlooville
Hants
PO8 9FS

Printed and bound in Great Britain

PUNISHMENT EXERCISE

Kate Benedict

Chapter One

'Prepare her,' snapped a harsh female voice. Cassie staggered as she was thrust roughly into the unknown, her naked flesh flinching as it came into contact with the cold roughness of a concrete wall. Heart pounding, she cowered in the darkness forced on her by the black velvet blindfold. Where was she? And how was she to be 'prepared'?

Echoing footsteps retreated and silence fell. She held her breath, her back against the wall, her face turning blindly and desperately in every direction. Was anyone there? Something hot, hard and smooth brushed against her lips and she flinched again.

'Welcome to the House of Fun,' sniggered another voice – male this time – and the blindfold was ripped away. Cassie blinked in the dim light and gazed fearfully round the – the dungeon? Torches flared in cressets on the grey stone walls, and she swallowed as she looked at the instruments of torture that hung from them. A long marble table – altar? – stood in the middle of the floor. At each corner dangled rusting manacles, attached to the wooden frame. She shivered uncontrollably.

Her frightened gaze returned to the man who had ripped off her blindfold and she shuddered at the smile on his thin lips. Dark, curly hair tumbled over his brow and he would have been good-looking if it hadn't been for the hidden cruelty behind that smile. That and the coldness of his eyes. His oiled skin glistened in the torchlight and he wore only a thin loincloth, which bulged ominously.

She remembered the thing that had brushed against her lips and shuddered again. He was obviously enjoying himself, her fear acting as an aphrodisiac.

'Where am I?' she gasped, then flinched under the stinging slap that made her head reel. She looked at him, wide-eyed, her hand cradling her cheek, biting back the whimper that rose to her lips.

'Slaves don't ask questions,' he sneered. 'They do as they're told.' He reached down, grabbed her arm and hauled her roughly to her feet.

'Careful, Peter,' came an amused voice from the shadows. 'We don't want to damage the merchandise. It lowers the price.' Cassie looked hopefully in the direction the voice had come from, then her heart sank again as the meaning of his words penetrated her dazed mind. As he emerged from the darkness, she could see he wore a similar skimpy loincloth. He had the fair, clean-cut good looks she associated with pictures she'd seen of the *Waffen SS*, and from one strong hand drooped a thin, vicious-looking whip, which he flicked idly against his thigh as he looked her over.

There would be no unexpected last minute rescue from that quarter.

She opened her mouth to repeat her question, then closed it again quickly as the first man – Peter? – raised his hand once more.

'Good,' purred the second, his German accent confirming her suspicions. 'She is a quick learner.' He frowned. 'Bring her into the light. I wish to examine her more closely.'

Cassie cowered back, trying to cover her breasts and pubis, to preserve the last shreds of her modesty. It was useless. Peter seized her arms and twisted them behind her back, forcing her quivering breasts to jut proudly. He pulled her backwards so that her body bowed, her hips thrust forward in a parody of desire, her legs forced apart by the pressure, the lips of her sex opening as if to welcome a lover. She closed her eyes as a hot flush of shame washed over her.

'Nice,' said the second man softly. His eyes ran over her body, lingering on the heavy breasts, the narrow waist, the curving hips and the proud mons veneris under its modest covering of delicate curls. 'Very nice indeed.'

He stepped forward and raised the whip, butt first, and she gasped again. The handle of the whip had been carved lovingly – and perversely – into the shape of a rigidly erect penis. Smiling, he ran it softly up her inner thigh. It reached her sex and he parted the moist lips further, running the thick, smooth grip teasingly up and down against the soft entrance to her body. Against her will, she felt the first quickening of a painful desire. Then his face changed, his wrist twisted and she moaned as the first inch of hard wood pierced her.

'A sweet fruit,' he said thoughtfully. 'But not yet ripe for the plucking.' He raised his eyebrows. 'Peter?'

Cassie staggered as Peter released her for a moment – but her freedom was illusory. Before she could move his arms snaked round her, pulling her tight against him, trapping her own arms again between their bodies, her hands pressed tightly into his crotch, cradling the heavy weight of his balls. His hands squeezed her breasts, kneading and fondling the soft white flesh. She moaned with pain as he pinched her nipples until they stood out, red and swollen. He chuckled as she writhed, trying to escape the strange mixture of pain and pleasure his attentions were producing – and succeeded only in grinding her hands more firmly against the bulge in his loincloth.

'Please... please...' she whimpered.

'See, Heinz? Now she is begging for it,' boasted Peter. His tongue flicked into the cup of her ear, his hot breath making her shiver. 'And who am I to deny such a pretty lady?' One hand withdrew for a moment, reached down and fumbled with his loincloth till she could feel the thick hard length of his prick, nudging against her buttocks.

'Slowly, Peter, slowly,' commanded Heinz. 'Our orders are to prepare her, not to ravish her.' One eyebrow lifted sardonically. 'Our pleasures will come later.' He leaned forward and took one swollen nipple between his lips, his teeth grazing it as he teased it gently with his tongue. Against her will, her eyelids fluttered and she could feel herself moistening. He twisted his hand and the handle of the whip eased a little further into her wetness.

Then he bit down and she screamed as a feeling so intense that she could not tell whether it was pain or pleasure stabbed through her like a thunderbolt. She jerked and the whip handle, lubricated by her juices, slid all the way home. A moan escaped her lips and Heinz grinned. He withdrew it slowly then thrust it back again and again, watching as the expression on her face changed. Now her moans were those of pleasure. She began to writhe against the thrusting cock behind her and the instrument inside her, the pressure of her orgasm beginning to gather. Still smiling, Heinz withdrew the whip completely and stepped back. Her body sagged, her eyes opened and she gazed at him in a mixture of fear and disappointment.

'Later,' he promised, holding her eyes as he raised the whip handle to his lips and delicately licked the juices that coated it. 'Later you'll have everything you want–' his smile widened '–and more.'

'Bring her,' he said briskly to Peter, and her terror returned. What were they going to do to her? She struggled, digging the heels of her bare feet against the rough floor as Peter took her arm and pulled her in the direction of the marble table in the centre of the room.

'No… no…' she whimpered as her dragged her towards it, her frightened eyes taking in all the horrible details. Was that really rust on those dangling chains – or was it something worse? And what were those stains on the pitted marble surface?

Losing patience, Peter scooped her off her feet and carried her towards it, her hands beating futilely against his broad shoulders. With a grunt he lowered her onto it, her warm flesh flinching from the cold surface. She tried to swing her legs off it, but his strong hands pulled her back, their grip on her ankles vicelike as he spread-eagled her and forced first one leg and then the other into the cold clasp of the waiting manacles at the foot of the table. She forced herself into a sitting position and her flailing arm struck him a glancing blow. With a sneer, he pushed her viciously backwards, clipping her wrists easily into the ones at the top.

Panting, she lay there, her body spread out before them like an offering. She pulled uselessly against the confining chains in an attempt to break free.

'Naughty, naughty,' chided Heinz, flicking her nipples painfully with his forefinger. 'And naughty girls have to be punished, don't they?' He reached into a leather pouch at his waist, pulled out a cut-throat razor and opened it slowly. The dim light glinted wickedly on the blade as he turned it backwards and forwards, admiring it. Cassie froze, only her eyes moving as they gazed in horrified fascination at the deadly, glittering toy.

'Wha... what are you going to do?' she whispered through dry lips.

In answer he burst into peals of laughter. 'Why... nothing,

my pretty one.' His free hand stroked the soft cleft of her sex, his thumb finding the sensitive bud of her clitoris, his middle finger parting her lips and sliding gently in and out of her vagina. 'Silly girl. Did you really think I would spoil such a beautiful body?' He turned his head. 'Peter. Are you ready?'

She followed his eyes to see Peter approaching the table, carrying a tray. A bowl of water stood on it, tendrils of steam rising from its surface. Beside it stood several items she couldn't make out, no matter how she craned her neck. He laid it at the foot of the table, just out of reach of her jerking foot.

'Excellent,' he said. 'Now we shall begin.' He snapped his fingers. 'Peter?'

Peter stepped forward, a look of concentration on his face as he picked up the first item. Her eyes widened, trying to see what he held, then closed in terror as his hand descended to her lower body. Holding her breath, she bit her lip and waited for the agony to begin.

She gasped in surprise and relief as, instead of a surge of pain, she felt hot wetness as Peter lathered the mass of tiny curls that covered her mons veneris. The bristles of the shaving brush, stiff yet soft, swirled and teased, seeking out every crease and fold of flesh, leaving a trail of delicious sensations behind it. She whimpered as a bead of sudsy water trickled tantalisingly slowly down the cleft of her sex, tracing a path, like the delicately teasing finger of a lover. Peter chuckled as her hips rose involuntarily, trying to make the sensation last.

Then she froze again as Heinz leaned forward, the razor in his hand. Her mouth opened to protest and he laid a finger against her lips. 'Trust me, little one.' He laid the open blade against her smooth skin and, with deft movements, began his task.

It was exquisite torture. Her skin seemed to have a million nerve-endings, each of them demanding attention as the sharp blade slid over them, leaving the ultimate nakedness in its wake. The cold air seemed to press against her overheated flesh like a living thing. She whimpered again, willing her body not to move in case the kiss of the blade became a bite instead of a caress. Time stretched infinitely as her whole body centred on the contradictory sensations radiating from her groin.

'There,' said Heinz, in satisfaction, stepping back and admiring his handiwork with the dispassion of an artist gazing at a sculpture. 'Now the clients can see exactly what they are buying.' Cassie's chest heaved, the full globes of her breasts quivering, their nipples jutting against the cold air. Her spread legs revealed the pouting lips of her shaven sex, parted to show the glistening pink interior.

Peter was not quite so unmoved. His cock stood at attention again, its head swollen and purple, thrusting out from the skimpy loincloth. 'The oil now?' he demanded, licking his lips in anticipation. At Heinz's nod, he reached eagerly for the small bottle that stood on the tray. Smiling down at Cassie, he tipped a few drops from its narrow neck onto her clitoris. Her body jerked and his smile widened.

His hand spread the oil over her smooth nakedness, lingering, exploring, teasing, while he laughed at her feeble attempts to close her thighs against his onslaught. She twisted to one side, trying to escape, but he pulled her back roughly. His hands gripped the top of her thighs, pulling her cunt open like a fig, and he buried his face in her musky wetness, his tongue swirling round her throbbing clitoris then darting deeper until she moaned with unwilling desire.

'Shall I continue?' asked Heinz, in amusement. 'Since

you seem to be... er... busy.' He picked up a small pot from the tray, dipped delicately into it and applied the rouge to Cassie's nipples, rolling them firmly between thumb and finger till they swelled against his touch, hard and scarlet-tipped. She tossed her head from side to side, trying to escape from her own traitorous body. It was no use. She was trapped between the teasing tongue and the tormenting fingers. All she wanted now was a hot, hard, thrusting cock – or two – to release her from this maddening mixture of pain and pleasure.

'Please,' she begged, this time not from fear but from frustration. 'Please...'

'Enough!' snapped Heinz, taking his hands from her breasts. Peter lifted his head reluctantly. 'Our orders say that she is not to be taken. Enjoying that sweet cunt is the privilege of her purchaser.'

Deprived of the excruciating pleasures her body longed for, Cassie moaned and quivered, her back arching as her hips writhed against the cold marble. 'Fuck me!' she demanded, eyes glittering with desire. 'What are you waiting for? Fuck me now!'

'It is forbidden,' said Heinz regretfully as his eyes lingered on the juicy slit between her legs. 'Much as I would enjoy accepting your invitation, the preparation must go on.'

'What do you mean?' she demanded, her body stilling as apprehension swept over her again. 'What are you going to do?'

In answer, he held up a short length of triple gold chain, as thick and heavy as that on the handcuffs hanging on the dungeon wall. At each end there was a kind of toothed clasp, similar to the clasp of a clip-on earring. He jangled it, smiling cruelly. 'It is time to lock the gate.'

Her body shrank away as he leaned forward, holding a

clasp in each hand. 'Hold her,' he snapped in exasperation as she attempted to twist away. Peter's hands gripped the tops of her thighs again, this time holding her painfully in place as Heinz went about his business.

She shrieked at the twin stabs of pain as the clasps gripped the tender lips of her sex, drawing them together, half-concealing her vulva in a kind of golden chastity belt – then closed her eyes as it dulled to a rhythmic throbbing, matching the thudding beat of her heart. She groaned as she realised that the pain, far from dousing her desire, was wakening it again, each pulse sending quivers of feeling from her groin to every part of her body.

A smile touched her lips. So they thought the game was over, did they? That a piece of gold chain could stop her getting what she wanted? Well, they were wrong. She would break that iron resolve and make sure they disobeyed their orders. Then they'd see what happened next, when her 'purchaser' discovered that his little package had been opened already and he'd been fobbed off with second-hand goods.

She lowered her eyes in mock submission. 'Unchain me now,' she whispered. 'I'll be good.' She hid a smile as the manacles were unlocked and she was free again. Swinging her legs over the side of the table, she put her feet to the floor and staggered against Peter, her arms slipping round his neck to steady herself. 'Sorry,' she purred, deliberately pressing her body tight against his. It was his turn to gasp as the swell of her breasts and the hard buds of her nipples pushed against the smooth, oiled surface of his chest. Smiling wickedly, she ground her groin against his, feeling the rigid throb of his prick against the softness of her belly.

She stepped back and allowed her hand to trail down his body until it reached his cock, feeling the warm hardness yearning towards her. Her fingers wound round it and she tugged gently, the skin moving smoothly up and down over the swollen, purple head. He gasped again, his hands reaching for her breasts.

'What are you doing?' demanded Heinz, stepping forward and reaching for her to pull her away.

Without stopping her tantalising movements, she reached out and cupped his heavy balls through the thin material of his loincloth. He moaned as her hand slid upwards and she could feel his cock stirring and hardening, till it was as stiff and unyielding as Peter's.

He moved closer to her, eyes glinting dangerously, and she smiled exultantly, glorying in her power over them both. Peter's cock thrust against her, his fingers kneading her breasts, her nipples jutting out between them. Heinz leaned forward, his tongue sliding over their tender tips.

'Undo the clasps and you can both have me,' she moaned. 'One after the other.' Her expression was triumphant. 'You know you want to.'

Heinz stepped back so suddenly that she staggered. His eyes narrowed. 'So that's your game, my pretty,' he hissed. 'Well, it won't work.' He reached forward again and pulled her towards him. He dragged her across the room, sat down and flung her face down over his knees. She screamed as his hand came down spitefully on her buttocks, the tender flesh quivering and reddening under his harsh ministrations. Each stroke sent a wave of agony through her abused body. Finally, he let her go and she crouched at his feet, whimpering with a mixture of pain and frustration.

He grinned down at her. 'We have learned our lesson, have we?' She nodded in humiliation. 'Good,' he said. 'And for good girls there are also rewards.' One hand caught the back of her hair and pulled her face towards his lap, while the other fumbled at his loincloth. His erection sprang out. He thrust his hips forward and its swollen head brushed her lips. 'Here is yours.'

She cringed back. Everything had gone wrong. She was supposed to be in control, not them. 'You can't,' she protested. 'You're not allowed to.'

'Oh, but I'm afraid we can,' purred Heinz. 'There is more than one gate to paradise. One may be locked against us, but there are others.' He grinned over her shoulder. 'Are there not, Peter?'

There was a grunt of agreement as Peter dropped to his knees behind her and she whimpered in terror as his harsh hands pulled her buttocks apart. 'No... no! You can't,' she whimpered as his fingers stroked the soft pucker of her anus. 'No one's ever done that to me.'

'A virgin,' chuckled Peter. 'Looks like it's my lucky day.' She struggled to escape, then squealed as his hand swept down in a stinging slap, reddening her cheeks and making her flesh ripple. His grip tightened and she gasped as he slipped a finger between the chains that guarded her vulva, withdrew it, lubricated with her own juices, and began to work it into her arse. She clenched her muscles frantically, but instead of deterring him, it had the opposite effect. 'Hot and tight,' he groaned, pushing further in. 'Just the way I like it.'

He removed his questing finger and Cassie closed her eyes in relief.

Too soon.

As Heinz sat watching through half-closed eyes, his hand idly stroking his erection, Peter bent to his task again. Still holding her buttocks apart with one hand, he oiled his cock, then Cassie felt it pushing painfully at the secret entrance to her body. Just when she thought she could stand no more, it gave and she screamed as the head of his prick pierced her tender flesh.

She held her breath as he stopped for a moment, before renewing his onslaught. She groaned with a mixture of fear and twisted pleasure as, inch by slow, tormenting inch, the full length of his turgid cock slid into her, stretching and filling. His hands snaked round her body, fondling her erect nipples as he began to move, slowly at first, then faster, his heavy balls slapping between her thighs, making the golden chains jingle, the clips tugging at her swollen labia.

She began to moan, writhing her buttocks and pushing back into his thrusting hips, each movement sending him deeper inside her. Her mouth opened as she gasped for breath.

Heinz seized her tangled mane again, pulling her roughly between his knees. 'You randy little bitch,' he chuckled, thrusting his throbbing cock up into her defenceless mouth. 'You love it, don't you?' She moaned in agreement and his eyes narrowed. 'Suck it!' he ordered.

She needed no second telling. Eyes closed in shameful bliss, she clamped her lips over his pulsing prick, her tongue running in teasing circles round its sensitive rim, then darting to flick its blind eye. She cupped his balls, her head rising and falling as she sucked like a leech, taking it as deeply as she could without choking then sliding back until only her lips gripping the ridge of its swollen head prevented its escape.

Her breasts jiggled and swayed as Peter thrust faster. She groaned with pleasure as she greedily sucked one swollen cock while another pounded into the hidden channel of her body. Ripples of fire radiated through her, until she was nothing but a mindless mass of sensation, her orgasm building inexorably.

She screamed as her body exploded into release, only

the two men's hands and bodies preventing her from collapsing. Peter's cock jerked inside its clutching cocoon, sending wave after wave of warm wetness into her. At the same time Heinz's prick tightened and spasmed. Spurts of salty come splattered against the roof of her mouth and trickled down her throat. She swallowed, licking her lips, as sated and relaxed as a well-fed cat.

She stretched and yawned, her breasts still rosy with the flush of orgasm, then smiled at the two exhausted men.

'Well,' said Heinz, in astonished respect, 'the slave has become the mistress.' He smiled, and this time it reached his eyes. 'Whatever price is paid for you, it will be worth every penny,' he murmured. 'You were made for sex. I envy the man who buys you.'

Peter stumbled to his feet, then grinned and reached down to help her up.

With a screech of rusty hinges, the door banged open.

Chapter Two

'What is going on?' demanded a strident female voice that Cassie recognised as that of her earlier tormentor. Her mouth twisted in apprehension as she took in the sight of the woman glaring at them with cold, pale blue eyes. Almost six feet tall, her heavy breasts strained at the mannish shirt she wore beneath a stark black suit, and her hair was pulled back so tightly that it looked painted onto her skull. She held a short leather quirt in her right hand, which she slapped incessantly against the palm of the other. It was the only sound that broke the uneasy silence.

She strode into the centre of the underground room and stood there, taking in Cassie's dishevelled appearance and the guilty looks on the faces of Heinz and Peter.

'I asked you a question,' she hissed. 'Must I repeat myself? What has been going on?'

'Nothing, Frau Hilde,' muttered Heinz. 'We were merely preparing the slave for auction, as instructed.' He forced a smile. 'She is ready now.'

Frau Hilde walked slowly round Cassie, her lips curled lasciviously as she took in the long, smooth thighs, the rounded hips and pert buttocks. Finally, she stood facing her, and Cassie flinched as the leather quirt tapped gently against the side of her left breast, making the flesh shiver.

'Pah!' snorted Frau Hilde. 'Men! You are useless. You still have not rouged her tits.' Cassie glanced down. Her nipples, soft now, were bare of the coloured unguent Heinz had applied so lovingly, rubbed off by her recent exertions. Frau Hilde glared at Peter. 'Pass me the pot of rouge,' she ordered. He jumped to obey.

Impatiently, she twisted the top off, flinging it to the floor and scooping out the coloured paste. Cassie suppressed a cry as unrelenting fingers pinched and kneaded her nipples, rubbing in the rouge. Horrified, she realised that her treacherous body was beginning to respond again, her aching flesh rising and hardening beneath Frau Hilde's rough touch, her thighs loosening in anticipation.

A smile crossed the hard face; the fingers lingered, becoming delicate and teasing. 'It takes a woman to please a woman,' murmured Frau Hilde. 'When this is over, I will prove it to you.' Cassie shivered.

Frau Hilde glanced regretfully at the man's watch on her wrist and became brisk again. 'But we are running out of time. You must be dressed.'

Cassie breathed a sigh of relief. Thank God! At least she wouldn't have to stand naked on the auction block. She watched eagerly as Frau Hilde rummaged in a wooden chest that stood against one damp wall. 'Here,' the woman snapped, flinging a scrap of silky material at Cassie. She caught it and waited for the rest.

'Well?' demanded Frau Hilde. 'What are you waiting for? Get dressed.'

'I can't wear this,' protested Cassie, holding it at arm's length. 'It's far too small.'

Frau Hilde's eyes narrowed. 'You dare to argue with me?' she asked softly. Her knuckles whitened on the quirt and Cassie swallowed.

'No, Frau Hilde,' she said meekly, stepping into the skimpy garment and struggling to pull it up. Only once it was on did she realise how bad it actually was. A grotesque parody of a Roman toga, it hung from one shoulder, and was cut so low that one full breast, with its scarlet nipple, was fully exposed. The hem was so short that it barely touched the tops of her thighs, revealing tantalising glimpses of her shaven slit every time she moved – her only covering the triple net of gold chains, which jingled as she moved. She groaned inwardly. This was worse than being naked!

'Excellent,' said Frau Hilde in satisfaction. She bent to the chest again and retrieved a tangle of metal. First came manacles for wrist and ankle, joined by a short length of chain which barely allowed Cassie to take short, halting steps. Then a thick metal collar which she fitted round Cassie's throat. The final humiliation came when she clipped another length of chain to the collar and tugged it viciously. Cassie staggered, her breasts swaying.

Frau Hilde smiled. 'Excellent,' she repeated. 'Now we shall go.' Her smile widened. 'Your audience is waiting, my dear.' She tugged the chain again and Cassie was forced to follow, Heinz and Peter falling in behind as she was led through the door into a maze of narrow passageways.

It seemed to take forever before they reached a heavy wooden door, studded with iron and ornately carved with obscene images. They halted before it. 'Just one more thing, my dear,' smiled Frau Hilde. Cassie squealed as the woman's hand rose and fell, delivering several stinging slaps to her quivering rear. 'A rosy bottom is so appealing, don't you think?' she smirked.

Cassie glared at her with hatred, her fear forgotten for the moment.

But it returned in a rush when the door swung open. There was a blast of overheated air and a babble of conversation, then everything fell silent. Cassie hung back, but a push in the back propelled her, stumbling, into the room.

Her eyes widened in amazement. At first glance, it looked like the reception room of an expensive but old-fashioned hotel. Ornate gilt chandeliers hung from the ceiling, light reflecting off their dazzling crystals and the matching crystal glasses on the linen-covered tables. The rich red carpet was set off by the silk wallpaper, where oil paintings hung in exquisite, gilded frames. The clientele matched its setting. Women in designer dresses delicately sipped their wine, while their dinner-jacketed partners held oversized brandy glasses. There was the expensive glitter of diamonds around white throats and the more subdued gleam of gold Rolexes on male wrists.

It was only when she peered closer did the flaws in this picture of respectability become evident. Only when she peered closer could she see that the oil paintings on the wall depicted scenes of appalling depravity: women coupled with women; men coupled with men – and both coupled with each other and an assortment of mythical beasts in a tangle of limbs and rampant sexual organs.

But it was the elegantly dressed people sitting around the tables who drew Cassie's horrified eyes.

She saw an elderly aristocratic woman, whose expensive dress completely exposed her breasts – surprisingly smooth and creamy under the raddled throat. Her companion, a heavy-lidded boy, young enough to be her grandson, had one arm draped casually over her shoulders, toying idly with her swollen nipples as he sipped his drink.

At another table, two girls, so alike they could have been twin sisters, kissed passionately, their tongues entwining, while their grinning escort sat between them, his fingers thrusting busily between their thighs.

A stunning, full-breasted woman, in a short scarlet satin dress that clung to every voluptuous curve, leaned back, laughing at something the dark-haired man with her had said. As she crossed her legs, there was a brief flash of what lay beneath her dress, and Cassie gasped at the outline of a huge penis bulging against the silken knickers. 'She' was a man!

Beyond 'her', a solitary man sat, ordering a drink from one of the smiling waitresses in their neat uniforms. Nothing unusual – apart from the fact that as he ordered, one hand was jammed up her skirt, while the other played with the massive erection that jutted from his open flies.

Cassie swayed, dizzy from the heat, the smoke, the smell of expensive perfume and the heavy scent of sex barely hidden beneath it all. No wonder they'd made her wear this parody of a toga. No wonder it was a slave auction. The whole place reeked of the decadence of a Roman orgy.

She might have fainted if a vicious pinch hadn't brought her swiftly back to reality. 'Move,' hissed Frau Hilde, planting a hard hand in her back and pushing her forward. Eyes focused on the distant dais, Cassie placed one reluctant foot in front of the other and shuffled forward awkwardly. With every movement the jangling chains between her legs tugged at the delicate flesh of her labia, producing a dull, throbbing sensation; painful yet exciting.

Silence fell as she wove her way through the close-packed tables. Greedy eyes devoured her humiliation and greedier hands reached out to sample the merchandise, fondling the soft skin of her thighs and buttocks as she passed, each touch inflaming the forbidden pleasure that pulsed through her. With alarm she realised that some dark part of her was revelling in their perverted attentions.

The walk to the podium seemed to last forever – yet still ended too soon. As she reached the bottom of the steps and began to stumble up them, she could see her tearstained predecessor being bundled through the heavy velvet curtains at the back of the stage. The girl's 'purchaser', a satisfied grin on his fat red face, was already fingering her obscenely as he pushed her ahead of him, ignoring her wails of protest. Cassie shuddered. That could have been her. That would be her!

Straightening her back, she shook off her fear and stood proudly in the centre of the stage, boldly surveying her tormentors. Who would be her buyer? That elegant man staring at her narrowly through a haze of cigarette smoke, the signs of cruelty and self-indulgence already marked on his handsome face? The thin-lipped woman wearing a severely cut dinner suit instead of a dress, her cropped grey hair glistening with gel? That couple, holding hands and giggling while they both eyed her lustfully? Who?

Her eyes drifted to a shadowy corner and she paused. The hawk-faced man in the wheelchair, flanked by two burly minders, seemed strangely out of place. His gaze was dispassionate, uninvolved – as if he was an explorer watching the incomprehensible rituals of some obscure tribe. She wondered what had brought him there.

'Lot ten, ladies and gentlemen,' boomed a voice from behind her. She jumped, forgetting everything but the situation she was trapped in. Grinning, the 'auctioneer' strode to the front of the stage, bowed to the audience and indicated Cassie with a flamboyant wave of his arm. 'A young female slave, blonde, twenty-two years of age. Ready to be trained to fulfil your every whim.' His grin widened. 'What can I say, ladies and gentlemen? An exquisite piece of flesh. Absolutely exquisite.'

Cassie cringed as he stepped up beside her, pulling her tangled blonde hair back. He ran his tongue slowly up her neck, rolling his eyes comically at the audience as he did so. Her skin crawled at the trail of slimy wetness the slug-like tongue left in its wake.

But much worse was to come.

'Just look at these luscious tits, ladies and gentlemen,' he went on. He cupped them in turn, jiggling them in his palms as if he was weighing fruit in a market. His thumbs stroked their sensitive tips, bringing them instantly erect, and he licked his lips salaciously. That tongue slithered out again and slobbered over the exposed nipple, and Cassie shuddered under his sordid ministrations. His sickly cologne swamped her and made her feel a little queasy. He looked up and smiled at the audience, his lips smeared with the rouge Frau Hilde had applied so carefully. 'See, ladies and gentlemen? A randy little filly, just waiting to be serviced by the right stallion–' one eye closed in an exaggerated wink '–or mare, if your tastes run in that direction.'

He jerked his hips against her in a parody of sex and his hands travelled lower, tweaking the skimpy skirt aside to reveal her shaven sex, half-hidden by the golden chains and still gleaming with the oil with which Peter had anointed her earlier. There was an appreciative murmur from the audience.

Stepping behind her, he slipped his hands around her waist before sliding them down her trim belly to her vulva. The fingers of one hand tugged on the chains, pulling her swollen lips apart, while the middle finger of the other wriggled in between them and plunged deep into the most secret part of her, sliding in and out slowly and tantalisingly, while his thumb stroked her clitoris.

Her eyelids fluttered closed and she sagged against him, her knees weakening. The audience was forgotten as tendrils of heat spiralled up from the base of her belly. Her hips began to move, pushing against his hand, trying to force the maddening finger deeper into her receptive body.

He withdrew abruptly, and she moaned with disappointment, teetering on the verge of an orgasm. His fingers glistened with her juices. He closed his eyes in ecstasy as he slipped them into his mouth, sucking till every last drop was gone. Opening his eyes again, he smacked his lips theatrically for the benefit of the audience, and sighed. 'Mmmm. Finger-lickin' good!'

There was a ripple of laughter and Cassie flushed with humiliation again. She bowed her head, her tousled hair mercifully concealing her flushed cheeks.

'Right, ladies and gentlemen,' said the auctioneer briskly. 'Now what am I bid for this beautiful piece? You've already seen what you're getting for your money. Gentlemen – the right price and that hot little cunt can be sucking every last drop from your cock.' He paused meaningfully. 'And ladies, just think what that tongue and those sweet lips could do to you–' he flipped the hem of Cassie's skirt again, flicked her rosy slit and raised his eyebrows to show what he meant '–or you could do to them.' He winked. 'You pays your money and takes your choice.

'And speaking of money,' he went on, 'do I hear one thousand pounds to start me off?' A hand shot up. 'Thank you, sir.' He looked around the assembled company. 'One thousand pounds, ladies and gentlemen. Any advance on one thousand pounds? Do I hear two? Thank you. And three?'

Dazed, Cassie listened as the bids rose and a group of debauched men and women bid fabulous amounts of money for the privilege of fucking her – whether she wanted it or not. It was like some grotesque nightmare from which she couldn't escape.

She shook herself and her lips tightened with determination. Three-quarters of the money being bid would come to her – to be added to her rapidly growing account. They might abuse her body, but they couldn't touch her mind, and it would all be worth it in the long run. She smiled grimly. Money bought power – and power brought revenge.

She tossed back her tangle of blonde hair and peeked around the room through demurely lowered eyelashes, swaying her hips enticingly and throwing her shoulders back so that her breasts jutted and swelled proudly. As a direct result the bidding rose by another two thousand, and she smiled inwardly.

But as she stood there, her body half-naked, her eyes looking out upon the sea of avid, lustful faces beneath her, her mind was elsewhere, drifting back in time.

Back to when it had all started.

Chapter Three

'Three more days,' gloated Lyn, stretching luxuriously. 'Just three more days till freedom.' She grinned. 'Eight weeks' holiday with nothing to do but lounge around relaxing. No early morning rises, no school bells, and, best of all, no kids.'

'And no money, either,' grumbled Cassie. 'It's all right for some, but I'm on a short-term contract, remember? If I don't work I don't get paid. I'll need to get a job over the summer or else sit on the dole till the new term starts.'

'Sorry, I forgot,' said Lyn. She brightened. 'Still, I'm sure you'll find something.' She grinned. 'It might be quite fun. Like a vacation job when we were at college. Maybe you could get a job as a barmaid.' She raised an eyebrow. 'Just think of it. All the gorgeous well-heeled blokes you'll meet, serving up their iced drinks.'

'All the drunken lager louts I'll have to chuck out at closing time, more like.' Cassie grinned back. 'But you're probably right. I'm bound to find something – and it's not as if it's forever. Just until term starts again.'

The bell rang and they both groaned. 'No rest for the wicked,' muttered Lyn, picking up her folder. 'The continuing saga of 3C and the semi-colon. Exciting stuff. I'll think about you enjoying your free period while I'm trying to thump grammar into the little darlings.'

'Free period? You've got to be joking,' moaned Cassie, getting slowly to her feet. 'Bob's still off. I've got to take his sixth-year boys again.' She tugged down the hem of her shorts. 'Fifteen horny seventeen-year-olds. Fifteen walking packages of acne and raging hormones. We're talking Testosterone City here.' She giggled. 'Maybe I should invest in a chastity belt to protect my honour.'

'Fifteen laps of the gym and a cold shower should take their minds off things,' chuckled Lyn over her shoulder as she headed out of the staff room. 'Get rid of all that energy. Anyway, better go before 3C start dismantling the classroom. See you later.'

Reluctantly, Cassie followed suit. She wasn't looking forward to the next forty minutes. It was all very well joking about it, but a pack of baying seventeen-year-old boys could be pretty intimidating. Most of them were taller and stronger than she was, for a start. She straightened her shoulders and grinned. Still, she was older and nastier, thank God. One step out of line and she'd flay them with her tongue. Flinging her bag over her shoulder, she headed for the gym.

She was almost there, when she was stopped by her head of department. 'The period bell has already gone, Miss Grey,' she said, looking pointedly at her watch. 'You should be in the gym by this time.'

'Sorry, Miss Carr,' Cassie apologised. 'I'm on my way. Anyway,' she defended herself, 'it isn't really my class. I'm only taking it because Bob's off.'

'That's no excuse,' snapped Miss Carr. 'If anything happened while the class was unattended, you would be held responsible. Now get a move on.'

'Yes, Miss Carr,' said Cassie meekly. 'No, Miss Carr, three bags full, Miss Carr,' she muttered rebelliously under her breath, as she hurried on. God, she really hated that woman. Head of department or not, there was just something about her. The dark, cropped hair. The muscular thighs in the tight shorts. That damned whistle hanging round her neck. She was like a caricature of a butch lesbian gym mistress.

Actually that might not be too far off the mark, Cassie thought. There had been rumours – and she'd seen for herself the way the woman hung around the showers when the girls were getting changed, ostensibly to make sure they weren't 'carrying on'. Carrying on? Hah! She should be so lucky.

The gym was still deserted when she walked in. Scuffling noises and adolescent male voices coming from the adjoining changing rooms revealed the whereabouts of her missing class. She strode across the hall and banged on the door. 'Right, boys,' she snapped. 'Get a move on. We haven't got all day.'

There was silence, followed by a muttered comment she couldn't quite make out and a chorus of guffaws. She banged on the door again and they filed out, grinning at one another. She folded her arms and glared at them. 'Down on the floor,' she ordered. 'Ten press-ups. Now!' Reluctantly they did as they were told, while Cassie looked on, tapping her foot.

'Sorry, miss,' came a lazy voice. She jumped and looked towards the door of the changing rooms, where the owner of the voice was lounging, with only a towel wrapped around his waist. He smirked. 'Seem to have forgotten my PE kit again... miss.' His eyes ran over her, lingering on the long legs beneath her white shorts, and she found herself wishing she'd worn her baggy tracksuit instead.

She glared at him. Robert Channing. She might have known. Damn the boy. Seventeen years old and he had the smug self-confidence of someone twice his age. Hardly surprising; if she remembered rightly, his father was one of the richest men in Britain and a member of the board of governors, as well. On his seventeenth birthday he'd driven into school in a brand new Porsche convertible that put everything in the staff car park to shame. Spoilt brat!

To add insult to injury, he was gorgeous. And didn't he just know it! When he walked past, sixth-year girls drooled and dampened their knickers. Cassie took in the broad tanned chest, the muscular thighs, the dark hair falling over the blue eyes, and snorted. Well, hard cheese! It wasn't going to work on her. He'd got away with that feeble excuse last week, but not this time. As far as she was concerned, he was just another snotty kid, pushing his luck.

'I'm sure we can find you something to wear, Robert,' she said smoothly. 'I think there's an old pair of shorts in the lost property locker. You can have those.'

He stood up straight, the smirk disappearing. 'I'm not wearing somebody else's cast-offs,' he protested.

'I'm afraid you are, Robert,' she insisted. 'Unless you fancy a walk down to the office. Oh, and while we're at it,' she went on, 'you can write out "I must not forget my PE kit" two hundred times. Maybe that'll improve your memory in future.'

There was a tense stand-off for a few moments, a silent battle of wills, and then, to Cassie's relief, he sulkily yielded and did as he was told.

Despite his obvious resentment, the rest of the period went without incident – much to Cassie's surprise. Once the boys had changed and gone off to their next class, she decided to sneak in for a quick shower herself. Class 2B, who usually used the gym, were out on the playing fields, so the place would be deserted until they came back in. At least she hadn't lost both her free periods. She'd have a shower, grab a cup of coffee and make a quick getaway at home time.

Humming, she slipped out of her clothes and dumped

them on a bench. Reaching back, she pulled out the band that held her ponytail and shook out her hair, then picked up her shampoo and stepped under the spray. She sighed with pleasure as the hot water hit her, her nipples rising and hardening as the bubbles from her freshly lathered hair ran down and dripped off the points. Soaping her hands, she ran them over her breasts and down her smooth flanks, enjoying the slippery feel against her skin. Spreading her legs slightly, she rubbed the bar of soap round her vulva, her pubic hair curling in a wet, soapy tangle round the proud rise of her mons veneris. A picture of Robert Channing's smooth young body flashed into her mind, and she dismissed it quickly. She grinned. You could get fired for that sort of thing. Still, you couldn't get the sack for fantasising. Delicious possibilities ran through her head. Her eyes closed and her breath came faster.

'Ah, Miss Grey, there you are. I've been looking for you.'

Cassie's eyes widened in shock and she dropped the soap, reddening as if she'd been caught in a compromising situation. 'Mi... Miss Carr,' she stammered. 'You gave me a fright. I didn't hear you come in. I'm just taking a shower.'

'I can see that,' snapped Miss Carr. Her eyes ran over Cassie's body, taking in the tight rosy buds of her nipples, the flushed wet skin, and the smooth thighs. Unconsciously, her tongue flickered out to lick her thin lips. Aware of the other woman's avid scrutiny, Cassie reddened even further, her hands automatically moving to try and conceal her nakedness.

'What did you want me for?' she asked, horribly aware of her vulnerability. Carefully avoiding Miss Carr, she stepped out of the shower and grabbed up her towel, pitifully grateful for its meagre cover.

'Mr Armstrong sent me along to speak to you,' announced Miss Carr. 'He wants to see you in his office after school.'

'But... but what for?' asked Cassie. Surely she couldn't be in trouble for dealing with Robert Channing? Even if he'd found time to use his posy mobile phone to complain to his father, she hadn't done anything wrong in confronting him. She'd only been doing her job. Bewildered, she looked at Miss Carr for a clue.

'I'm sure Mr Armstrong will tell you that himself,' she smirked. 'Just be in his office at a quarter past four.' Turning on her heel, she stalked out, leaving a speechless Cassie gaping after her.

'Don't worry,' said Lyn, when they met up in the staff room at four. 'It's probably just to sort out the renewal of your contract for next term.' She smiled reassuringly. 'You never know, it might even be good news. Maybe he's going to offer you a permanent post.'

'Oh, God, I hope so,' muttered Cassie. 'Have you seen the size of my overdraft?' She groaned. 'And there's the rent to pay as well. That doesn't stop even if I have joined the ranks of the temporarily unemployed.' Then she brightened a little. 'Still, you might be right. Wouldn't it be great if you were.'

'Fingers crossed,' grinned Lyn, holding up both hands. 'Anyway, I'll do the shopping and get the tea in. I'll see you back at the flat and you can tell me all about it then.'

The minute hand seemed to crawl round as Cassie sipped her coffee and nervously watched the clock. At ten past four she got up and walked through the deserted school; at quarter past, she was standing outside the door of the headmaster's office. Nervously she raised her hand and knocked.

'Come in,' he boomed.

Swallowing, she did as she was told.

'Ah, Miss Grey,' he smiled. 'Do take a seat.' He shuffled the pile of papers in front of him, then leaned back in his chair and folded his hands neatly over his paunch. 'Now, Miss Grey, as you know, you have been working here on the basis of temporary contracts, renewed at the start of each school year.' He peered at her over the top of his glasses, and she nodded hastily. As if he needed to tell her that! 'And I'm sure you're also aware that, like most schools nowadays, we have to stay within a strictly limited budget.'

Cassie's heart sank. This was not the kind of conversation that was going to lead into 'but, despite all that, I'm delighted to be able to offer you a full-time permanent position'.

And it didn't.

'So I'm afraid that under the circumstances, we shall not be renewing your contract next term.' He cleared his throat and shuffled his papers again. 'The school will be extremely sorry to lose you,' he said, oozing sympathy and sincerity, 'and I personally wish you every success in finding a new position elsewhere.'

Cassie gaped at him, thunderstruck. She'd thought that he'd been going to cut down her hours, tell her that she'd have to work part-time rather than full-time – but not this! Find what new position elsewhere? There weren't any. The dole queues were full of out-of-work graduates. Even if there had been jobs, they'd all been advertised ages ago – and snapped up by people straight out of college.

Tears welled up in her eyes. 'But... but what am I going to do?' she asked. 'I really need this job.' She looked at him, her tone pleading. 'Isn't there any other way? Couldn't I go part-time or something?' She brightened, forcing a smile. 'Or what about class support? I know it's not really my line – but I'm prepared to do anything, if it keeps my job.'

He raised his eyebrows. 'Anything?' he enquired.

'Anything!' she reiterated. She crossed her fingers. He was looking interested now. Perhaps things weren't completely lost, even yet. She regarded him hopefully.

He ran a hand over the few remaining hairs that were carefully combed across his head, then leaned back and smiled. 'Well, well,' he smirked. 'That's certainly an interesting proposition. I may just take you up on it.'

It was the word 'proposition' that did it. That and the way he was eyeing her up and down. Her mouth fell open. Surely he didn't mean what she thought he meant – did he? Good grief! He was repulsive. He was twice her age for a start, and the bald head and the pot belly didn't exactly increase his appeal. She suppressed an uncertain giggle. Of course he didn't mean anything of the kind. He was well past it. She must have got the wrong end of the stick. 'Er... exactly what did you have in mind, Mr Armstrong?' she asked politely, and cautiously.

He leaned forward so suddenly that she flinched. 'I think you know very well what I have in mind, Miss Grey,' he leered. 'You scratch my back, and I'll scratch yours.' The leer widened. 'Though possibly "back" isn't quite the right word.'

She felt sick. He had meant it! 'How dare you!' she gasped, stumbling to her feet. 'I wouldn't sleep with you if you were the last man on earth.' Head held high, she walked to the door.

'Please yourself,' he said indifferently. 'I'm sure a bright girl like you will soon find another job.' He paused meaningfully. 'Of course, it might be more difficult without a decent reference.'

She stopped dead with her hand on the door handle, and her shoulders sagged. Damn the man! He was right. Unless he gave her a reference, she was well and truly scuppered. She quickly weighed up her options. If she walked out of the door, she was walking straight onto the dole queue. If she did what he was blackmailing her into, she would keep her job. When she got right down to the bottom line, she didn't really have any options.

Turning, she walked back and sat down. 'All right,' she said, staring at him with contempt. 'You win. I'll do whatever you want.' Her stomach churned as she looked at him. He was disgusting, but it would probably all be over within ten seconds flat – and then she could walk out of there and forget all about it, knowing she still had a job and could pay her rent and bills.

'A wise decision,' he wheezed, sweat breaking out on his large forehead as the excitement clearly got to him. He stood up and walked around the desk, and she couldn't help but notice – with a sickening feeling in the pit of her stomach – the obscene bulge tenting his corduroy trousers. She closed her eyes and steeled herself against the feel of those clammy plump hands crawling all over her.

But he didn't touch her.

'Get to your feet, girl,' he snapped. Surprised into obedience, she did as she was told. 'Now, go to the sofa,' he ordered, pointing to the couch normally used by visiting parents, 'and bend over the arm.' When she hesitated, he pushed her forward so that she lost her balance and fell, face down. Before she had a chance to push herself up again, he had darted round with surprising speed and secured her wrists firmly with a lanyard from a box of gym equipment in one corner. As she struggled to stand up he ran another one through her linked wrists and tethered her to the arm at the opposite end of the couch.

He stood back and regarded his handiwork with satisfaction. She was sprawled helplessly face down, her head halfway along the couch. The arm pressed against the lower part of her belly, forcing her bottom in the air.

She threshed frantically, trying to plant her feet on the carpet to gain some leverage, but the angle she was lying at thwarted her. At last she gave up and strained to stare up at him. 'Wh-what are you going to do?' she gasped. 'And aren't you even going to lock the door? Wh-what if someone comes in?' Her eyes closed in shame at the thought of being caught like this.

'Forget the door,' he snarled. 'There's no one here but us.' His lips twisted in a sneer. 'No white knight to come galloping to your rescue.' He stepped behind her and she felt his hands tugging the hem of her skirt up, to reveal her tiny white cotton knickers. There was a pause, filled with the sound of his wheezy breathing, then he drew those down to her ankles, exposing her to his gloating gaze.

She clenched her buttocks, trying to hide herself, but his appreciative chuckle showed that all she'd succeeded in doing was tantalising him further. She heard the sound of a zip and his belt hitting the floor, and bit her lip, waiting for the assault.

But again it didn't come. Instead, she heard him moving away. She twisted her head, trying to see what he was doing, then he reappeared and she froze in horror. From the waist up he was still the respectable headmaster, in jacket, shirt and tie. But from the waist down he was something from a Freudian nightmare. From beneath his protruding stomach jutted an enormous prick, totally disproportionate to his height. It was almost ten inches long and its swollen purple head bobbed as he walked, as if it had a life of its own.

But horrifying as that was, it was the object he was holding that made her flinch. He was clutching a thin cane, bending it between his hands as he smiled down into her frightened face. 'Someone didn't do their homework,' he hissed. His eyes were glazed with lust and increasing beads of sweat stood out on his forehead. 'That was very naughty. And naughty girls must be taught a lesson, mustn't they?'

He stepped behind her and she heard the cane whistling through the air, then her body went rigid as pain exploded through her. A fine white line appeared across her quivering buttocks, then turned scarlet as the blood rushed into the abused flesh. She whimpered as the cane rose and fell again – and then a third time.

'Not again! Please, not again!' she sobbed feebly. 'Do anything you want, but please don't hit me again.' Her bottom felt as if it was on fire and she squirmed, trying to escape the pain, barely feeling the questing finger that ran down between the deep valley of her buttocks and pushed its way between her swollen labia. But as it advanced and retreated, she did feel herself moisten, the waves of scorching pain changing subtly to waves of simmering pleasure. Against her will, she sighed, humiliated by her own wanton need.

The finger was withdrawn and she felt him spreading the lips of her vulva with one hand as he pushed the thick head of his cock against them. She moaned as his enormous organ drove its way into her, sliding slowly into her welcoming wetness. He grunted with pleasure and gripped her hips as he began to move back and forth, sinking deeper and deeper with every thrust. She pushed back, meeting each thrust with one of her own, whimpering as she teetered on the verge of an explosive orgasm... then froze as the door squeaked a little and slowly opened.

Miss Carr stood on the threshold, taking in the scene before her. Cassie blushed and cringed with utter shame, her humiliation complete as an amused smile touched Miss Carr's thin lips.

The headmaster clearly felt no such embarrassment. Cassie groaned in disbelief as from the corner of her straining eyes she saw him beam at the newcomer. 'Ah, Miss Carr,' he panted, continuing to grind his hips against the beauty tied and helpless before him. 'Come in. I'm chastising a disobedient girl. Perhaps you would care to assist me.'

'Certainly, Mr Armstrong,' she purred. 'I'd be delighted.' To Cassie's dismay, she strode across the room and perched herself on the couch, directly in front of her. Cassie shrank away from her, impaling herself even more firmly on the grotesque weapon behind her. She was trapped.

Miss Carr squeezed her talon-like hands between Cassie and the sofa, inside her blouse, and pushed her bra down and cupped her breasts, twisting the nipples between her fingers. She then smiled and stood up, her hands reaching for the buttons on her own shirt. She shrugged it off, unhooked her own bra, then slid out of her skirt and underwear, revealing a tight, muscular body. Although her breasts were small, huge brown nipples stood out like gnarled fingertips. Her greying pubic hair reminded Cassie of a scouring pad.

Still smiling, she knelt in front of her poor victim and thrust her groin into her face. As she sank back on her thighs the lips of her sex parted, revealing the moist, pink interior. 'Lick me,' she ordered gruffly.

Cassie recoiled. 'I won't...' she protested. 'You can't make me.'

There was a chuckle behind her and she felt Armstrong withdraw. He walked round and stood in front of her, his cock glistening with her juices, the cane back in his hand. He looked down at her and tapped the cane against his palm. 'Oh, I think we can,' he grinned. The cane swished through the air, and Cassie squealed as it cut viciously into her already tender flesh, reawakening the slumbering pain. Fresh tongues of fire licked her delicate skin.

'I'll do it! I'll do it!' she yelped. She leaned forward and gingerly inserted her tongue in the musky vulva in front of her face. Miss Carr spread her legs wider and Cassie licked tentatively at the tight bud that protruded from its hood of flesh. Armstrong watched avidly, his cock swelling even further, its tip tight and shiny. Unable to control himself, he took up his previous position. Again Cassie felt herself split asunder as he forced his way into her, grunting and heaving, every movement forcing her nipples against the harsh material of the couch and pushing her face further into the gaping cunt before her.

Her traitorous orgasm began to build again and she moaned as she lapped and sucked at Miss Carr's sex, copious juices coating her chin. Miss Carr arched her back, thrusting herself forward, stroking her own nipples as she revelled in Cassie's attention.

Armstrong gave one final, enormous thrust, and Cassie felt his huge cock throb and spasm inside her, triggering her own explosive climax. Miss Carr writhed for a few more seconds, then she, too, whimpered and collapsed.

Cassie lay, sobbing with shamed relief, her eyes closed, too humiliated to look at her tormentors. Even when she felt her wrists being untied, she didn't move. Eventually she had to. Slowly she sat up and began to adjust her clothing. Finally, she forced herself to raise her eyes.

Armstrong was sitting behind his desk as if nothing had

happened. Carr was dressed and sitting calmly, a cigarette between her lips. They looked smug and self-satisfied, and Cassie hated them both. Stiffly, she got to her feet and glared at Armstrong.

'I take it this means I can keep my job,' she croaked.

Armstrong gave her a look of astonished innocence. 'Whatever gave you that impression, my dear?' he chuckled. 'I'm afraid it's got nothing to do with me. The board of governors makes the decisions. I'm merely the message boy.'

Cassie gawped at him. 'But... you said...' Her voice trailed off as the full horror sank in. The bastard! He'd used her desperation to make her submit to his sexual whims and now he was sitting there, smiling at her as though butter wouldn't melt. Well, he wasn't going to get away with it. 'I'm going to the police,' she said, her voice hardening. 'You won't be a headmaster for much longer once I tell them what's just happened.'

He looked back at her calmly. 'Go ahead,' he said. 'Do you really think they'd believe you?' He shook his head. 'Somehow I don't think so. After all, it's just your word – the word of someone who has just lost their job and might just possibly bear a grudge – against that of Miss Carr and myself.' He raised an eyebrow. 'Now, which of us do you think they'd believe?'

Cassie gulped as the full realisation of how stupid she'd been slowly dawned. He was right. There was nothing she could do. The police would think she was making it all up just to get her own back for being paid off.

'Poor Cassie,' he said with mock sympathy. 'Just like your namesake, Cassandra. Doomed by Apollo always to tell the truth – and never to be believed.' He smiled patronisingly. 'Now, why don't you admit that you secretly rather enjoyed it, and then run along like a good girl and stop complaining? Hmm?'

Tears welling, she rose and fled the room, their mocking laughter echoing in her ears. She stumbled into the staff room, shut herself in the ladies' toilet and glared at her reflection in the mirror. The flush of orgasm stained her cheeks and she still could feel the memory of Armstrong's thick cock throbbing between her legs. Her humiliation was complete. She had enjoyed it – and that unpalatable truth made her hate them even more.

Standing there with the taste of another woman still on her lips, like some twisted sacrament, Cassie vowed that one day she would be avenged.

Chapter Four

'For God's sake, Cassie! Get up off your backside and do something,' exclaimed Lyn in exasperation, glaring at her flatmate. 'You've barely moved since I went out this morning.' She sighed. 'It's been almost a month now, and you've been lying around like a sack of wet washing ever since you got paid off. You can't just sit there forever.'

Cassie hunched her shoulders protectively and gazed listlessly at the cartoon on the television, hoping Lyn would leave her alone.

But she didn't. 'Come on, love,' she said gently, sitting down beside her. 'Losing your job's not the end of the world. I know it's a knock-back.'

Cassie smiled bitterly. Knock-back? Knock-up was more like it. Lyn didn't know the half of it. She wasn't the one who'd been screwed. Literally! A brief vision of Armstrong, leering down at her as he stroked his grossly swollen erection, flashed in front of her eyes and she shuddered.

Obliviously Lyn ignored her and went on. 'But you've got to get over it. Try and find yourself something else.'

'I *have* tried,' she protested. 'There's just nothing out there. I'm either overqualified or inexperienced or born in the wrong phase of the moon.' She snorted. 'Maybe I should put in an advert myself: "Second-hand gym teacher. Only slightly used. No reasonable offer refused".'

'Look, I hate to go on about this,' Lyn persisted, 'but you're going to have to find something soon. The rent's due and I don't have enough money to carry the both of us.'

Cassie shivered. She didn't need telling. This morning's post had contained a charming letter from her bank manager, suggesting that they meet to 'sort out' her overdraft – so obviously a bank loan to tide her over was out of the question. Her credit card was maxed out to the limit so, no doubt, she could look forward to letters from them in the near future, too. She smiled ruefully. If things went on like this she'd soon end up living in a cardboard box! But then at least she wouldn't have to worry about the damned rent!

'I got tonight's paper on the way home,' said Lyn. 'Why don't we go through it together and see if there's anything suitable?'

'Why not,' agreed Cassie, her voice betraying a hint of sarcasm. 'Apart from the minor detail that there won't be. There hasn't been so far.' She grabbed the paper and flicked through to the *Situations Vacant* section, which seemed to consist of a meagre couple of columns. 'Now let me see…' she said with mock interest. 'How about a job working in a burger bar? Oops, sorry. "Would suit school leaver".' She shook her head. 'Somehow I don't think they mean me. Severe acne's probably one of the qualifications.

'Or how about this one?' she went on. '"Telesales personnel required. Commission only". That would certainly keep the wolf from the door, wouldn't it, flogging double-glazing over the phone? Or, even better, "Technical engineers wanted for positions in the Far East". Maybe I could go drilling for oil in Iran. Bulletproof vest provided.' Her voice rose. 'Spoilt for choice really, aren't I?' She flung the paper down. 'See? I told you. There's absolutely nothing here. It's hopeless.'

'There's got to be something,' said Lyn, picking up the

discarded paper. There was silence as she scanned the columns and began to come to the same dispiriting conclusion as Cassie. Then she paused. 'Hang on!' she exclaimed. 'What about this?' She stuck the paper under Cassie's nose and pointed at a boxed advert. 'Look. "Good Companions. Young, attractive women required for escort agency. Excellent remuneration".'

Cassie stared at her in disbelief. 'An escort agency? You've got to be joking. You know what that means, don't you? It's just a fancy name for a call-girl set-up.' She shook her head. 'I might as well invest in hooker boots, lycra hot-pants and a see-through blouse, and set up soliciting on the street corner!'

'Don't be daft,' said Lyn. 'A call-girl outfit? With a name like "Good Companions"? It sounds like something cosy from the Thirties. Anyway, they'd hardly be advertising in the paper if they were, now would they? Everything has to be above board these days, or else they'd get prosecuted.' She smiled. 'You'll get paid for being wined and dined and all you'll have to do is be nice to lonely businessmen.'

'Exactly *how* nice?' muttered Cassie.

'Look,' said Lyn in exasperation. 'Beggars can't be choosers. It's a job – and let's face it, the way your finances are just now, you should be grateful for anything. Anyway, they can't make you do anything you don't want to do, now can they?'

Cassie scowled. A month ago she might have agreed. Now she wasn't so sure.

'Come on,' coaxed Lyn. 'Why not ring up and give it a try?'

'Okay,' Cassie agreed reluctantly. 'I'll call them first thing tomorrow. It's after five, they'll be shut now.'

'You'll ring right now,' ordered Lyn, sensing victory.

'It's not an office. It's an escort agency, remember? They're probably only just opening.' She stuck the phone under Cassie's nose. 'Come on, call. Before you lose your nerve.'

'Oh, all right,' grumbled Cassie, reaching for the handset. 'Read out the number and I'll dial.'

'Well?' demanded Lyn, when Cassie hung up.

'I've got an appointment for eleven o'clock tomorrow,' she said grudgingly. 'To see if I'm "suitable".' She glared at Lyn. 'But if it's some kind of seedy operation, I'm walking straight back out again.'

'It won't be,' prophesied Lyn. 'Now come on,' she ordered, hauling Cassie to her feet and tugging her towards the bedroom. 'Let's go through your wardrobe and pick out an outfit. You want to look your best. You want to make a good impression.' She ran her eyes disparagingly over Cassie's baggy T-shirt and washed-out leggings, and grinned. 'They're not going to offer you a job if you look like a bag lady.'

At quarter to eleven next morning, Cassie was standing nervously in front of the building where *Good Companions* had their office. Lyn had insisted on overseeing her as she dressed, making sure she put on the smart charcoal suit she'd picked out the night before.

'Stockings and suspenders?' Cassie had protested, holding up the offending items. 'Why can't I wear tights? This skirt's short enough as it is. I don't want to give them any wrong ideas.'

'They'll make you act differently,' Lyn had insisted. 'Prim and proper on top – seething volcano underneath. It's a great combination, trust me. You want this job, don't you?'

'I suppose so,' Cassie had mumbled sulkily.

'Then do what your Auntie Lyn tells you,' Lyn said

patiently. 'It's worked for me in the past, and it'll work for you now.' She grinned. 'Oh, and put on those black lace knickers of yours too. We might as well go the whole hog.'

Obediently, Cassie had slipped them on and sat half-naked in front of the mirror while Lyn put her hair up in a chignon and applied her make-up. Finally, Lyn stood back and admired her handiwork. 'There,' she said with satisfaction. 'You'll knock 'em dead. Now put your suit on – and don't smear your make-up.'

Cassie looked up at the office block towering over her. It was both frightening and reassuring at the same time. Frightening because she didn't know what to expect, and reassuring because she could not believe that some seedy call-girl operation would have its office in such an expensive and respectable building. Taking a deep breath, she pushed her way into the revolving door.

It spat her out on the other side, into an imposing foyer. Thick pile carpet covered the floor. On one side there was a bank of lifts, on the other a curved marble staircase and in the centre, facing the door, a long mahogany reception desk, apparently manned by refugees from *Vogue*. Grateful for Lyn's insistence that she wore her smartest suit, she took her courage in both hands and approached the reception.

'*Good Companions*, madam?' said one of the exquisitely dressed receptionists in a languid cut-glass accent. 'Certainly. Their suite is on the third floor.' She pointed to the bank of lifts with a perfectly manicured finger. 'Turn left when you leave the lift and it's at the end of the hall.'

Thanking her, Cassie made her way across the foyer.

The lift seemed to take forever, giving time for the butterflies in her stomach to breed several more generations. Despite this, it arrived at the third floor far too soon for Cassie's liking. Stepping out into yet more ankle-deep carpet, she turned left. Ahead of her, as promised, lay the offices of *Good Companions*, the name emblazoned on the frosted-glass door in flowing golden script. Taking a deep breath and needlessly straightening her skirt, she forced herself to walk up and open it.

The reception area could have contained her whole flat quite easily. Black leather sofas crouched against three walls, and the receptionist was yet another Sloane clone. 'Eleven o'clock appointment, madam?' The receptionist checked her book and favoured Cassie with a polite smile. 'That's fine. You're a little early. Please take a seat and Mr Harris will see you as soon as possible. There are magazines on the coffee table.'

Once seated, with the latest copy of *Cosmopolitan* on her knee, Cassie had a chance to look around. There were two women already waiting. One was middle-aged, but the other was in her early twenties: a bleached blonde with a hard face, a low-cut blouse and a skirt that barely skimmed the cheeks of her backside. All Cassie's fears rushed back. If this was the kind of person they were looking for, then she'd been right; this was nothing but the cover for a glorified knocking-shop.

'Miss Cane?' said the receptionist. 'Mr Harris will see you now.' Cassie suppressed another nervous giggle. Miss Cane? What was the betting her first name was *Kandy*? Miss Cane gave her a dirty look, deposited her chewing-gum in a crystal ashtray, and minced carefully across the carpet in her stiletto heels.

She was out again in two minutes flat. 'And you can stuff yer bleedin' job!' she snarled furiously over her shoulder, stomping out and banging the door so hard behind her that the glass shuddered.

The receptionist raised a cool eyebrow. 'Mrs Watts?'

she said silkily. 'Mr Harris will see you now.' The middle-aged woman rose and disappeared into the inner office.

She was out almost as quickly, looking as if she was about to burst into tears. Cassie swallowed nervously, her increasing anxiety beginning to make her feel queasy. It didn't exactly bode well for her prospects. As the receptionist nodded towards her, she put down her magazine, straightened her skirt again, and walked forward with an air of confidence she didn't really feel.

It was like stepping into a different world. Somehow she'd expected something even more opulent than the reception area. Something pink and fluffy. Soft seats padded in satin. Ruched curtains. All the trimmings of a courtesan's boudoir. Instead it was like a hi-tech laboratory. Fluorescent lights gleamed off polished surfaces and the thick carpet gave way to standard heavy-duty office floor covering. Three computers flickered softly beside a bank of filing cabinets. In the middle of the room stood a strictly functional black desk.

The man behind the desk came as quite a surprise as well. He looked as if he'd be more at home on a rugby field than in an office. His nose had obviously been broken at some point, then badly set. This, together with his designer suit, olive skin and the dark hair falling over his forehead, reminded Cassie vaguely of a Mafia hit-man in a gangster movie. He reached into the desk drawer and she wouldn't have been in the least bit surprised if he'd suddenly pulled out a machine-gun.

Instead, he produced a perfectly harmless notepad. 'Take a seat, Miss Grey,' he invited. 'I'd just like to take a few details.' His voice was surprising, too; light and cultured, in stark contrast to his appearance. She smiled back uncertainly and sat down, primly smoothing the hem of her skirt back over her knees.

'Now,' he went on, 'if you could just tell me a little about yourself. Your interests. What you were doing before you applied for this job. That kind of thing.'

'Well,' she began. 'I was a teacher. I mean I *am* a teacher, I just haven't got a post at the moment. I was paid off because of budget cuts.' A picture of herself, tied over the arm of the sofa, her face buried in Carr's crotch while a grunting Armstrong thrust into her, flashed onto her mental screen. She shook her head to dismiss it and forced herself to go on. 'I enjoy reading and music – classical as well as popular.' She smiled at him brightly. 'I like visiting museums and art galleries. Eating out. That sort of thing. Oh, and I've been abroad. I can speak a little French and German.' She smiled. 'Not that much, but enough for a pretty basic conversation.'

He leaned back and looked her over, unsmiling, for so long that she began to get nervous again. He obviously didn't like her. 'I'm sorry,' she said, starting to rise. 'I've wasted your time. This whole thing has been a mistake from start to finish.'

He sat up and leaned forward, gesturing for her to take her seat again. 'Nonsense,' he said. 'You're exactly what we're looking for. Attractive, well-dressed–' he looked approvingly at her suit '–and above all, bright and articulate.' He leaned back again. 'Our clients are successful businessmen. They need someone who can dress well and carry on an intelligent conversation. Someone who's not going to let them down in public.' He smiled at her again. 'I think you'd be ideal. Particularly with a smattering of two foreign languages. Excellent.'

He suddenly became businesslike. 'We charge our clients two hundred pounds for the pleasure of your company for an evening. Out of that, *Good Companions* takes fifty per cent. Anything over and above that, which a gentleman may care to give you, is yours. Any questions?'

Cassie blushed. It all sounded too good to be true. One hundred pounds for simply going out with someone? There was bound to be a catch somewhere. But how could she put it diplomatically?

'Er... and that's all I'd have to do?' she asked tentatively. 'Go out with the clients for a meal or to the theatre? Just keep them company?'

He sat bolt upright, apparently offended. 'Of course,' he snapped. 'That's why it's called *Good Companions*.' His expression hardened. 'I hope you're not implying anything else.' He grimaced with distaste. 'I'm afraid Miss Cane was under the impression that the services we provide went a little further than that. I had to tell her that her kind of talents were not required here.'

Cassie blushed even more. Damn! She'd probably just thrown away any chance of getting a job. She looked at him apologetically, and, to her relief, he was smiling again.

'Still, that doesn't concern you,' he said. 'I can understand why you might be worried, but I can assure you that everything we do is completely above board. We are an escort agency, and that's all you'll be required to be. A pleasant, undemanding companion for visiting businessmen. A meal, a show, and then safely home to your own little bed – with a nice cheque in your handbag to boot.'

Feeling reassured, Cassie allowed herself a first relaxed smile of the interview.

'Oh, just one more minor detail.' He paused, and her heart sank. What now? Maybe he was going to ask if she spoke Swahili or something and the job would fly out the window. She looked at him anxiously. 'You do have suitable evening wear, don't you?'

'Oh, yes,' she exclaimed. 'That's no problem.' She suppressed a grin. If she didn't now, she soon would have. Stuff the bank manager! She was going out to hit the shops as soon as she left the building.

'Does that mean I've got the job, then?' she asked. He nodded and relief flooded her. At one hundred pounds a night she'd soon have her credit card and overdraft paid off. Not to mention the rent. Everything was working out beautifully, at last.

She held out her hand to him as she stood to go. 'Thank you, Mr Harris,' she beamed. 'I look forward working for you.'

'And I you,' he smiled, shaking it politely. 'I'm sure it will be a long and mutually satisfying relationship.'

His polite veneer disappeared as soon as she had left the room, but by that time it was too late. Cassie was already halfway across the outer office, with a cheerful wave for the receptionist and a pitying smile for the other hopefuls seated nervously on the leather sofas. Nothing could go wrong now. She'd got the job and it sounded brilliant. She could hardly wait.

Chapter Five

'You got the job,' predicted Lyn smugly. 'I knew you would. Told you the smart suit and the sexy underwear would do the trick.'

'How'd you guess?' grinned Cassie, depositing a pile of expensive-looking carrier bags on the sofa and slumping down beside them. 'The shopping spree give it away, did it?'

'Well, no, actually,' confessed Lyn. 'The agency was on the phone while you were out. You've got your first client already.' She picked up a sheet of paper from beside the phone and waved it under Cassie's nose. 'I took down all the details.' Cassie grabbed for it and she laughed and whipped it out of reach.

'Your client is a Mr James Garret,' she announced in an affected voice. 'He's a company director with a computer firm and he's in town to attend a convention. Your instructions are to meet him at the *Connaught Hotel* at eight and go out to dinner with him.' She grinned. 'Lucky sod! Fancy someone paying good money to take you out and feed you! He must be mad.'

'Don't be so damned cheeky,' giggled Cassie, throwing a cushion at Lyn's head. 'I'll have you know I'm a valuable commodity. Men will be beating a path to my doorway for the privilege of my company.' She pulled a face. 'Anyway, what kind of a man has to pay to take a woman out? He's probably a nerd with glasses like bottle bottoms and the conversational skills of a dead parrot. You know what computer blokes are like. The last time he spoke to a female was probably on the Internet. It'll be bloody hard work.'

'Oh yeah,' said Lyn sarcastically. 'Bloody hard work. Stuffing your face in a posh restaurant and knocking back wine from fancy crystal glasses. I'm glad I don't have to do it. I couldn't stand the pace!'

'If it's so wonderful, why aren't you volunteering?' said Cassie dryly. 'Anyway, my feet are killing me. Make me a nice cup of coffee, then I'll try on my new stuff and you can give me your opinion.' She smiled wryly. 'I spent a small fortune. This job had better work out so I can pay for it all, before the bank manager catches up with me.'

'Well, what do you think?' asked Cassie, twirling round to give Lyn the full benefit. 'Will this do?'

'That looks great,' admitted Lyn enviously. Cassie admired her reflection in the mirror and smiled. The dress, in gunmetal-coloured satin, clung to her like a second skin, showing off the soft curves of her body. As she moved, the light caught it, and the colour changed from grey to silver, highlighting the smooth length of her thighs and drawing the eye to the triangle where they met. The prim effect of the high neckline was contradicted by the way her nipples jutted proudly, outlined by the silky material, and the way the dress was cut almost to the cleft of her buttocks at the back. Her smile widened. Though she said it herself, she looked pretty good.

'You look like an incredibly expensive courtesan,' Lyn went on. 'Or the mistress of some foreign diplomat.'

Cassie's ego deflated rapidly. 'Thanks a lot!' she muttered crossly. 'Why don't you just say "hooker" and have done with it? I wanted to look elegant and sophisticated, not give the bloke the wrong idea.'

'Oh, for God's sake, stop being so touchy,' said Lyn in

exasperation. 'That's not what I meant and you know it. You look classy – but sexy at the same time. Now stop complaining, put on your new shoes and walk across the room so I can see the whole effect.'

Cassie slipped on the expensive grey leather shoes and did as she was told, her pert bottom swaying enticingly as she moved.

'Not bad,' grinned Lyn. 'Not bad at all. Pity I'm straight, otherwise I'd fancy you myself.'

For a moment the breath caught in Cassie's throat and she was back in Armstrong's office, Carr's hands groping at her breasts, teasing and tormenting her. With face scarlet, she rounded on Lyn. 'That's disgusting!' she spat. 'Don't you ever say anything like that to me again!'

'Take it easy,' protested Lyn, hurt and surprised. 'I was only kidding. I didn't mean it. What on earth's got into you today? I'm frightened to open my mouth in case you jump down my throat.'

'Sorry,' muttered Cassie, slipping out of her new clothes and back into her comfortable old jeans and T-shirt. 'I shouldn't be taking it out on you.' She forced a smile. 'It's just nerves. I mean, it's all very well joking, but I've never even met this guy. He could be Jack the Ripper or some kind of pervert for all I know.'

'Don't be daft,' said Lyn, reassuringly. '*Good Companions* seems to be a pretty respectable set-up. They probably vet their clients before they take them on.' She grinned. 'Think about it. They wouldn't last very long if their escorts kept getting bumped off, now would they?'

'You're right.' Cassie sighed. 'I'm just being silly. James Garret is probably a perfectly nice bloke, looking for a bit of company because he's on his own in a strange town.' She grinned. 'I'll bet he's almost as nervous as I am.'

'More so, if he knew the mood you were in.' Lyn

chuckled. 'One false move and you'll probably punch the poor guy's lights out! And bang goes your new career.' She shook her head. 'Don't worry, Cassie, you'll be fine. In six hours' time you'll be wondering what you were ever nervous about.'

It was the longest six hours of Cassie's life. The thought of the coming rendezvous hung over her like a cloud of impending doom, and she couldn't settle to anything. Finally, at about five o'clock, she got up from the chair in front of the television, where she'd been sitting gazing blankly at the screen. 'Well, better start getting ready,' she announced.

'Oh, I quite agree,' grinned Lyn. 'You really need to put in three hours before you're presentable. Don't want the poor bloke taking one look, then turning tail and running.'

Cassie stuck out her tongue and flounced out of the room. She took great satisfaction in using up the last of the hot water, filling the bath to overflowing and helping herself to Lyn's expensive bath lotion into the bargain. With a sigh of satisfaction, she slid below the foamy surface and relaxed, leaning back against the bath pillow. Maybe this wouldn't be so bad after all. For all she knew, this Garret guy could be tall, dark and handsome. For several minutes she indulged in a pleasant fantasy in which he wined and dined her, swept her off her feet and ended the evening by making mad, passionate love to her on white silken sheets.

Eyes closed, she idly caressed the slippery crests of her nipples where they poked softly through the bubbles, feeling them harden under her fingers – then she grinned and sat up. Chance would be a fine thing! Picking up the soap, she scrubbed herself briskly. Finally, she used the shower attachment to wash her hair and sluice away the last of the soap from her body, shivering as the cool water ran down between her thighs.

Dabbing herself dry, she dropped the towel and stood in front of the mirrored tiles, looking at herself. She was flushed and rosy from the heat, beads of moisture still clinging to her skin where she hadn't quite reached. Turning, she looked over her shoulder to check her rear view. She slapped her bottom and smiled when the firm flesh merely quivered gently. She shivered as the sting of her hand against her cheek set a familiar tingle running through her loins.

A thought struck her as she remembered something she'd read, God alone knew where. Hardly likely to be in one of her women's magazines, that was for sure. Grinning wickedly, she sat on the edge of the bath and spread her legs. Gently parting her labia, she dipped one finger into her own moisture, withdrew it, glistening, and carefully dabbed it behind each ear, like perfume. She giggled. There. He wouldn't know what had hit him. Why bother with expensive scent to attract the opposite sex, when Mother Nature had done the job so much better?

An hour later, hair dried and make-up on, she examined herself again. Her dress clung even more tightly to her damp skin and her dark stockings and high heels accentuated the smooth length of her legs. She fastened a pearl pendant around her neck, put in the matching earrings, pouted her scarlet lips and blew a kiss at her reflection.

'Mmm, you look amazing,' said Lyn, when Cassie swanned into the living room and pirouetted in front of her. 'He can't complain that he's not getting his money's worth. Tell you what, I'll even let you borrow my velvet evening jacket. Just don't spill wine down it or I'll kill you.' She disappeared into her bedroom and reappeared with it, slipping it over Cassie's shoulders and stepping back to admire the effect.

'Lovely,' she said, with satisfaction. 'It sets off the whole outfit. Now,' she went on briskly, 'have you got your keys? Purse? Emergency tenner in case he makes a pass at you and you need to get a taxi quick?'

'Oh, for heaven's sake,' protested Cassie. 'You sound just like my mother. You'll be asking me next if I've been to the bathroom and if I've got a clean hanky. I'll be fine. What can possibly go wrong?' She jumped as there was a knock at the door. 'That'll be the taxi,' she said, going to answer it. 'I ordered it for half-past seven.' She smiled back over her shoulder, a little uncertainly. 'Wish me luck – and don't wait up.' With a final wave, she disappeared, her high heels clattering down the stairs.

She didn't feel particularly confident as she stood in front of the hotel, where the taxi had dropped her. The people going in and out had that understated elegance peculiar to the very rich, the women wearing expensive mink coats and stoles, despite all the efforts of the anti-fur campaigners. Lyn's velvet jacket suddenly seemed very small beer indeed, and she was aware that her pearls were cultured instead of the genuine article.

She shook herself. This bloke worked with a computer firm, for God's sake. He wasn't the heir to the bloody throne! He was paying for her company – and he was damned lucky to be getting it, too. Straightening her shoulders, she strode through the doors and up to the reception desk.

'I have an appointment with Mr James Garret,' she announced imperiously. 'He's meeting me here at eight.'

'Certainly, madam,' said the receptionist. 'Mr Garret's still in his room. I'll let him know you're here.' She pointed to the leather chairs dotted around the foyer. 'Please take a seat. He'll be with you shortly.'

Head high, Cassie walked across the carpet and selected one. Seated, she crossed her legs, picked up a magazine and pretended to read, as she scanned the people coming and going.

Five minutes later the lift doors slid open and a tall dark man came out and headed in her direction. Mmm. Not bad. Not bad at all. Cassie pasted a welcoming smile on her lips and prepared to get to her feet.

But he walked straight past her and she subsided in disappointment. Damn! She might have known it was too good to be true.

'Er... Miss Grey?' A tentative voice made her jump and she turned to see its owner. Her heart sank. The comical description of her potential client she'd dreamed up with Lyn was almost spot on. He was skinny and at least two inches shorter than her. Watery eyes peered through thick glasses, and thinning red hair combed carefully over a freckled skull completed the picture. She shuddered inwardly. She needed the money and even if he had terminal halitosis, she was still duty bound to be charming to him.

'That's right,' she smiled, holding out her hand. 'Call me Cassie. You must be James. I've been looking forward to meeting you.'

He took her hand in his sweaty one and smiled back, revealing a mouthful of bad teeth. 'Great,' he said enthusiastically. 'We can go for a drink in the hotel bar and get to know each other, then I've booked us a table at the French restaurant round the corner.' Taking her arm, he led her across the thick carpet and pushed open the swinging door. As they entered, Cassie thanked her lucky stars for the subdued lighting.

'Now, what'll you have?' he asked, rubbing his hands. 'How about a nice big snifter?' Cassie suppressed the desire to ask for a triple brandy and settled for a ladylike Campari and soda instead. Sipping it daintily, she cudgelled her brains for suitable small talk.

She needn't have bothered. James – 'Call me Jimmy' – talked quite enough for both of them. He regaled her with the riveting details of his life, his ambitions, his job, and enough computer information to set up her own company. She smiled until her face hurt and nodded in what she hoped were the appropriate places.

'Right then,' he grinned, when they'd had a couple of drinks. 'How about a spot of grub now?'

Grub? Cassie was appalled. What the hell were they going to eat? Tripe and onions? Pie and mash? Jellied eels? She smiled in agreement and got to her feet. Still grinning, he ushered her out of the hotel lounge and they set off for the restaurant.

If the drinks had been bad, dinner was worse. Cassie drank more wine than was good for her as she picked at the food on her plate. Her appetite had mysteriously disappeared as he chomped his way determinedly through his meal, mouth open, treating her to a delightful view of his semi-masticated food. It was like sitting opposite a cement mixer. And he talked. Oh, how he talked. On and on, spraying crumbs over thc pristine linen tablecloth, until Cassie felt like screaming. It was one of the worst evenings of her life.

Finally – thank God – it came to an end.

'Marvellous,' he burped, flinging down his stained napkin. 'We'll have another drink at the hotel and then I'll square up with you.' Cassie gave him the first genuine smile of the evening. Once she got that cash in her purse she'd be off so fast he wouldn't see her for dust!

'That would be lovely,' she said, finding it increasingly difficult to appear attentive. 'I've really enjoyed our evening together.'

Clearly flattered, he beamed at her and snapped his fingers for the waiter, while Cassie cringed inside.

On the walk back to the hotel, Cassie staggered slightly and suppressed a giggle. She really shouldn't have had all that wine on an empty stomach. Never mind, she'd get a taxi home and fall straight into bed. She stumbled again as they re-entered the hotel lounge, and this time couldn't keep the giggle in. 'Better not have any more,' she chuckled. 'I think I've had enough already.' Despite her protest, he came back with what looked like a double and placed it carefully in front of her. 'You're trying to get me drunk,' she protested – then swallowed it regardless.

'Right, now,' he announced, reaching into his inside pocket. 'How much do I owe you?'

'Two hundred pounds,' said Cassie, suddenly embarrassed at the mention of money. Why couldn't the agency collect the fees and save all this awkwardness. What if he got stroppy and created a scene?

But he didn't. 'Cheap at twice the price,' he grinned, and Cassie sighed with relief. Then his expression changed. He groped around in his pocket for a few more moments then smiled apologetically. 'I'm sorry, my cheque book must be in my case. I've only got my plastic here. Come up to my room and we'll sort it out there.'

A warning bell rang dimly in the back of Cassie's brain, but she ignored it. What harm would it do? He'd been a perfect gentleman all night – well, if you didn't mind the horrible table manners. She giggled. Anyway, she was taller than he was; she could probably snap him over one knee, like a dry twig. 'Okay,' she agreed, tottering to her feet and following him to the lift.

'Thank you,' she smiled, accepting the cheque he wrote out in his room. 'It's very pleasant here,' she said, looking around, swaying a little. 'Do you stay at the Connaught oft–' Her words were cut off as he pounced on her, his mouth slobbering down on hers as he dragged her towards him. One hand groped at her buttocks while the other fumbled at her breasts, kneading and squeezing. Despite the amount of alcohol she'd consumed she managed to squirm free and push him away.

'What do you think you're playing at?' she gasped. 'I'm an escort, not some kind of a whore!' She looked down at her dress, where his clammy hand had left a clear print on the silky fabric, and alcohol-fuelled rage overwhelmed her. She hadn't even paid for it yet. Before she knew it, she'd lifted her hand and administered a stinging slap to his leering face.

His reaction took her aback. Instead of curbing his ardour, it only seemed to inflame him further. 'More!' he panted, the rapidly swelling bulge in his trousers revealing his excitement. 'Hit me again!'

Cassie, who'd been about to do exactly that, dropped her hand and stared at him nonplussed for a moment, then a feeling of power swept through her. Raising her hand, she slapped him again. Twice. Hard.

'Oh, yes,' he moaned, 'do it again.'

A quiver of excitement flickered in her groin. She suppressed it firmly. 'No,' she said boldly.

His eyes opened and he looked at her beseechingly. 'Please, mistress,' he grovelled. 'I'll pay you.'

The feeling of excitement returned and she could feel her nipples becoming tight and engorged, pressing against the soft satin of her dress. It wasn't this feeble specimen she saw before her, it was George Armstrong, the day he and Miss Carr had done what they liked with her; used her body for their own sick gratification and then cheated her with utter disdain. A vengeful smile lifted the corners of her mouth. He'd pay all right. Oh yes, he'd pay.

'Strip!' she ordered, slapping him again. Whimpering, he hurried to obey her, tearing the buttons from his shirt in his haste. In no time he stood before her naked, his erect penis pulsing eagerly. She took in the skinny legs and the incipient pot belly. 'You're disgusting,' she sneered. 'Aren't you?'

'Yes, mistress,' he quavered. His eyes flickered hopefully to a case lying on the bed. 'Are you going to punish me?' Following his gaze, she investigated, suppressing a gasp as she eyed the contents. The pervert had enough equipment to set up his own dungeon! She pulled out a short whip with several thin lashes and flicked it experimentally against her palm. He shuddered in horrified anticipation.

'Oh, yes,' she said softly. 'I'm going to punish you all right. Bend over.'

The lashes whistled through the air and half a dozen red weals sprang up on his scrawny buttocks. He jerked and moaned. 'Thank you, mistress,' he whimpered.

Her arm rose and fell again, her breath coming faster with excitement. The crotch of her knickers was wet now, and her nipples were so swollen that even the soft material of her dress was unbearable. She slipped the straps off her shoulders and gasped as the satin slithered slowly down her body.

Legs wide, she stood over him, clad only in her high heels, stockings and skimpy knickers, tapping the whip dangerously against her hand. 'Lie down on the bed,' she ordered. He did as he was told, gazing up at her with fearful delight, his cock so stiff it might have been made out of steel. 'Put your hands up against the headboard,' she snapped, taking a pair of handcuffs from his case. She ran the chain between the bedposts and clicked them on his wrists, then did the same with each ankle in turn, leaving him helpless.

'And what shall I do with you now?' she purred, stroking her nipples as she stared down at him. She trailed the lashes of the whip slowly over his raging erection, and he moaned again. She slid her fingers slowly between the wet lips of her sex, beginning to move them in and out and laughing cruelly as his fascinated gaze followed every movement, his hips thrusting futilely at the empty air. 'Stop that!' she snarled, smacking the side of his prick with her open hand so that it sprang almost comically from side to side. 'You move when *I* tell you.'

Still smiling, she knelt on the bed, straddling his body, the tip of his cock barely grazing the parted lips of her vulva. When he tried to thrust towards her she twisted his nipples viciously till he whimpered and subsided. 'That's better,' she purred. 'You're here for my pleasure, not yours.' She twisted again. 'Aren't you?' she demanded.

'Yes, mistress,' he whined.

She lowered herself onto his rigid cock, engulfing it slowly. She gasped as it slid deep into her, then she raised herself and plunged down again and again. Her surrogate revenge was complete. He didn't even exist any more, except as an instrument for her pleasure. Her hair fell about her shoulders as she tossed her head back, moaning, her hips bucking faster and faster as she rode him triumphantly to a shuddering climax, barely noticing his.

Once her pleasure had subsided she stood up and stretched luxuriously, looked down at him with total indifference, and began to put her clothes on, ready to leave.

Clearly alarmed, he tugged futilely against the handcuffs.

'Undo me,' he pleaded. When she ignored him, alarm turned to anger. 'Come on,' he snarled. 'Joke's over. You can't just leave me like this.'

'Can't I?' Cassie smiled, slipping on her shoes. 'Oh, I don't know. It might give the hotel staff a good laugh.'

'Take everything in my wallet,' he begged. 'There's five hundred quid in there. It's yours, all of it. Just take these handcuffs off me. Please. Think of my job. Think of my wife.'

'You weren't thinking of your wife earlier, were you?' said Cassie tartly. Still, she took pity on him. Not quite enough to forgo the money he'd promised her, though. Smiling, she tucked it into her handbag beside his legitimate cheque, before finally unlocking the cuffs. He was still trying to untangle himself when she blew him a kiss and let herself out.

Safely home in her own bedroom, she looked at the wad of notes in her bag with sheer disbelief. What on earth had she been thinking of? She giggled tipsily. Well, it was his own fault. If he hadn't given her quite so much drink, she'd never have gone to his room in the first place – let alone done anything else. And he could hardly complain. She'd given him exactly what he wanted – and made him pay for it, too. That would teach him. That would teach them all.

Still clutching the money, she fell into the first decent night's sleep she'd had since that day in the headmaster's study.

Chapter Six

She woke up next morning with a splitting headache, a mouth like the bottom of a birdcage and the feeling that something had gone disastrously wrong. Groaning, she rolled over – and came face to face with a wad of notes lying beside her on the pillow. For a moment she looked at them in disbelief, then snippets of the previous evening began to filter back into her consciousness. Her eyes widened in shock. Oh, no! She couldn't have! A faint, pleasurable throbbing between her thighs hinted that she had – and thoroughly enjoyed it into the bargain. She sagged back onto the pillows and groaned again.

There was a light tap at the door and Lyn's face appeared. 'Hi,' she beamed, coming into the room carrying two cups of coffee. 'Time to wake up, sleepyhead. It's almost twelve. I looked in earlier but you were sound asleep.' She plonked herself down on the edge of the bed and grinned. 'But I couldn't wait any longer. Curiosity was killing me. Come on. Tell me all. How did last night go?'

Cassie sat up, pushed the money well out of sight under the sheet and accepted the hot cup gratefully. 'Oh, it was all right,' she muttered, sipping the coffee in order to avoid Lyn's eyes.

'And that's it?' demanded Lyn. 'Your first date with an escort agency and all you can say is, "it was all right"?' She grinned. 'Well, that's not good enough. I want all the gory details. What was he like? Tall, dark and handsome? Small, bald and ugly?'

'He was just average,' muttered Cassie. Lyn opened her

mouth to demand more, but Cassie forestalled her. 'If you must know,' she burst out, 'I can't remember all that much about it.' She blushed guiltily. 'I had a bit too much to drink.'

Lyn looked at her in dismay. 'You're joking,' she said. 'You know what you're like with alcohol. Two wine gums and you're brain-dead.'

'I was nervous,' protested Cassie. 'I couldn't help it.' She glanced at Lyn defensively. 'You'd have been the same if you were the one being paid to go out with a strange bloke.'

'I suppose so,' agreed Lyn. 'Never mind,' she added, 'I'm sure everything went okay. If you'd been dancing naked on the tabletops you'd probably have heard about it by this time.'

Cassie suppressed another groan. Dancing naked was the least of her worries. Beating the shit out of her first client, handcuffing him to the bedposts and fucking his brains out didn't exactly bode well for her future career as an escort, did it? She smiled wryly. Oh, and let's not forget the blackmail, while we're at it. Still, as the saying went, he'd 'asked for it', so he could hardly complain when he got it. The agency would never find out, so why worry?

This comforting thought gave her a fresh burst of energy. Swinging her legs out of bed, she grinned at Lyn. 'I'll try and remember the details next time,' she promised. 'In fact, I'll take notes. In the meantime, I'd better get a move on.' She glanced at the clock on the bedside table. 'The day's half gone already and I want to get down to the bank.' She looked up in appeal. 'Any chance of you making another cup of coffee while I get dressed?'

Grumbling, Lyn left her to it.

Her mood had improved even further by the time she got back from the bank. Her overdraft hadn't exactly disappeared, but the five hundred pounds had made a reasonable dent in it – and she still had another hundred to come, once she took the cheque into the agency offices. She was humming as she clattered up the stairs to the flat.

'There was a phone call for you,' called Lyn, as she let herself in. 'That bloke from the agency. The number's on the pad. You're to call back as soon as you get in.'

Cassie's heart sank. What did he want? Maybe Garret had complained after all. No, it was probably about the cheque. Perhaps she should have popped round with it after she'd been to the bank. With a nagging feeling that something wasn't quite all right, she picked up the phone.

She was smiling with relief when she hung up. She'd been right. It was about the money. 'Don't bother about starting tea,' she called through to Lyn. 'I've got to go straight back out again. Apparently they like you to hand the cheque in the day after you've been out with a client. That way they can keep the books straight and stop you running off to the Bahamas with the company profits.' She grabbed her handbag and stuck her head round the kitchen door. 'In fact, don't bother cooking at all,' she grinned cheerfully. 'I'll pick up a Chinese takeaway on the way home to celebrate my new-found solvency.'

It was almost half past five by the time she reached the office building, and the revolving door was disgorging a steady flow of workers into the street as she pushed her way in the opposite direction. The remaining receptionist looked pointedly at the ornate clock on the wall as Cassie hurried across the foyer.

Cassie ignored the hint. 'I have an appointment,' she lied, bypassing the desk and heading straight towards the lifts. 'They're expecting me.'

In the offices of *Good Companions*, the secretary was also preparing to leave. Her coat was already on and she was carefully tying a scarf round her neck. She looked at Cassie with disfavour. 'Sorry, madam,' she said, as she leaned over to click on the answering machine. 'I'm afraid we're closed. Monday's always a quiet day, so the office shuts at five-thirty. You'll have to come back tomorrow.'

Cassie looked at her in dismay. Damn! She'd come all this way, just to get pipped at the post.

The door to the inner office opened. 'That's all right, Caroline,' smiled Mr Harris. 'I called Miss Grey in. Don't worry. Off you go. Just lock up on your way out and I'll let her out later.'

Cassie gave her a triumphant smile as she walked past her into Mr Harris' office. Caroline shrugged, collected her handbag and switched off the lights, before locking the door behind her.

'Take a seat, Miss Grey,' said Mr Harris, settling himself behind his desk. 'Sorry to have called you in like this, but it is company policy to collect any remuneration the day after.' His smile hardened. 'I'm sure *you* wouldn't think of it, but some of our less scrupulous ladies have decided on occasion to – how shall I put it? – cut out the middleman.'

'Good heavens,' said Cassie, genuinely shocked. 'It never even crossed my mind. It's just that I didn't know.' She scrabbled in her handbag, produced the cheque, and handed it over. 'Here it is.' She smiled at him. 'Sorry. Now I know the routine it won't happen again.'

'Good… good,' he said thoughtfully, taking it and sticking it carelessly into a drawer. From the same drawer he took out a thick sheaf of twenty-pound notes, counted out five and laid them in a neat stack on the desk in front of Cassie. She reached for them, but he drew them back, just out of reach. Cassie swallowed. The gesture reminded her of a cat, cruelly toying with a mouse.

'Now,' he smiled, leaning forward. 'How did your first assignment go? Any problems that you'd like to discuss?'

Cassie blushed. 'Er... no,' she muttered. 'Nothing I couldn't handle.' She smiled, relaxing a little. 'In fact, I thought it went rather well.' She reached for the money again, and this time he allowed her to take it. She tucked it into her bag and prepared to rise.

'Not quite yet,' he said softly – and there was something in his voice that made her very aware that she was sitting behind locked doors with this man. In a virtually empty building. He was still smiling, but there was a shark-like quality about it that unsettled her.

'I'm sorry,' she said, scrambling hastily to her feet. 'But I really do have to go now. My flatmate will be waiting for me.'

'I said, not quite yet.' And this time there was no mistaking the menace in his voice. 'There's something I'd like you to see.' He reached for a switch set into the desk and clicked it on. Cassie gasped as a screen on the wall behind him suddenly sprang into life. Sighs and whimpers filled the room. Cassie took one quick look at the writhing bodies and shut her eyes, clapping her hands over her ears to shut out the sounds of sexual ecstasy.

'Switch that off,' she moaned. 'It's disgusting. How dare you show me pornography? Why are you doing this to me?'

The soundtrack died and his amused voice managed to cut through the protective barrier of her hands. 'Pornography, my dear? You do yourself a disservice.' He chuckled. 'As to why I'm doing it – may I suggest that you look a little more closely at the participants?'

Cassie opened her eyes and took a cautious sidelong glance at the screen, where the performance continued in silence. Head tossed back, the woman plunged and reared, impaled on the rampant penis of the man chained to the bed. The camera zoomed in on a close-up of the swollen cock as it slid in and out, trailed over the heaving, sweat-beaded breasts, then locked onto the woman's face as her mouth opened in her moment of release. Cassie went white as it dawned on her that she was looking at herself.

'Recognise anyone?' came Mr Harris' sly voice.

She stared at him in horror. 'How did you get that video?' she whispered. 'It's impossible. There was no one else there.'

He smiled dismissively. 'That's not important. Shall we just say that chambermaids are not particularly well paid? It's amazing what a small bonus can arrange.' He shrugged. 'It's just as well you didn't use the en-suite, and our satisfied little client fell asleep as soon as you left, so she could make her exit undetected.'

'Wh-what do you want?' choked Cassie. 'I haven't any money. You know that. You're wasting your time if you think you can blackmail me or something.' She smiled bitterly. 'Why do you think I had to get a job working as an escort in the first place?'

'Oh, I'm not interested in your money, my dear,' he said. 'I've got a little proposition to put to you, that's all.'

Cassie got to her feet and glared at him defiantly. 'I don't want to hear your proposition. I'm no whore! Stuff your damned proposition – and your damned job! I'm out of here!' She gathered her tattered dignity about her and walked quickly towards the door.

'Prostitution... grievous bodily harm... blackmail.' Harris gloated over the words, stopping her in her tracks. 'Need I go on?' he asked in amusement. 'I'm sure Mr

Garret could be persuaded to press charges – for a small fee.' She turned to stare at him in horror. He smiled cruelly. 'You were a teacher before coming to us, weren't you? In a position of trust? In charge of young, impressionable minds? And presumably you hope to be a teacher again, once you're over this little bad patch?' The smile vanished as he leaned forward and placed his elbows on the desk. 'How far do you think you would get with a criminal record?'

Feeling numb, Cassie retraced her steps and sat down again. 'I'm *not* a whore,' she repeated, but this time there was no defiance there.

His mocking laugh made her cringe. 'But my dear, we've already established what you *are*. Now we're merely haggling.' His grin was wolfish. 'Now, back to my little proposition.' He pointed to the screen where the video loop had begun again. 'You obviously have a talent for this kind of thing.'

Cassie shuddered as her half-clad alter ego raised a whip, smiling with drunken glee.

'Please, switch it off,' she whispered. He clicked the switch again and the screen flickered into blessed darkness.

'As I was saying,' he went on, 'I merely wish to utilise your natural abilities. *Good Companions* is a perfectly respectable agency.' He paused meaningfully. 'However, we do have one which caters for – how shall I put it? – more *specialised* tastes.' His voice became brisk and businesslike. 'I would like to offer you a position with that. Now, what do you say?' His smile was benign.

'I don't have any choice, do I?' she said dully.

'Good. I'll take that as a yes, shall I?' His smile widened. 'You won't regret it. Your first assignment will be most lucrative. I'm authorised to offer you a flat payment of ten thousand pounds for one month of your time.' He looked up at her astounded face. 'Plus seventy-five per cent of anything else you earn during that period.'

A reluctant smile touched her lips. With money like that, her problems would be over. And after all, how bad could it be? It was only a month and she'd already proved that she could do it. In fact, becoming a dominatrix might be quite fun.

'Done,' she agreed, holding out her hand to shake on the deal.

He looked at her proffered hand in amazement. 'Oh no, my dear. I'm sure you can do much better than that.' He grinned and licked his lips.

'What do you mean?' she asked, puzzled.

'I mean,' he said, getting up from behind his desk and advancing upon her, 'that I expect to sample the merchandise before I give my final approval.'

For a moment she shrank away, realising what he was after. Then she gritted her teeth. For ten thousand pounds she could put up with almost anything.

Harris perched arrogantly on the edge of his desk, arms folded, watching closely as her shaking fingers reached for the buttons on her blouse and began to fumble them open, revealing the lacy bra beneath. It strained to contain her breasts and squeezed her cleavage tight as she shrugged the blouse from her smooth shoulders and then reached back to unfasten the flimsy piece of lingerie. It fell away, and Harris loosened his tie, his calm veneer cracking just a little as her mouth-watering breasts burst free. She dropped the bra to the floor, and then unzipped her skirt. It slithered down her stockinged legs and joined the small pile of warm material, leaving her standing in only her black stockings and knickers. She bent, her generous breasts swinging forward, and the knickers joined the rest of her discarded clothing.

'Leave the stockings on,' he said huskily.

Her hands clenched at her sides, she stood silently under his scrutiny. His eyes ran over her body, taking in the lovely breasts with their soft tips, the swell of her hips, the proud pout of her vulva with its covering of blonde curls.

'Not bad,' he conceded. 'Not bad at all.' He reached forward and pinched each of her nipples in turn, smiling as she gasped and they sprang erect. 'But that's even better.'

He slipped off his expensive jacket and began to undress, too. Cassie's eyes widened in dismay. It was like watching his layer of civilisation being stripped away to reveal the wild animal underneath. Dark, wiry hair covered his chest and shoulders like a pelt, and a thick line of it bisected his stomach, leading her hypnotised eyes downwards to what hung below.

She gasped again. His thick cock lay curled against his thigh, heavy and menacing even in its dormant state. As she looked, it jerked and stirred, slowly engorging in front of her horrified eyes, like some huge and venomous snake getting ready to strike. He saw her reaction and smiled as he reached for her, pulling her towards him. One hand expertly cupped and fondled each breast in turn, while the fingers of the other pushed between the cleft of her buttocks, her attempts to wriggle free forcing her body against his. She could feel the full length of his hardness against her soft belly, and whimpered at the size of him. He would tear her apart if he put that inside her!

But it seemed he didn't intend to. 'On your knees,' he ordered. She tried to pull away, but he was quicker, grabbing her shoulders and jerking her towards him. Despite her feeble struggles, he pushed her inexorably downwards. One fist tangled cruelly in her hair, he forced her face towards his groin. There was a momentary reprieve as he pulled her head backwards and grinned down into her eyes. 'Nice and slowly,' he said, eyes half closed with lust. 'And don't even think about biting.' His other hand gripped his prick and he thrust it forward, rubbing its plum-coloured head against her tightly closed lips.

She gagged as the pressure forced them open and his engorged penis slid into the warm cave of her mouth, virtually choking her. Her tongue pushed against the intruder, sliding over the slick skin. 'Oh, yessss,' he whispered his encouragement. 'That's it.' He withdrew slightly, then pushed inside even further. 'Come on, baby,' he moaned. 'Give it to me.'

Despite herself, Cassie felt the first quivers of excitement as his cock slid in and out between her lips. Her tongue swirled round its tip, and he moaned again. Jerking her head back she broke free, then leaned forward and ran her tongue down the full length of his throbbing shaft to the heavy balls beneath, taking first one and then the other gently into her mouth.

With a groan, he yanked her to her feet and flung her on the desk, his mouth seeking her breasts, sucking and biting, forcing her thighs apart to bury his fingers in the delicious wetness between them. It was her turn to whimper as his thumb teased the swelling bud of her clitoris, sending heat spiralling through her body.

He looked like a satyr as, eyes glinting, he stood up and gazed down on her spread-eagled body, stretched out before him like a sacrifice. Parting her labia with one hand, he inserted the head of his shaft into her vagina and bore down with all his strength. She shrieked with a mixture of pain and pleasure as his phallus sheathed itself in her flesh.

For a moment he paused, and she could feel the whole

heavy weight of him, filling her completely, then he began to move again and all thought was lost in the sensations rushing through her. Her hips writhed, trying to force him even deeper, meeting each thrust with a counterthrust of her own. One flailing arm triggered the switch on the desk and the screen sprang back into life, the scene they repeated, over and over, a mirror image of the one in the office.

On the wall, Cassie straddled a supine body, using it for her own pleasure. On the desk, she was splayed out and fucked unmercifully. The moans and whimpers from the video blended with the real ones until they were indistinguishable from one another. On screen, the camera zoomed in on the image of a rigid prick thrusting into her vagina, at the same time as another did the same in real life. Cassie was lost in sensory madness and as the cock inside her exploded, spurting its copious juices, she screamed, her cry lost amongst all the others.

The switch clicked off and silence fell, apart from their ragged breathing. Cassie stretched lazily, her limbs heavy with satisfaction, and raised an eyebrow at Mr Harris. 'Well?' she asked huskily. 'Did you enjoy your free sample? Do I get the job or not?'

He barely had the strength to nod. He staggered to his chair and collapsed, his penis deflating rapidly. Then he lifted his head and gazed at her in evident admiration. 'You little whore,' he exclaimed softly. 'You enjoyed every minute of that.'

Recovering himself, he dragged on his trousers and sat down again, watching as Cassie slid off the desk and began picking up her clothes and putting them back on. He reached into the drawer, produced a cheque book, wrote quickly, then tore out the cheque and handed it to her. She looked at it.

'I thought you said ten thousand,' she protested. 'This is only for five.'

'Half now and half when the month is over,' he said. 'Together with anything else you make during that time.' He ran a hand through his hair, smoothing it down, beginning the metamorphosis back into the respectable businessman. He cleared his throat. 'A limousine will pick you up tomorrow evening and take you to your destination to begin your assignment.' He smiled at her, the transformation complete. 'I wish you every success,' he said formally.

'Thank you,' she said, smiling back demurely, as if they hadn't just finished screwing each other's brains out on the desk between them. 'I'll do my best.'

He rose and escorted her to the door of the outer office, opening it to let her out. Without a backward glance or another word, she walked past him and left.

With the cheque tucked safely in her handbag, she was astonished to see that only an hour had passed. Good grief. How could her whole life have changed in such a short time? She grinned. She'd pick up the Chinese takeaway, get back to the flat, and Lyn would hardly even notice she'd been gone.

Then her expression became bitter. The money she made with this assignment would take her one step further towards her revenge. She smiled coldly. A dominatrix; what a delicious touch of irony.

Now she would have the whip hand. Quite literally.

Chapter Seven

'You're going to do what?' spluttered Lyn, almost choking on a mouthful of chicken fried rice. 'You must be out of your tiny, cotton-picking mind. Go off God knows where, with God knows whom, to do God knows what?' She glared at her flatmate. 'For all you know you might end up in the back of beyond, chopped up into tiny pieces, and I'll never see you again.'

'Don't be ridiculous,' snapped Cassie. 'Everything's perfectly above board.' She sighed inwardly. She could hardly tell Lyn that she was going off to make a career out of literally whipping strangers into a sexual frenzy, now could she? Her mind raced as she tried to think up a plausible explanation for disappearing for a month. Then she grinned. Got it!

'I'm only going to be a companion,' she lied, crossing her fingers behind her back. 'The client's an elderly gentleman. A widower. All he wants is someone presentable to take to various social functions. What is it the Americans call it? A piece of arm-candy.' She grinned at Lyn. 'He's seventy-eight, for God's sake. What do you think he's going to do? Rape me?' She shook her head. 'Somehow I don't think so.'

Lyn was only slightly mollified, the disapproving expression still on her face. 'Are you sure about this?' she asked anxiously. 'I mean, if you're really skint, *I* could always try and get a bank loan. You could pay me back once you got another job.'

'That's really brilliant of you,' Cassie said softly. 'I do

appreciate it.' She shook her head again. 'But there's no point in both of us ending up in debt, not when I can sort everything out myself. And what's a month? It'll go past in no time. In fact, I'll be back before you've even noticed I've gone.'

She grabbed the bottle of champagne she'd bought on the way home, and waved it enticingly under Lyn's nose. 'Now stop worrying. Have another top-up and we'll drink to my new career.' She giggled as she filled Lyn's glass, slopping the fizzy champagne over the rim, then refilled her own. She raised it in a toast. 'Here's to the good ship *Cassie*. God bless her and all who sail in her.' She knocked it back and grinned. She was on her way – and if she had to smack a few bottoms to get what she wanted, then who cared? More power to her elbow.

Next morning she was up bright and early, despite a lingering headache. There was a lot to do before she left.

'I'm off down the bank again,' she called, sticking her head around Lyn's bedroom door and addressing the bump under the duvet. 'Anything you want while I'm out?' There was a muffled groan from beneath the bedclothes. 'I'll take that as a no,' she said breezily. 'See you later then.'

Closing the door quietly behind her, she tiptoed out of the flat.

Once the cheque had been safely deposited and she'd got over the shock of the bank manager actually smiling at her for a change, she set off for the shops. Two hours later she'd acquired an expensive suitcase, a selection of luxurious underwear from one of the most exclusive shops in town, and a pair of Italian leather trousers.

Her next stop was in a less salubrious area. Litter blew about her feet as she walked down the dead-end street and she began to question the wisdom of carrying expensive-looking shopping bags into such a deserted area. When she reached her destination her eyes widened, as she stared in disbelief at the display in the sex shop. There were two dummies in the window. One wore a skimpy outfit, consisting of crotchless, blood-red nylon knickers and a matching peephole bra. The other had on a black leather basque, with thin leather strips leading from the top to a studded collar around the neck. A whip hung from the lifeless hand and an array of luridly coloured vibrators were arranged in a semi-circle at its feet. Cassie shivered. How tacky could you get?

She peered in through the door. Against the far wall drooped a semi-deflated sex doll, its arms and legs spread, its mouth a gaping, scarlet hole. There was a puff of nylon pubic hair glued to the V of its plastic crotch. Cassie stared at it. Who in their right mind would buy something like that? An unwelcome picture of some sad bastard humping sweatily at it sprang into her mind, and she dismissed it with a shudder. Whoever said, *'Of all sexual perversions, chastity is the strangest'* had never seen this thing!

'Can I help you, darlin'?' came a voice, making her jumped. The assistant, a pimply youth with a feeble attempt at a moustache, was lounging at the door, smirking at her. He took a half-smoked cigarette out of his mouth and grinned at her, revealing rotting, nicotine-stained teeth. She shuddered inwardly.

'Er... no, thanks,' she stammered. 'I was just passing.' She turned and fled hurriedly, horribly aware of him staring after her.

'Bleedin' tourists,' he muttered, taking a final drag of his fag before dropping it and stubbing it out underfoot, before turning back into the shop.

It was five minutes before Cassie slowed down. There was no way she was going into a place like that. It was disgusting. If they wanted her to dress up, then they'd have to provide the gear. She wasn't going anywhere near any more sex shops. Maybe it would be like being a waitress; uniform provided. The feeble joke failed miserably to cheer her up. She shivered again. Perhaps this wasn't such a good idea after all. What difference was there between her and that doll dangling on the wall? None at all. Someone bought you and you got fucked. That was what it boiled down to.

She shook herself. This was ridiculous. There was a big difference. She was the one in charge. She'd be the one dishing out the treatment, not the one on the receiving end. She smiled. Anyway, going by a programme she'd seen on television the other night, she probably wouldn't even have to sleep with them. A dominatrix did exactly what she pleased.

Her smile vanished. Anyway, there wasn't any point in having second thoughts. She'd already taken the money and by the time her overdraft cleared, there wouldn't be much left. She needed that other five thousand. And there was one other little detail. She had the sneaking suspicion that Mr Harris would not take too kindly to a last minute change of heart. If he had the connections to bribe a chambermaid to take videos in one of the most expensive hotels in London, what other connections did he have? Lyn's remark about disappearing permanently didn't seem quite so unlikely in the clear light of day.

She felt suddenly cold, despite the bright sunlight. No, she'd just have to go through with it, no matter what. She felt a sudden longing for Lyn's sensible conversation and the safety of their comfortable flat. Shifting her bags to one hand, she raised the other and hailed a taxi.

'Thank goodness you're back,' said Lyn, as soon as Cassie walked in. 'That Mr Harris has been on the phone three times while you were out. The last time he rang he sounded a bit narked. You'd better call back right now.'

Her stomach lurched. What now? Cassie picked up the phone and dialled the number with shaking fingers.

'*Good Companions*,' said the genteel voice at the other end of the line. 'How may I help you?'

'Er... it's Cassie Grey,' she said nervously. 'Mr Harris has been trying to contact me. I'm returning his call.'

'Certainly, Miss Grey,' said the voice. 'I'm afraid he's speaking to a client at the moment. Would you care to hold?' Before she could answer there was a click, and an electronic version of Vivaldi's *Four Seasons* began to play shrilly in her ear.

She had almost reached screaming point when it blessedly clicked off again and a familiar voice spoke.

'Cassie,' he said heartily, 'good of you to call back. I'm afraid there's been a slight change of plan. The limousine will be round to pick you up this afternoon, instead of this evening. Probably around three. I hope you can be ready by then.'

'But I've still got things to do—'

His voice changed, cutting her off. 'I said, be ready,' he repeated coldly. 'I do hope there's not going to be any problem. I'd hate to think I'd have to... exert any undue pressure.'

'No problem,' said Cassie weakly. 'I'll be waiting.' The line went dead and she stared at the receiver in dismay, a sinking feeling in her stomach. What the hell had she let herself in for?

Even packing her new suitcase with her expensive new underwear didn't lift her depression. Folding the silky garments and laying them carefully on the top of her case, she couldn't help thinking about the circumstances under which she'd be wearing them. What would her 'clients' be like? What if they were old? Or fat? Or ugly? Even worse, what if it was someone like Miss Carr? Could she force herself to do *that* again? Her mouth flooded with the memory of the taste of another woman's juices, and she felt physically sick.

'Lunch is ready,' called Lyn. 'You'd better eat something before you go. You don't know what time you're going to arrive.' She sniffed in disapproval. 'Wherever it is you're going.'

Cassie closed the case, clicked the lock and went through to the kitchen. 'I'm not hungry,' she protested, staring at the plateful of chicken salad Lyn plonked in front of her. 'I couldn't eat a thing.'

'Force yourself,' ordered Lyn.

Reluctantly, Cassie picked up her fork and poked at the food. She put it down again and glanced anxiously at Lyn. 'What time is it, anyway? I don't want to keep them waiting.'

'Oh, for God's sake,' moaned Lyn. 'It's only half-past one. They won't be here for another hour and a half. Now eat your lunch and stop worrying. You've got plenty of time.' She took a forkful and stuffed it in her own mouth to demonstrate.

Cassie picked up her fork again and slowly began to follow her example.

'Hang on,' grinned Lyn, leaping to her feet. 'I've got the very thing.' She disappeared into the living room and returned, triumphantly waving the bottle of cheap brandy she'd brought back from her last holiday. It gurgled enticingly. 'Just enough left for a glass each,' she announced, checking the remaining few inches. 'Good job it was stuck at the back of the cupboard or it would've evaporated by this time.' Rummaging in the sink, she dug out their glasses from the night before, ran them under the tap, then filled them with the coarse spirit. 'There you go,' she said, handing one to Cassie. 'A bit of Dutch courage to keep your pecker up. Cheers.'

'We'll turn into a pair of raddled old alcoholics, if we're not careful,' grumbled Cassie. 'I've had two hangovers in as many days.' And perhaps 'keep your pecker up' wasn't the most comforting choice of words under the circumstances. She giggled nervously. Still, at least she hadn't said 'bottoms up'!

Cassie accepted the glass and took a sip. The fiery liquid burnt a warm trail all the way down to her stomach and she felt instantly more cheerful. 'Thanks,' she said. 'Maybe I could eat something, after all.'

The food seemed to settle her stomach. After washing the dishes she took the remains of her brandy into the bedroom and began to get ready, while Lyn sprawled on the bed and chatted to her.

'You look great,' she said enviously, as Cassie twirled in front of the mirror in a blue silk shirt and her new leather trousers. 'You'll knock their eyes out. Come on, sit at the dressing table and I'll do your hair for you.' Picking up the brush, she began to run it through Cassie's long blonde curls, tugging at the tangles.

'Ouch,' muttered Cassie. 'Watch what you're doing. It's hardly going to improve my appearance if I end up bald.'

'Shut up and stop complaining,' Lyn chuckled. 'By the time I've finished you'll look gorgeous.' She tied back the heavy mass of curls with a black velvet ribbon at the nape of Cassie's neck and stood back to admire her handiwork. 'There. Very classy. What do you think?'

Cassie turned her head from side to side, checking her

reflection. Small tendrils sprang loose, framing her face. 'Not bad,' she agreed. She pouted into the mirror. Her eye-shadow matched her shirt, making her eyes look bigger and darker, while the soft rose lipstick made her lips moist and inviting. 'I'll pass.' She reached across, picked up her deodorant, raised her shirt and sprayed on another liberal application. It would be a shame to spoil the effect by sweating like a pig through sheer nerves.

Finally she got up and pulled her dark velvet jacket out of the wardrobe and slipped it on, flicking her curls out from beneath the collar. 'All set,' she announced.

'Just in time, too,' said Lyn, peering out from behind the curtain into the street. 'That looks like your car now.'

Cassie hurried over to join her, staring down to where a sleek black limousine was parking outside the flat. She felt a wave of apprehension wash through her. It reminded her unpleasantly of a hearse drawing up. The windows were tinted, making it look as if there was no one driving. As it sat at the kerb with its engine running, Cassie was reminded of an image from a horror film she'd once seen about a car that was possessed by the devil. The demonic vehicle had sat at the kerb, patiently waiting for its next victim. She dismissed the thought hurriedly.

'Well, better go,' she said, with forced cheerfulness. 'Don't want to keep the man waiting.' She flung her arms round Lyn and hugged her. 'Thanks for everything.' She stepped back and smiled into her friend's worried face. 'And don't look so woebegone. It won't be long till I'm back.' She smiled, with more reassurance than she really felt. 'Be good – and if you can't be good...'

'...Be careful,' finished Lyn. She looked at Cassie, suddenly serious. 'You be careful,' she said. 'If you don't like the job, just up sticks and come home. Remember what I said about my getting a bank loan. If the worst comes to the worst, we'll work something out.'

'I'll be fine,' said Cassie. 'Don't worry.' She grabbed her case. 'I'll see you in a month. Take care of yourself.' With a final wave over her shoulder, she hurried out of the flat and clattered down the stairs to the waiting car.

As she came out, the driver's door opened and the chauffeur got out. Cassie's eyes travelled up – and up – his body in amazement. He must have been six foot five at least. The grey jacket of his uniform strained tightly over massive shoulders, and thick black hair curled on the strong wrists that jutted from beneath the cuffs of his immaculate white shirt. Equally black hair grew low on his forehead, overhanging deep-set brown eyes, and his thighs bulged under the thin material of his grey trousers. He looked positively Neanderthal; as if he should be dressed in wolf skins, carrying a club and beating off sabre-toothed tigers, instead of wearing a neat uniform and driving an expensive limousine.

'Miss Grey?' he enquired in a cultured voice that belied his appearance. Cassie nodded. 'My name's Parker.' Cassie suppressed a nervous giggle. Wasn't that the name of Lady Penelope's chauffeur in that puppet programme? His eyes twinkled as if he'd read her thoughts, and she relaxed slightly. 'May I take your luggage?' he asked politely.

She handed over her case and watched as he placed it carefully in the boot, then came back and held open the back door for her.

'Thank you,' she smiled, climbing in. The door clicked closed behind her and she sank into the comfort of the soft leather seat. As they drove away she saw Lyn's pale face as she waved down from the bedroom window.

Cassie took a deep breath. For better or for worse, she was on her way.

Chapter Eight

As the sleek car purred its way out of town and into the suburbs, Cassie took in her present surroundings. It was the first time she'd been in a limousine, and she was very impressed. She stroked the smooth upholstery and smiled. It was even softer than the Italian hide of her trousers, and the whole car had that indefinable scent of sheer luxury. The smell of new leather mingled with the scent of polish. Ghosts of exclusive perfume lingered in the air, mixed with traces of expensive cigars and the faint aroma of Napoleon brandy. And something else. Surreptitiously she sniffed the air. What was it?

Then it came to her, and she gasped in recognition. Underlying everything was the animal scent of sex. The inside of the limousine smelled the way she imagined an expensive bordello would – all the perfumes of the world failing to mask the rank corruption underneath. The hand that was absent-mindedly stroking the soft leather recoiled. God alone knew what had gone on in this back seat!

Her whirling thoughts were interrupted by a disembodied voice and she jumped, her eyes seeking its source. 'Would madam care for a drink?' it enquired again, and she saw that it came from a small speaker, set beneath the glass that separated the driver from his passengers.

'Um... yes, thank you,' she replied. 'That would be lovely.' The little bit of Dutch courage provided by Lyn before she left had worn off. She could certainly do with another dose or two.

'If madam would look at the panel in front of her,' went

on the driver, 'she will find the cocktail cabinet.' Cassie gasped. Cocktail cabinet? Good grief – this car was better equipped than her flat! She searched the panel until she found a small button. She pressed it and gasped again as a concealed section of the panel unfolded silently to form a small table. In the hidden section sat a selection of crystal glasses and an array of bottles. Her eyes widened as she read the labels of famously expensive drinks. Talk about how the other half lived. She and Lyn were grateful when they could afford a bottle of supermarket generic!

Shakily, she poured herself a stiff vodka, added one of the selection of mixers and took a healthy swig. She sighed with relief as the alcohol effectively drowned the butterflies fluttering around in her stomach. Relaxing into the opulent leather, she gazed out of the window at the passing scenery.

The suburbs had long since given way to countryside. As the car purred smoothly along, effortlessly eating up the road, Cassie could see nothing but fields and trees stretching away for miles into the distance. Occasionally they slowed to pass through a picture postcard village, with thatched cottages and gardens rampant with flowers – but even these became fewer and farther between. The landscape became bleaker and her nervousness returned. What the hell was she letting herself in for? She didn't even know where she was going. She took another mouthful of vodka.

'Er... is it much further?' she ventured.

The driver's head turned partially, and for a moment the deep-set eyes met hers in the rear-view mirror. 'Not long now,' he assured her, and for some reason the simple words sounded ominous. She shivered. Lifting the glass to her mouth, she discovered that the contents had mysteriously disappeared. She poured herself another.

The light was beginning to die from the sky when they finally turned off the main road. The car slowed as it began to bump along what seemed to Cassie to be nothing more than a glorified cart track, and it dawned on her that she hadn't seen a single house for at least the last half-hour. Stunted trees, blown into twisted shapes by the wind, lined the sides of the track. She nibbled her lip anxiously. All it needed now was a pallid shape flitting silently through the undergrowth and you had the perfect set-up for a spine-chilling ghost story.

As they turned the last bend in the track she saw the house. A wave of sheer terror ran through her. It stood, its gothic turrets silhouetted against the rising moon, like a caricature of every haunted mansion in every horror film she'd ever seen. No way was she going in there!

'Stop the car!' she ordered. 'I've changed my mind. I'm getting out.' The limousine continued inexorably towards the house.

'I don't think so,' said the driver, his disembodied voice issuing from the tiny speaker. He turned to grin at her, and the fading light caught his face at an odd angle. For one horrific moment Cassie could see the bony skull leering satanically at her from beneath the flesh. She cringed back against the soft leather, then fumbled for the door handle and pulled. She pulled hard.

But nothing happened. She tugged again and again, her hands slipping with nervous sweat against the smooth metal. Nothing.

The driver's grin widened. 'Childproof locks,' he explained. 'Don't want you falling out and hurting yourself, now do we?' There was a crunch of gravel as he drew up in front of the house and pulled to a stop.

She cowered down into the corner, gripping the door handle so hard her knuckles turned white. As he opened the door and reached in to pull her out, she lashed out, fingers hooked into claws. Her sharp nails raked the back of his hand and she felt the skin split beneath them.

He swore under his breath and glared at her as he sucked his bleeding hand. 'You're going to regret that... madam,' he said softly. Undaunted, he reached in again.

It was useless. Despite her struggles, he lifted her out as easily as if she was a kitten. One massive hand circled the top of her arm and she kicked uselessly against the gravel as he practically carried her into the house and deposited her on her feet again.

Angrily shaking herself free, she looked around. Her eyes widened. She was standing in an enormous, marble-floored hall, so huge that it dwarfed even the heavy oak furniture that stood round the walls. A tapestry hung from one wall and she quickly averted her eyes from the scene of writhing half-human, half-animal bodies it depicted in salacious detail.

A portrait of a woman hung from another. The smooth, innocent features were belied by the knowing smile on the lips and the look of cruelty in the cold painted eyes that stared down at Cassie. She gasped as she realised that the pale hands held not a scroll, as she'd first supposed, but an ornately carved ivory dildo, the thumb idly caressing its bulbous tip.

High heels tapped across the marble floor and Cassie turned. The approaching woman ignored her completely. 'Thank you, Parker,' she said, nodding to the chauffeur. 'That will be all for the moment. You may go.' He inclined his head briefly in acknowledgement, turned on his heel and went out through a door in the wall beneath the tapestry. Cassie gulped as the last contact with her previous life – no matter how unpleasant – disappeared.

She turned back to discover that the woman's attention

was now focused on her. Small, piggy eyes, set in a dough-coloured face, ran in a calculating fashion over Cassie's body, lingering on her slim legs and the way her blue silk shirt strained over her full breasts, and Cassie decided she'd preferred it when she was being ignored. Finally, as if Cassie had passed some kind of examination, the woman gave a satisfied nod and smiled coldly at her.

'If you will come this way, Miss Grey,' she said, 'the committee will see you now.'

Cassie hung back. What was the woman talking about? What committee? She fumbled for some kind of excuse to stay exactly where she was – and finally found one. 'Wh-what about my case?' she blurted. 'It's still in the boot of the car and all my clothes are in it.' She straightened her back and attempted to look haughty. 'I can't possibly meet the committee looking like this. Please show me to my room, have my luggage brought up and I'll meet them after I've showered and changed my clothes.'

The woman's harsh laughter startled Cassie. 'Oh, my dear,' she chuckled. 'I really don't think you'll find that necessary. Clothes are the least of your worries.' Her face hardened. 'Now, are you going to do as you're told and come with me, or do I have to call Parker back and have him carry you?'

The thought of being manhandled by that revolting Neanderthal was quite enough to reduce Cassie to instant obedience. Holding on to the tattered remnants of her courage, she followed the woman meekly across the marble floor and up the huge winding staircase, her eyes focused on her back. The well-cut suit couldn't disguise the bony hips beneath, swaying in a parody of sexiness as the woman climbed the steps. Cassie might have been amused by the contrast between the dark stockings and the shiny high-heeled shoes and the sexlessness of the creature wearing them – if she hadn't been quite so scared.

The upper hall seemed endless. As they passed open doors, Cassie risked a peep in, at rooms of unimaginable luxury; four-poster beds, hand-painted wallpaper, antique furniture. The place reeked of money, and of the decadence of another age, when wealth could buy anything. Apparently it still could, thought Cassie bitterly.

At last they reached a large mahogany double door. The woman stopped, knocked, and waited respectfully for an answer. There was a muffled 'Come,' and she opened it, ushered Cassie in, then stepped back and stood with her hands clasped neatly in front of her.

Cassie looked around. In contrast to the bedrooms, this could have been the boardroom of any successful modern company. Utilitarian grey carpet covered the floor. Two computers stood in one corner, screen-savers flickering. A row of filing cabinets stretched the length of one wall. Cassie was unpleasantly reminded of Mr Harris' office, and was relieved to see there were no video screens.

But what drew her eyes was the long boardroom table that sat squarely in the middle of the room. Behind it, staring at her, five men were seated, pens and folders neatly placed in front of them. She suppressed a nervous giggle at the incongruity of the situation. What were they going to do? Test her shorthand?

She found out soon enough.

'Take your clothes off, Miss Grey,' ordered the man seated at the centre of the table. 'We haven't got all night.'

She gawped at him in astonishment. 'Certainly not,' she snapped.

He looked at her and sighed, as if his request and her disobedience were simply a typical but minor problem in his busy working day. He waved an imperious hand at the woman standing against the wall. 'Help Miss Grey disrobe,' he suggested. 'She seems to be having some difficulty.'

The woman stepped forward eagerly. Cassie took one look at her avid face and shivered at the thought of those bony fingers fumbling at her body. Despite being confused and reluctant, she slowly began to comply with the audacious demand. As slowly as possible, she slipped her jacket from her shoulders, dropped it to the floor, and started to unbutton her shirt.

Once she was naked, her hands went automatically to cover her breasts and pubic mound. But the woman wrenched them roughly away.

Hands clenched at her sides, she stood exposed in front of them, flushed with humiliation. She closed her eyes. What now? Were they going to hold her down on the table and take her, one after the other, while that bitch stood in the corner and gloated?

Nothing happened, and so she cautiously opened her eyes. Instead of circling her like marauding wolves, as she'd imagined they would, they were still seated exactly where they had been, regarding her with a mixture of calculation and indifference. Their dispassionate eyes took her in as though she was a marble statue, or a piece of fine bloodstock they were considering buying. One was even scribbling on his notepad. Cassie felt subtly insulted by their lack of reaction.

Eventually the man in the middle spoke again. 'Excellent,' he said. There were nods of agreement. 'We'll put her in as lot twenty-one. She should bring in a good price.' He put his pen down, leaned back, and smiled at the woman. 'That's fine. You can take her away now.'

Cassie shook the woman's hand off her arm and stared from one dissipated face to the other, forgetting her nudity.

'What the hell do you mean, lot twenty-one?' she demanded.

'Lot twenty-one,' he repeated slowly, as if she was mentally deficient. 'In the slave auction.'

'But, I'm not a slave,' she protested, aghast. She drew herself up, glared at them and attempted to sound authoritative. 'I'm a dominatrix,' she stated, without conviction, and without really understanding what she was saying. 'People obey *my* orders. Or face the consequences.'

Their laughter punctured her defiance. The man in the centre shook his head. 'I'm afraid you're mistaken, my dear,' he chuckled. 'Slaves take orders, they don't give them.' His laughter drained away as quickly as water down a plug hole, and his face became ugly. 'And I suggest you start right now, by doing what you're told, without question.'

'I won't,' snarled Cassie. 'I'm leaving.' She grabbed her clothes and held them in front of her. 'I'm putting these on and getting out of here.' She glared around the circle of amused faces. 'And don't try to stop me.'

'Oh dear,' sighed the man. 'Some girls never learn, do they? It looks as if we'll have to take drastic measures.' Smiling insincerely, he leaned forward and pressed a small button on the desk.

The door swung open and Parker stood there, almost filling the doorway. A small whimper escaped Cassie's throat.

'Miss Grey seems a little reluctant to conform to our wishes,' smiled the man. 'Take her to her quarters please, Parker.'

For a moment she stood, frozen to the spot, then she fled to a corner and stood, back against the wall, prepared to defend herself.

But it was useless. A grinning Parker simply knocked her arms aside, scattering her clothes, before he swept her, naked and helpless, over his shoulder, the coarse material of his jacket scraping against the tender flesh of her nipples. Kicking and screaming, she was carried out, her humiliation completed by the laughter that followed her undignified exit. The last thing she saw as the door closed behind her was the gloating expression on that horrible woman's face.

'Put me down,' she wailed, as Parker strode along the corridors. Her hands beat a futile tattoo against his back.

'Stop that damned squalling,' he growled. 'Nobody's going to hear you.'

She screamed again, then gasped in shock as his massive hand smacked against her backside. Her buttocks quivered and reddened as he slapped her again and her screams died away to whimpering sobs.

Finally, he stopped in front of a shabby, white-painted door, fumbled for a key and pushed it open. Striding across the small room, he dumped her unceremoniously on a narrow iron cot. She glared up at him from tear-blurred eyes, her breasts heaving.

'There,' he leered. 'Madam's boudoir. I trust you'll be comfortable. Don't hesitate to complain if you're not satisfied by the service.' With a grin he left the room and Cassie heard the key turn in the lock.

Arms clasped round her shivering body, she looked around. A wire-covered bulb cast a harsh light on her surroundings. The room was small, and windowless. Her hopes of escape quickly disintegrated. Apart from the cot, there was no other furniture, and the carpet was stained and worn. Behind a screen in one corner there was a toilet and a small washbasin. She breathed a sigh of thankfulness and padded across to relieve herself, then stood for ten minutes, washing her aching body in a vain attempt to remove the hateful touch of Parker's fingers. Finally, she crawled under the thin covers and sobbed herself to sleep.

When she woke she had no idea where she was. It was pitch black and her hand automatically reached for her bedside light. But, of course, it wasn't there. Eyes straining to pierce the darkness, she cowered as the memories of the day trickled back into her consciousness.

Then she froze. Something had woken her. What was it? She listened, barely daring to breathe. Nothing. She began to relax, then stiffened as she heard it again. Low voices and the sound of quiet footsteps. She cringed against the iron bedstead as the key turned and the door swung slowly open.

A light shone in her eyes and she was blinded. The door closed again and the darkness settled on her like black velvet. She held her breath and heard heavy breathing and the sound of muffled amusement.

She screamed as a hand slid under the cover and seized her ankle. Another hand covered her mouth, muffling her cries as she was dragged from the cot and pulled to the floor. Her arms were hauled above her head and pinioned to one leg of the cot, as her other ankle was seized and her legs were pried apart.

She moaned as an obscene tongue began to trace a wet path up her inner thigh. Someone was going to fuck her and she couldn't even see who it was – didn't even know if her attackers were men or women. She shivered uncontrollably as the tongue spiralled higher, leaving a snail-trail of coldness behind it.

Hands found her breasts and began to fondle them. She whimpered as her nipples were pinched viciously until they stood erect, then another mouth descended upon them, sucking greedily at first one and then the other, tongue rasping across their engorged tips till she thought they were going to explode. She moaned again, this time with reluctant pleasure.

She twisted her hips, trying to avoid the other invading tongue as it advanced towards her vulnerable centre, but all that did was bring her closer in contact with the seeking mouth. Hands clawed her buttocks, raising them and pulling the soft lips of her vulva wide apart. She whimpered as her swelling clitoris was licked and teased and she felt herself falling into a maelstrom of sensation. Her hips writhed again, but now she was no longer trying to escape but to push her eager cunt closer to the source of the maddening pleasure.

A hand joined the tormenting tongue and for a moment she winced as persistent fingers slid roughly into her, then her inner walls closed wetly round them and she gave herself up to the delicious surge of feeling as they pushed in and out.

There was a series of muffled groans and she could feel them changing positions. The tongue and fingers withdrew and her legs were pulled up as heavy thighs forced themselves between hers, pushing them even further apart. Something hot and hard nudged against the soft wet entrance of her body, then she shrieked as it thrust home, almost splitting her apart.

She was silenced as a thick wet tongue, tasting of her own juices, forced itself greedily between her lips and the hands on her breasts renewed their attack. She moaned into the mouth clamped on hers. Every inch of her flesh was being touched and stimulated. It was unbearable. Was that a man's chest pressing against her or another woman's breasts? With mounting shame, she knew she no longer cared who was the source of this exquisite mixture of pain and pleasure – only that it continued.

The huge prick continued its pounding, filling her with its weight and heat. Her hips rose and fell, matching every move until she thought she would go mad with sensory overload. Then there was one final, massive thrust and she could feel her assailant erupting inside her as she exploded too.

She collapsed, panting, against the worn carpet as her visitors withdrew, untied her aching wrists and left as silently as they had come, the door closing behind them.

When her breath had finally reverted to normal, she heaved herself to her feet and staggered towards the basin, to sponge her ravaged flesh with cold water. She thanked God there was no mirror. Even in the darkness her cheeks would have been luminous with remorse. How could she? She didn't even know who she'd fucked. What kind of person could revel in such shameless animal enjoyment? Shuddering, she crawled back under the covers.

She had no idea what time it was when she woke again. The light was on and a covered tray sat on the floor near the door. She seized it eagerly, eating and drinking ravenously despite the fact that the coffee had a skin on it and the food was cold and congealed to the plate. The meal she'd shared with Lyn before she left seemed to have been days ago. Eventually satisfied, she washed herself again and sat on the edge of the bed to wait.

Hours passed and she was hungry again, before the door finally opened. She looked up apprehensively. The woman was standing there, with Parker looming behind her. Cassie blushed; had it been them during the night? She searched their faces for clues, but they merely stared back impassively.

'It is time,' said the woman. 'Will you do as you're told this time, or do I have to get Parker to help you again?'

Cassie shuddered as she remembered the humiliating way she'd been carried along the corridors like a sack of coal. Whatever she had to face, she'd face it on her own two feet with what was left of her dignity. 'I'll do as I'm told,' she conceded humbly.

'Good,' said the woman, with a smile of satisfaction. 'Put this on.' She flung a black velvet blindfold at Cassie, who obediently tied it over her blonde curls, wincing as she caught strands of hair in the knot. Deprived of vision, she was tugged to her feet and pulled unceremoniously from the room and along the corridors.

She shivered as the air became chilly against her naked body. The carpet beneath her bare feet gave way to wood, then finally to rough stone and twice, when she stumbled against the walls, she felt cold dampness against her skin. Where were they taking her now? It felt as if they were descending into the bowels of the earth.

Eventually they stopped, and Cassie heard the creaking of rusty hinges. 'Prepare her,' snapped the woman's harsh voice – and she was thrust roughly into the unknown.

Chapter Nine

'Aaaah!' Cassie jumped as a smart slap on her buttocks brought her sharply back to the present. She groaned inwardly. Her memories hadn't been enjoyable, but they were marginally less unpleasant than the situation she was in now. The audience tittered as she brought her hands up automatically, trying to cover herself – and was stopped with a jerk by the manacles round her wrists. The auctioneer tugged at the collar round her neck as if she was a disobedient bitch.

He grinned at the sea of leering faces. 'Any advance on eight thousand pounds, ladies and gentlemen? No? Very well. Going once... Going twice... Sold!' He pointed into a shadowy alcove. 'To the gentleman in the corner.'

Cassie peered frantically across the smoky room, trying to make out the features of whoever had been prepared to pay such a huge amount of money for her, but she could see nothing more than a dark, hunched shape.

The auctioneer winked and slid his hand under Cassie's skimpy costume, flicking up the hem. 'Would sir like her delivered?' His eyebrows rose suggestively. 'Or would he care to unwrap her now?'

Cassie cringed as she remembered the poor girl before her, sobbing in pain and humiliation as her new purchaser manhandled her publicly for the amusement of himself and his friends. Was that going to be her fate as well?

She sighed with relief as a pale hand emerged from the shadows and waved dismissively, before withdrawing into the smoky gloom again. A fleeting look of disappointment crossed the auctioneer's face as he snapped his fingers and her escort stepped forward and flanked her again. Thwarted, he contented himself with one final, stinging slap, jiggling the smooth globes of her behind and bringing another titter from the audience, as Heinz and Peter turned to lead her through the red velvet curtains behind the stage.

It was blessedly cool and quiet away from the crowded room, but Cassie didn't have time to appreciate it as the two men hurried her along wordlessly. Her bare feet slapped against the cold floor of the corridors as she tried to keep up with them. At last they reached another door, opened it, pushed her inside and locked it firmly behind her.

The room she found herself in now was very different from the cold narrow cell where she'd spent the previous night. Thick carpet covered the floor and a midnight-blue chaise longue, covered in heart-shaped cushions in lurid shades of pink satin, stood against one wall. The opposite wall consisted almost entirely of a huge mirror, and the ceiling above the king-sized bed was mirrored, too, reflecting the rumpled black satin sheets below. Money obviously couldn't buy good taste, Cassie thought. The whole room was like the set of a cheap blue movie.

Investigating further, she padded across the room and slid out the top drawer of the small cabinet beside the bed – then wished that she hadn't. She gazed in horror at the contents. Two small whips lay, coiled neatly, beside a massive black dildo, a selection of ribbed condoms and a tube of lubricant. She closed it again quickly then shivered as she noticed the leather cuffs dangling from the posts of the bed. This was no fantasy. This was the real thing!

She would have liked to dive underneath the covers, close her eyes and pretend none of this was happening, but there was no way she was getting between those black satin sheets. Instead, she tiptoed back across the room and curled herself into the corner of the chaise longue, clutching one of the heart-shaped pillows against her for comfort.

Then she froze. What was that? Holding her breath, she strained to hear more clearly.

From the room next door came the smack of leather on skin, followed by the noise of flesh slapping against flesh. Faint whimpers were almost drowned out by animal grunting and the rapid squeaking of bedsprings. Sickened, Cassie covered her ears, trying vainly to drown out the sounds of lust and abuse that seemed to go on forever. Finally, there was a long groan of male satisfaction. Five minutes later a door opened, closed again, and silence fell, broken only by soft sobbing.

She tapped against the wall and the sobbing stopped for a moment, then continued, worse than before. Cassie groaned as her attempts to communicate were frustrated. If only there was someone to talk to, perhaps she wouldn't feel so afraid. Then she heard footsteps outside the door and the idea of company didn't seem quite so appealing. She cringed back into her corner, clutching the cushion even tighter, a shield, no matter how useless, against what might be coming next.

She peered fearfully at the door as it creaked open. As her brain processed the information her eyes were taking in, she thought the small shackled body that shuffled in belonged to a child. But the truth quickly dawned on her. Despite the lack of height, she was looking at a full-grown man. She gasped. If she stood up, he'd be lucky if he came up to her ribcage. Then she caught his eye and blushed at her own rudeness, realising she was staring.

'Sorry,' she muttered, as the door closed again.

'No problem,' he said. 'It gets a lot of people like that.

Doesn't bother me any more.' He walked across the room and hopped up on the chaise longue beside her, settling down companionably. 'Just don't call me a PORG, though,' he muttered. 'It gets right up my nose.'

Cassie looked at him, puzzled. 'PORG?' she asked. 'What's a PORG?'

'"Person of restricted growth",' he snorted derisively. 'God! I can't stand all that politically correct crap. I'm not ashamed of what I am. Call me a dwarf and have done with it, that's what I say.' He stuck out a hand. 'Tom,' he introduced himself. 'Tom Patterson.' He winked. 'Or "Tom Thumb" if you prefer my stage name.'

Cassie relaxed, grinned back and shook the proffered hand. 'Cassie Grey,' she said, aware of the irony of polite introductions under the circumstances, but unable to think of anything else appropriate to say. 'Nice to meet you.'

Now that she was over the initial shock, she could take him in properly, and was amazed to find that he was actually rather good-looking, with blue eyes and black curly hair. The skimpy Roman kilt he wore showed off strong shoulders and a smooth, broad chest. In fact, if it hadn't been for the stunted legs, dangling six inches above the floor, he'd have been a thoroughly attractive man.

'Short, dark and handsome,' he said, the blue eyes shrewd, and Cassie flushed guiltily again. He leaned back and crossed his legs. The short kilt rode up his thighs and Cassie gasped again, this time in horrified awe. Like herself, he wore nothing underneath his costume and, despite his size, there was nothing stunted about the manhood he'd inadvertently revealed. His genitals hung like heavy fruit between his thighs, his penis enormous, even flaccid. Her flush deepened. My God! she thought. If it was like that now, what the hell would it be like if he was aroused?

His eyes followed her fascinated gaze and he grinned and flipped the short kilt down to cover himself. 'Compensation,' he explained, with a cheerful wink. 'I may be deficient in the leg department, but the Good Lord made up for it in other areas.' His face became more serious. 'Anyway, at the risk of sounding trite, what's a nice girl like you doing in a place like this?'

'Trying to make some money,' Cassie replied with a sigh, carefully omitting the debts, the blackmail threat and exactly what it was she wanted the money for. She smiled ruefully. He might not think she was quite such a 'nice girl' if he knew she intended to use it to get revenge on her former colleagues. 'What about you?'

'Ditto,' he said. 'I'm afraid I'm a bit too fond of playing the ponies – and lately I've done nothing but back glue factory rejects.' It was his turn to look rueful. 'The gentlemen I owe money to are getting rather insistent on having it paid back. Most inconsiderate of them.' He rubbed his legs and grinned again. 'These might not look much to you, but I'd still like them in one piece. And the job opportunities aren't what they were. Do you know,' he added indignantly, 'that I went for a role in *Snow White And The Seven Dwarfs* last Christmas, only to be told they were only employing *four* dwarfs? Bloody ridiculous,' he grumbled. 'I ended up doing the unexpurgated version for the blue movie business. Then the guy who organised that offered me good money for this job – so here I am.' He shrugged philosophically. 'No matter how bad it gets, it still beats hell out of having your legs broken by a couple of skinheads with baseball bats.'

They were so engrossed in their conversation that when the door opened again they both jumped. Cassie looked up apprehensively, wondering what was about to happen, then relaxed as another girl was thrust into the room. She stumbled, righted herself and stood glaring at the closing door, hands on broad hips.

'You boys better learn how to treat a lady right,' she yelled angrily, in a thick African accent. 'Or Tanisha voodoo you! She voodoo you good!'

Cassie gazed at the newcomer in fascination. She was almost six feet tall, heavily built, and her skin was so black it seemed to gleam with a blue sheen. Like Cassie, she wore a brief white toga, cut to reveal one breast. And what a breast! It swung like a watermelon, the dark, jutting nipple almost half the length of Cassie's thumb. Because of her height, her skirt was even shorter than Cassie's and Cassie could see that the nest of pubic hair was an almost perfect match for the tight black curls on Tanisha's head. She was magnificent. A glorious African queen, ready for battle!

Tanisha turned from the door, still glaring, and took in her companions. The frown vanished and was replaced by a huge grin that revealed perfect white teeth. 'You haven't got a fag, have you?' she asked, the African accent replaced by a perfectly ordinary English one. 'I'm gasping.' The grin widened as she indicated her skimpy outfit. 'And this thing doesn't have pockets.'

Cassie gaped at her in astonishment. 'You mean you're not from Africa?' she gasped.

'Africa?' Tanisha grinned. 'Try Birmingham.' The grin became malicious. 'But I bet I scared the shit out of those two sorry white boys.' She chuckled richly, the huge black body shaking with mirth, her breasts quivering with her laughter. 'Voodoo?' she snorted. 'I wouldn't know voodoo if it sneaked up and bit me on my big black behind!'

She strode across, eased Cassie aside with a nudge of one ample hip, and settled herself comfortably on the chaise longue. It sagged under her weight and Tom slid against her. She grinned and put a massive arm round his shoulders. 'You're a cute little one,' she said, giving him a squeeze that almost knocked the breath out of him. 'Come to Momma.'

Totally unfazed by Tom's lack of height or the situation they were all in, she began to chuckle again. 'Liquorice allsorts,' she gurgled. 'A bag of liquorice allsorts, that's what we are.' Their puzzled looks set her off again. 'Just look at us. All shapes, sizes and colours. The rich bastard that paid for us must have pretty catholic tastes. There's something here for everyone. Black, white, gay, bi. The lot.'

The pleasant feeling of companionship that had begun to warm Cassie disappeared rapidly at the thought. Going by Tom's face, the idea that they might have been purchased by someone who was equally into men and women hadn't crossed his mind until Tanisha's comment, either. He didn't look too happy about it.

'What do you think they'll do to us?' Cassie asked miserably.

'Whatever they damn well want, honey,' grinned Tanisha. 'You pays your money, you takes your choice.' She shook her head. 'And take it from me, the money they're paying, there's going to be some pretty funny choices. You wouldn't believe some of the things I've seen.'

Cassie didn't find this reassuring, and it must have showed, because Tanisha's grin disappeared and her expression became serious. 'Don't you fret, honey,' she murmured, patting her arm. 'It's not that bad. Just remember one little tip and you'll be fine. They can fuck with your body, but they can't fuck with your mind. Not if you don't let them.' Her lips twitched as the irrepressible grin began to creep back. 'It ain't voodoo, but it works.'

She winked. 'I'm still here, aren't I? Large as life and twice as ugly!'

The key clicked in the lock once more and they all looked up, expecting another 'slave' to join their motley crew. Instead, Heinz marched into the room, followed closely by Peter. Tanisha grinned at them and they eyed her warily. Heinz clapped his hands and glared at them.

'Right, on your feet,' he ordered. 'It's time to go.'

'Go where?' demanded Cassie. He ignored her question and hauled her to her feet. She winced as his fingers dug into her upper arm, leaving red imprints on the soft skin. She shook him off angrily. To think she'd had this man's prick in her mouth. The very thought made her sick. She should have bitten it off while she'd had the chance.

'Just do as you're told,' he snapped. 'Or perhaps you'd like to meet Parker again?' He leered at her. 'He seems to have taken quite a fancy to you.' Cassie shivered and avoided his eyes.

Tom hopped off the couch and stood beside her, his head barely reaching her tummy. His hands were clenched, but he was helpless. There were two of them and they towered above him. There was nothing he could do.

The only one who seemed unmoved by the situation was Tanisha. Still grinning, she uncoiled herself with insolent slowness, then crouched, forked her fingers in the sign of the evil eye and hissed at their two guards. She gurgled with delight when Heinz and Peter flinched away. Straightening up again, she smiled at them. 'Lead on, boys,' she drawled. 'Time's a-wasting.'

Carefully avoiding getting too close to their black tormentor, they led their captives through the labyrinth of corridors, until Cassie was hopelessly lost. After a while they reached a wooden door, locked and bolted against outsiders. Peter produced a heavy key and inserted it in the lock. The door swung open.

Cassie shivered as they stepped into the night. Clouds had covered the moon and there was the hint of rain in the air. She shivered again, the cold hardening her nipples into tight buttons. She clasped her arms round herself to try to keep warm in her skimpy costume.

'This way,' ordered Heinz. Her feet hurt as they were bruised by the gravel of the driveway, but the distance was mercifully short. As her eyes adapted to the dark, she could make out the waiting van. It was black and windowless. Peter pulled open the back door and they were forced to climb inside. Cassie whimpered as a rough hand groped at her genitals as she stepped up to enter, then she was pushed forward and fell onto the floor of the van. The door banged closed behind them.

'There you go,' said Tom, helping her up. In the darkness she fumbled her way to the side, where her grasping hands felt the outline of a seat. With a sigh of relief, she collapsed on it, feeling the warmth of Tanisha's body beside her. The van jerked forward and a wave of despair washed over her. Where were they going and what was going to happen next? She was hungry and exhausted – but far too frightened to sleep. The way she felt, she would never sleep again.

When she woke she was warm and comfortable – and for a moment she thought she was safely back home in her own bed. She yawned contentedly, then stiffened as she became aware of her surroundings. There was someone else beside her! Her head was pillowed on a large brown breast, her lips mere centimetres from the turgid black nipple, while a heavy arm was draped around her shoulder, the hand cupping her own left breast. The fingers were sleepily stroking Cassie's treacherous nipple, which, to her horror, was swelling in response.

She leaped out of the bed as if it was on fire.

Tanisha mumbled in her sleep, rolled over and began snoring gently as Cassie gazed around wildly. She must have fallen asleep in the van. Where the hell was she now?

The room was large and sunny, the window looking out over rolling parkland. The floor was thickly carpeted and the furniture, including the large double bed, was new and modern. A linen-draped trolley holding a coffee pot, cups, saucers, plates and an array of covered dishes, stood enticingly against the far wall. She might have been in a luxurious country hotel – if it hadn't been for the bars on the window and the fact that the door didn't have a handle on the inside.

The aroma of freshly made coffee drew her across to the trolley and a quick investigation of the covered dishes revealed a traditional country house breakfast. Toast, kippers, kedgeree, sausage, bacon, eggs. Cassie's eyes widened and her mouth began to water. At least they weren't going to starve her. Even the ominous fact that the cutlery was plastic, didn't spoil her appetite. She filled a plate and blissfully began to eat.

'Hey, save some for me!' protested a sleepy voice. 'Skinny little white girl, eating all the food,' Tanisha grumbled, sitting up in bed. She yawned, the magnificent bosom thrusting forward as she stretched and grinned at Cassie.

Cassie grinned back, filled a plate with everything on the trolley and carried it across to Tanisha, along with a steaming cup of coffee. Tanisha reached for it gratefully.

'Ouch!' She winced suddenly, then slid her hand under the bedcovers. 'What's this?' she demanded. She held up Cassie's gold 'chastity' chains, and a look of comprehension and distaste crossed her face. She flung them into a corner and reached for the food again. 'Thanks,' she mumbled, through a mouthful of bacon and eggs.

She had barely started when the door swung open. A hard-faced middle-aged woman wearing a dark housekeeper's uniform stood running her eyes over them. Cassie's recently raised spirits sank again. The woman's unfriendly expression was a million miles from welcoming. Cassie became suddenly aware that she was still wearing her Roman costume from the night before, and that it didn't cover much. One hand flew to tug down her hem and the other to cover her exposed breast.

'The master will see you now, Miss Grey,' she announced. 'Follow me, please.'

'But what am I supposed to wear?' protested Cassie. 'I can't go looking like this.'

'That's perfectly adequate, I'm sure,' came the uncompromising reply, much to Cassie's dismay. The woman's lip curled in a sneer. 'The master will wish to inspect the... merchandise.'

Still trying to cover herself, Cassie followed the woman.

The next few minutes were a nightmare. As Cassie walked along behind the woman, they passed several male servants. Greedy eyes followed her passage and comments and sniggers floated after her. It was a relief when they finally reached their destination and she was ushered into a dim, book-lined study. The woman closed the door behind her.

For a moment, before her eyes adjusted, Cassie thought the room was empty. Then she made out a dark silhouette against the lighter square of the window. It turned towards her and she could make out that the shape was a wheelchair. Its occupant swung round to face her.

She gasped as he wheeled towards her, then stopped

just outside the ring of light thrown by a lamp on the desk. Even from that distance she could see the thick scar that ran from under one eye to the side of the stern mouth, twisting his face into a permanent grimace. He ignored her reaction, and ran his eyes over her. The mouth twisted into something of a smile.

'Ah, the Roman slave girl look,' he drawled. 'Trite, but still amusing.' He put his hands together and looked at her across them. 'An inventive people, the Romans. Experts in decadence. Did you know that Roman whores did their best business in the corridors leading from the arena, after the games? Blood and lust,' he said thoughtfully, 'an interesting combination.' He smiled. 'Death is so stimulating, don't you think?'

Cassie looked at him, dumbfounded. A lecture on Roman history was the last thing she'd expected.

'Or take the Emperor Heliogabalous,' he went on, without awaiting an answer. 'A connoisseur of cruelty. Did you know he had his slaves suffocated with rose petals while they fornicated?' He shook his head. 'You do have to admire his style.'

'Oh yes, very stylish,' said Cassie tartly. She mimicked his scholarly tone. 'Did you know he was assassinated, along with his mother, by the Praetorian Guard?' She snorted. 'Obviously not everyone admired him as much as you seem to.'

He looked at her with new interest. 'An educated whore,' he murmured. 'How entertaining. I shall look forward to teaching you a few things your education *hasn't* covered.' He snapped his fingers. 'Come closer.'

Eyes dull, Cassie did as she was told. Without warning, one hand reached up and twisted her exposed nipple, while the other administered a stinging slap to her flank. She jumped back, tears bursting to her eyes.

'What did you do that for?' she whimpered.

He smiled. 'That's better,' he said, with evident satisfaction. 'Your eyes are bright, your cheeks are flushed, your chest is heaving – and at this moment you probably feel like killing me.' He shook his head in amusement. 'Don't you see? You are far more alive than you were ten seconds ago. And what has caused this miraculous transformation? The simple application of a little pain.' He smiled again. 'You will come to appreciate that over the next few weeks.'

'What do you want me to do?' asked Cassie, apprehensively.

The smile became bitter and he indicated the wheelchair with a wave of his hand. 'For me? Nothing. Fate has seen to that.' He gazed at her levelly. 'But even a chef who has lost his sense of taste may still create a banquet for others to enjoy.' He leaned back. 'I have business associates. Friends to whom I owe favours, and from whom I expect favours in return.' He shrugged. 'And people who have had their... appetites... satisfied, are so much more amenable, don't you find?'

He leaned forward, pressed a button on the desk and the door opened behind her. The housekeeper stood there, waiting. He gave Cassie one last twisted smile as he turned towards the window again.

'Oh, and do try to relax today, Miss Grey,' he advised. 'I'd like you nice and fresh for tomorrow.'

His next words were so bizarre that Cassie wasn't quite sure she'd heard him properly.

'You've been invited to a birthday party.'

Chapter Ten

His words puzzled her all the way back to the room – so much so, that this time she was totally oblivious to the salacious whispers that followed her passage. A birthday party? What the hell was he talking about? Perhaps the housekeeper could enlighten her. She glanced at the woman she had mentally christened 'Mrs Danvers', after the mother of all sinister domestic servants, hoping to see a sign of humanity on the harsh features, then sighed. Fat chance! The woman looked as if she'd be more at home in charge of a concentration camp rather than a big house in the country. Dejectedly, Cassie followed her along the corridor.

The image was reinforced when they arrived and 'Mrs Danvers' produced a massive ring of keys, before unlocking the door and pushing it open. Standing rigidly to the side, she waited until Cassie was safely in, before staring coldly at Tanisha and announcing, 'The master will see you now, Miss Smith.'

Despite herself, Cassie found herself grinning. Smith? Hardly the name she'd imagined for such an exotic creature as Tanisha. Tanisha grinned back, obviously reading her mind. She stuck out a pink tongue and, as she strutted past, flitted up her short skirt to give Cassie the benefit of her round backside. Cassie chuckled. Tanisha was irrepressible.

Left to her own devices, Cassie began to explore and was delighted to find that a door she'd thought led to a cupboard actually led to a separate shower unit. At least she could get clean. Slipping out of the detested Roman costume, she flung it into one corner, grabbed the shampoo and stepped under the steamy spray, sighing in ecstasy as the needles of hot water stripped away the feeling of grubbiness that clung to every pore.

Pushing her wet hair back with both hands, she found the soap and began to scrub herself, luxuriating in the stream of scented bubbles coursing down her body. Against her will, thoughts of the past few days drifted back into her mind. She'd been beaten, bruised and abused... and yet... and yet... there had been something strangely liberating about it all. Something darkly exciting about being reduced to nothing but an object of desire. No question of morality. No question of responsibility. No question of right or wrong. All that had been taken out of her hands. All that was left was the shameless animal pleasure of submitting, without thought, to a will stronger than her own. She shivered. What was happening to her? One minute she was terrified, the next she was aroused. It was as if she was turning into two separate people.

As if on cue, her nipples began to harden under the hot spray. Pictures flashed through her mind. James Garret, tied to the bed and whimpering as she rode him. Kneeling in front of Mr Harris as he fed his prick into her mouth and fucked her there. Heinz and Peter enjoying her at the same time; Heinz in her mouth, and Peter – of all the shameful places – in her bottom.

Her breath became shorter and one hand slid between her quivering thighs, stroking the tight bud of her clitoris, while her other hand caressed her breasts. Her eyes closed as her hand moved faster, her fingers plunging in and out. She moaned as she began to build towards a beautiful orgasm.

There was an answering groan and she froze, snatching

her hands from her body as if they'd been burned. She looked around frantically. The groan had been muffled but it had sounded close. She heard another one, and her eyes found the small hole that had been drilled in the tiled wall. She gasped in horror, turning scarlet with mortification. Someone had been watching her masturbating! Tossing himself off as he feasted his eyes on her naked body, like a dirty old man in one of those pay-slot cubicles you found tucked away in the back of sex shops. What a disgusting, scummy thing to do! She leaped out of the cubicle as if she'd been scalded, and fled, wrapped protectively in a bath towel.

She was still sitting on the bed, shivering, when the housekeeper escorted Tanisha back and slammed the door behind her.

'Great! There's a shower,' she grinned, taking in Cassie's damp condition. 'Any hot water left, or have you used it all?'

'You can't go in there,' protested Cassie, through chattering teeth. 'There's a peephole. Someone's watching.'

'So what?' muttered Tanisha, shrugging herself out of her costume. 'That's his problem.' Her teeth flashed in a grin. 'Pathetic wanker! Might as well give him something worth looking at.' Black breasts bouncing, she strode lithely into the shower room, totally unconcerned. Cassie heard the hiss of water, accompanied by a cheerful rendition of the latest number one hit. Ten minutes later, Tanisha reappeared, swathed in a white towel, dark skin glowing.

'I thought about plugging up the hole with soap,' she muttered as she rubbed her hair dry. 'But who am I to spoil his fun?' She peered out from under the towel and grinned. 'So I gave him a full frontal close-up instead.'

The grin widened. 'I should think he had a heart attack.'

Cassie smiled reluctantly. It was hard to stay terrified with Tanisha around. She had the happy knack of finding humour in even the most unpromising situations. She looked at her gratefully. Then a thought struck her. 'Well? What did you think of "the master"?' she asked, pulling a face.

Tanisha's grin disappeared. 'Let's put it this way,' she said grimly. 'After meeting that guy, I really needed a shower.' She shivered. 'There was something about him that made my skin crawl.' She shook her head. 'That face for a start – and the way he crept up on you in that wheelchair. Scared the shit out of me, I don't mind admitting.'

For some strange reason, Cassie found herself defending him. 'He can't help his face,' she protested. 'It's hardly his fault if he's been in some kind of accident. And I don't suppose you or I would be too happy if we were stuck in a wheelchair. It must be awful being paralysed and impotent.'

Tanisha looked at Cassie. 'He might not know it,' she said thoughtfully, 'but I don't think he is.'

Cassie gaped at her. 'What are you talking about?'

'When he was talking, I'm sure I saw his foot twitch,' said Tanisha. 'Not much – and I don't think he was aware of it – but enough to make me think he wasn't completely helpless.'

'And you'd know, would you?' muttered Cassie.

'I would actually,' agreed Tanisha. 'I used to be a sister on the spinal ward. I've seen it happen before. The body might heal, but the patient's still paralysed up here.' She tapped her head.

Cassie gaped at her, stunned by this new information. 'You used to be a nurse?' she gasped. 'So what are you doing here?'

Tanisha's rich chuckle filled the room. 'If you're going to be walked over and treated like shit,' she grinned, 'you might at least get well paid for it.' The grin vanished. 'I'll get paid more for one month in this place than I would in a year on the wards.' She glared at Cassie challengingly. 'Anyway, you're a fine one to talk. Didn't you say you were a teacher?' Cassie nodded. 'Well, there you are then. We've all got our reasons.

'Oh, and just one more thing,' she added. 'I wouldn't waste your pity on this supposed master of ours. Don't start thinking you're Jane Eyre and he's Mr Rochester. In a wheelchair or out of it, he'd still be a twisted bastard.' She looked hopefully at the door. 'Now, where's lunch? I'm starving!'

The door remained closed and Tanisha shrugged philosophically. 'Ah well, I was thinking of going on a diet anyway.' She clicked her fingers. 'Hey, I forgot to mention it. Guess who I saw.'

Cassie looked at her blankly. In this place? Who was there to see? Film stars? Politicians? She sighed. With what she'd been finding out about human nature, recently, neither would have surprised her.

Tanisha looked at her blank expression with exasperation. 'Tom,' she said. 'I saw Tom. Remember? Good-looking bloke? Little legs?'

Cassie's face broke into a smile. 'How was he?' she asked. 'And where did you see him?'

'In the pub,' said Tanisha sarcastically. 'Where do you think?' She shook her head. 'Honestly, you're hopeless. I met him in the corridor with a big bruiser on either side of him. They must have been taking him to see Channing, too. He looked fine.' Her lips tightened. 'Got to keep the merchandise in good order, haven't they? Nobody wants to buy bruised fruit.'

Luckily, lunch arrived at this point, before the conversation could go any further down that particular road. As the door closed behind the silent maid, Tanisha fell on the food like a ravening wolf. 'Steak,' she squealed, lifting the metal covers from the dishes. 'And baked potatoes.' She investigated further. 'And there's gateau for pudding. Brilliant, it's party time! At least we won't starve.' Humming cheerfully, she filled the two plates to overflowing, handed one to Cassie, and started tucking in.

Cassie looked at the food with distaste. Her appetite had deserted her at Tanisha's last words. Bruised fruit? She felt more like the slab of steak on the plate in front of her. A piece of meat, there for anybody who fancied sinking their teeth into her. And as for 'party time' – it had been an unpleasant echo of Channing's cryptic words. She tried to force down a mouthful of food, but it stuck in her throat. She laid the fork back on the plate.

'What's wrong with you, girl?' demanded Tanisha, looking at her sharply. 'You got to eat. Keep your strength up.'

Cassie picked up her fork again and poked half-heartedly at her food. 'He...' there was no question about who 'he' was. 'He said I was "invited to a birthday party",' she muttered. 'What do you think he meant?'

'Maybe you've got to jump out of the cake,' grinned Tanisha. 'Stark naked, with a feather up your bum!'

Cassie giggled at the idea and felt marginally more cheerful. Of course. Why hadn't she thought of that? Relief brought her appetite back and she actually managed to finish half her meal. Tanisha looked on with approval.

'That's better,' she said. 'Can't have you fading away. You're skinny enough already.'

Cassie grinned again. Skinny? Compared to Tanisha, she probably was!

Afterwards, the silent maid removed the remains of their food and they looked at one another. The rest of the day stretched out ahead of them like a desert, with nothing to do but think. Cassie shivered. This must be what it was like in prison. A horrible combination of boredom, lethargy, and underlying unease.

'Let's find some entertainment,' grumbled Tanisha, who obviously felt the same. 'Got to be something.' She padded round the room, opening and closing cupboards. Five minutes later, she'd found what she was looking for. 'Eureka!' she shouted, jubilantly, opening the door of a small cabinet to reveal a concealed television set.

'Great,' agreed Cassie, settling down on the bed. 'We can watch the soaps. At least it'll pass the time. Come on, put it on.'

Tanisha did as she was told. The screen flickered into life, and the two girls gaped at it in horror as the picture cleared. The scene was dark, lit only by torches. Against the wall of what looked like a dungeon, a naked girl was chained, her arms pulled cruelly upwards, so that she had to stand on tiptoe. As they watched, a hooded man stepped into the picture. The whip he was carrying whistled through the air and the girl jerked and moaned, a thin red line appearing on her naked back. He laughed and began to fumble with his leather codpiece. The camera homed in on his massive erection as he walked towards her.

'Switch it off,' moaned Cassie, shuddering.

The revolting scene disappeared.

'Guess telly's out then,' said Tanisha, clearly shaken by what they'd just seen. 'Better find something else to do.' She continued her search, finally holding up a pack of cards she'd found in a drawer. She pulled a face as she saw the obscene pictures on them. 'These are disgusting,' she muttered. 'But they'll have to do. If we sit around doing nothing, we'll go mad.'

The rest of the day dragged slowly by, as they played cards and chatted in a desultory fashion. Cassie would have sold her soul for a single episode of her favourite soap to take her mind off their situation.

Dinner arrived, then supper, and finally it was time to go to bed and, exhausted by doing absolutely nothing, escape into the oblivion of sleep.

They climbed between the sheets of the double bed and Cassie rolled into the hollow made by Tanisha's weight. Too tired to do anything about it, she snuggled into her comforting warmth. Tomorrow she would have to face the unknown – the birthday party – but for now, it was enough just to close her eyes and forget everything. In ten minutes she was asleep.

When she woke again Cassie was still curled up, catlike, against Tanisha's generous body. Her head was pillowed on one breast, her arm lay across Tanisha's waist and their legs were entangled beneath the twisted sheets. She could feel the heat pulsing from her groin. Tanisha moaned in her sleep, turned slightly and her hand fell on Cassie's breast, the fingers sleepily finding Cassie's waiting nipple. Her stomach flipped over at the feeling radiating from her breast and his time she didn't move away. She arched her back and stretched, feeling the full length of Tanisha's body against her own, her pubic hair brushing against Tanisha's smooth thigh.

There was a lazy chuckle and the fingers stroking her breast became more purposeful. Tanisha traced delicate circles round the hardening nipple and Cassie shivered with excitement. Before her eyes, Tanisha's black nipple stiffened. Tentatively, Cassie flicked it with her tongue and there was a moan of pleasure. Encouraged, she took it into her mouth, rolling it between her lips and tongue. Tanisha's other hand slipped between her legs and gently stroked the inside of her thigh, gradually moving higher. Cassie felt herself moisten and gingerly reached down to return the compliment.

She felt Tanisha's pubic hair and gasped. How strange it felt to touch another woman there. As she stroked the length of Tanisha's vulva, the lips parted beneath her touch and her fingers sank into soft, velvet heat. This must be what it felt like to a man, when he touched her. They turned to face each other and, as their hands moved in unison, their breasts pressed together, nipples rubbing tantalisingly against each other. Cassie gasped again, her breath catching in her throat, and Tanisha's lips came down on hers, her tongue pressing into Cassie's willing mouth.

She withdrew and smiled down at Cassie. 'Just wait, honey,' she breathed. 'You ain't seen nothing yet.' She withdrew her fingers and moved down Cassie's body, her heavy breasts swinging forward, trailing a twin path against Cassie's flesh. When she had reached her target, she gently parted Cassie's thighs and Cassie moaned as Tanisha's tongue pierced the soft heart of her flesh.

'Oh God,' she moaned, as her hips arched towards the source of pleasure. 'That feels wonderful.' Tanisha's chuckle vibrated against her, sending tiny ripples of sensation radiating upwards through her body. She moaned again.

Just then the door burst open and they sprang apart. Cassie's moan became one of frustration at her sudden deprivation. She sat up in bed, holding the covers protectively against her as the housekeeper wheeled in the breakfast trolley and gave them a disdainful look.

'Get up,' she ordered, sniffing in disgust and staring pointedly at Cassie. 'You've got work to do. Your costume's in that box on the bottom shelf of the trolley.' She left, slamming the door behind her.

'Miserable old cow,' snorted Tanisha. 'With a face like that, she's probably never been fucked in her life.'

Cassie shuddered. At that precise moment, she wished she could say the same. Ignoring the food, she picked up the box containing her 'costume'. Funny – it felt as if it was empty.

She lifted the lid, stared inside, and her eyes widened. For all the material it contained, it might just as well have been empty. 'I can't wear this!' she protested, holding up what looked like two lengths of ribbon with bows attached. 'How the hell is it supposed to go on?'

'I think one bit goes round your boobs and the other goes round your—'

'Okay, okay,' snapped Cassie. 'I get the idea.' Standing in front of the mirror, she tied one piece round her hips, so that the bow sat over her pudenda, hiding nothing. The other piece went round her breasts. The two bows perched perkily on top of her nipples. She stared at her reflection in dismay. 'I look ridiculous,' she muttered.

'Actually, you look rather fetching,' grinned Tanisha. 'I wonder when the cake's arriving.' Her grin widened. 'Good job it's you inside and not me. They'd need one the size of a truck to get me into it.' She looked at Cassie's worried face. 'Cheer up, there are worse things than leaping half-naked out of a cardboard cake. All you have to do is jump up, shout, "Happy Birthday!" and that's you. It's embarrassing, but it's not too bad.'

Half an hour later, the cake arrived, wheeled in on another trolley by two large gentlemen. Cassie looked at it in disgust. How tacky could you get? Under the leering eyes of the two men, she struggled into the cake and crouched down as the top was fitted back on. It was pitch black and she sincerely hoped there were air holes. It would definitely put a damper on the party if she suffocated! She forced a smile in the darkness. It might be a feeble joke, but at least it staved off the claustrophobia that threatened to overcome her.

She held her breath as the trolley rumbled along the corridors. Through the cardboard, she could hear the sound of a door opening. The trolley bumped across the threshold, then stopped. She could hear excited voices.

Counting to a hundred, she took a deep breath, gathered her strength, then leaped upwards, knocking off the top of the cake. 'Happy birthd...!'

Her voice trailed off in horror and she crossed her arms across her chest in a futile attempt to cover herself as she gazed into a familiar pair of eyes. Their owner was lounging in a chair, grinning at her.

'Hello, miss,' he said.

Cassie gawped at him, open-mouthed. She'd last seen Robert Channing on her last day at school – when she'd humiliated him in front of his friends. She swallowed nervously. Now it was her turn to be humiliated.

'Nice to see you again,' he smirked. His eyes crawled over her. 'And there's quite a lot to see, too, isn't there?' He grinned round and Cassie reluctantly followed his eyes. It was worse than she'd thought. She'd been too taken aback at first to notice his two friends. They were staring at her, wide-eyed.

'Get out of that stupid thing,' Robert ordered. 'I want to look at you more closely.'

Cassie cringed back into the cardboard cake and faced him defiantly, trying to regain control. 'Don't be silly, Robert,' she said weakly. 'The surprise is over now. I'm sure you've got better things to do.' She smiled, struck by sudden inspiration. 'Isn't it time to open your presents?'

'You don't understand, do you,' he said softly. 'You *are* my present.' His grin became cruel. 'Mine. To do what I like with for my birthday.' He chuckled. 'Dad's always been good at buying presents.'

Cassie remembered the Porsche he'd driven to school on his seventeenth birthday, and it suddenly dawned on her who 'the master' was. Robert Channing senior. Pillar of the community. School governor. And someone so perverted that he would give his son a woman to use as an eighteenth birthday present. She closed her eyes in despair.

'Get her!' whooped Robert, and Cassie felt her arms seized as she was dragged bodily from the cake, the fragile ribbons snapping, so that she was totally naked. The two youths pulled her in front of Robert, who smiled as he produced a thin bamboo cane from behind his back. The smile became wider as he flexed it between his hands, then swung it, hissing, through the air. Cassie couldn't take her eyes off it. Her mouth had gone dry with fear and she flinched as the cane cracked against the table.

'You're not in class any more,' said Robert. '*I'm* the teacher now – and we know what happens to bad girls who don't do as they're told, don't we?' She opened her mouth to answer, but nothing came out. 'Don't we?' he snapped. Dumbly, she nodded. This was all a terrible, terrible dream. It must be.

'Good,' he drooled. 'Now we know who's in charge.' He crossed his arms and grinned at her. 'Stand up straight. Shoulders back.' She obeyed, staring over his shoulder as his eyes lingered on her heaving breasts. 'That's better,' he said softly. He walked slowly round her and she flinched again as the cane trailed slowly down her back, pausing at her full buttocks, flicking against her skin just enough to sting. Standing in front of her again, he ran it up her throat, forcing her head up. 'Very nice,' he said. 'Don't you agree, gentlemen?' Her eyes darted to the side, then closed to shut out the looks of avid lust on their young faces.

The cane began to move again, downwards this time. It slid over the upper slopes of her breasts, down to the soft fullness. She drew a jagged breath as the tip flicked remorselessly back and forth over her nipples. There was a groan from one of the boys as the soft pink flesh sprang erect.

She shuddered as the cane moved lower, over the smooth curve of her belly and down to her shaven pubic mound, tracing the cleft of her vulva. The tip slid between her thighs, parting her lower lips to reveal the moistness of her most private parts. She flushed with shame at the exposure.

'Excellent,' Robert purred, removing the cane. 'Now I think we'll have you do a few exercises for our entertainment. Jumps first, I think. Arms and legs nice and wide.' She shook her head and the cane whistled through the air. She gasped with pain as it stung her flank.

Gritting her teeth, she began. With each jump her breasts leaped and quivered and her vulva was exposed to their eager eyes. 'Fuck! It's better than reading porno magazines,' gasped one of the boys. 'You can see everything!'

A wave of shame and humiliation ran through her and she slowed down. The cane whistled again and she squealed.

'You don't stop till I tell you,' snarled Robert. Tears trickling down her cheeks, she continued.

'That'll do,' he ordered finally. 'Right. Legs apart and touch your toes.'

Face scarlet, she obeyed. There was an intake of breath as her breasts swung as she bent and straightened, while Robert amused himself by tapping time on her bottom with the cane. The threat of pain was quite enough to keep her obedient, but obedience wasn't enough for him. She squealed again as he brought it down on her quivering flesh – hard. She jerked upright and almost lost her balance.

'On the floor,' he ordered, pushing her down. 'I want ten press-ups now. Don't you remember, that's what you told me to do? Well, now it's your turn... miss.' He prodded her with his toe. 'Get started.'

Almost weeping with pain and humiliation, Cassie began.

'Look at her tits bounce,' crowed one of Robert's friends. 'And her arse.' The other one simply stood, licking his lips and grinning. A pang of fear ran through Cassie, sapping her strength, and she collapsed. She lay there, wishing she were dead.

'Help her to her feet, boys,' hissed Robert. 'She didn't finish her press-ups, so she's got to be punished.'

Whimpering, she looked from youth to youth, frantically seeking some compassion, but there was none. There was nothing but flushed faces and lustful eyes. She was pulled up again, led to the table and pushed down over it, arms spread, buttocks vulnerably exposed. The cane rose and fell, and she jerked and quivered as it smacked against her backside, biting into her tender flesh. She sank her teeth into her lip to prevent herself from crying out, but it was useless. As another hard blow reddened the cheeks of her bottom, a whimper escaped her. She closed her eyes, clenching her muscles against the expectation of another blow.

But it didn't come.

Instead, rough fingers fumbled at her, prising the lips of her vulva apart, thrusting their way into her body. She whimpered again and they withdrew – but her respite was brief.

'Turn her over,' came Robert's breathless voice. 'I want to fuck her.' She was rolled over, cruel hands gripping her wrists and ankles as her legs were pulled apart. Totally helpless, she lifted her head to see him fumbling with the zip of his jeans. He was going to screw her in front of the other two, and there was nothing she could do to stop him. She struggled to pull away, but it was hopeless. Panting with excitement, his friends held her down as he advanced on her, his swollen prick in his fist. She gasped; he might have only been a teenager, but he was certainly equipped like a man.

Her thighs were pulled apart and she could feel the smooth head of his cock pushing against her. With agonising slowness it forced its way in. She closed her eyes and tried to imagine Tanisha's fingers gently exploring her instead. Her body responded and the thrusting became easier as her juices began to flow.

Robert grinned down at her, his fingers painfully twisting her nipples. 'You like it, don't you, miss?' he gasped, ramming himself into her. 'Well, there's plenty more where that came from. I'm not selfish. When I'm finished, Ken and Allan can have a share.' All too quickly his youthful exuberance got the better of him and he groaned, shuddered, and fell away from her.

She lay there, legs splayed, with his hot come still trickling out of her. 'My turn,' demanded Ken throatily, pulling out his cock. Cassie groaned as he took Robert's place between her legs, slid into her and the merciless thrusting began again. It was impossible not to respond to the rhythmic pounding. As his hips jerked against her, two other pairs of hands roamed over her body, stroking and kneading. She moaned again. This time with pleasure at the sensations running through her. All too soon, he climaxed and collapsed, leaving Cassie still unfulfilled.

'I want her to suck me,' gasped Allan. He glanced at Robert. 'Make her take it in the mouth.'

Robert grinned at Cassie. 'You heard him,' he ordered, pulling her to her feet and twisting her arm behind her back. 'Suck him off.' He pushed her to her knees in front of Allan. A rock-hard prick was thrust in front of her face. Eyes closed to shut out their leering faces, she leaned forward and took it between her lips, and ran her tongue over its swollen head.

It was all too much for him, too. At the first touch he exploded, his seed bursting against the roof of her mouth. She whined in frustration, her body demanding to be satisfied. She was soaking now, her nipples rigid with thwarted desire. All she wanted now was to be given some sort of relief.

Her eyes widened as she looked up at Robert. He was naked now and ready again, the heavy cock in stark contrast to his slim, boyish body. Eagerly, she reached for it, running her hand up and down its smooth length. His eyes closed and he moaned. She pulled him down, lying back and spreading herself for him. As he slid into her again, she wrapped her legs round him, her hands on his clenching buttocks to pull him even further in, her hips rising to meet each frenzied thrust.

Fired by the display of lust, the other two were also naked and ready again. Robert gasped out his satisfaction and withdrew, watching as Allan knelt astride her shoulders, pushing his rigid young cock towards her mouth again. She took it greedily, licking and sucking its succulent length, while Ken knelt between her legs, tugging at his prick as he pushed his fingers in and out of her eager cunt. She moaned and jerked her hips, forcing them deeper inside her.

As Allan spurted into her mouth for the second time, Ken shuddered and pearls of semen beaded her heaving stomach. She screamed her own climax, and collapsed, satisfied at last.

There was a discreet tap at the door and the boys began to scramble back into their clothes. 'Who is it?' demanded Robert.

'The helicopter is here, Master Robert,' said a respectful voice. 'Your father is waiting.'

'I wish I could stay,' Robert said dreamily, smiling down at Cassie, lying naked and spent. 'But perhaps another time?' With a last regretful look at her, the boys finished their dressing and left, closing the door behind them.

Exhausted, Cassie pulled herself into a sitting position and looked around for something to cover her nakedness. She could hardly believe what was happening to her. She'd just been fucked by three young men – one of them a former pupil – and she'd revelled in every glorious, sweaty minute of it. If they hadn't left, she'd have done it again… and again, until she'd drained them dry. She moaned in self-abasement. She was becoming more and more shameless, each incident taking her a step further down the road of depravity. There was only one thing for it.

She would have to escape.

Chapter Eleven

'You're going to do what?' demanded Tanisha. 'You must be joking!'

'Escape,' confirmed Cassie. She was slumped on the bed, wrapped only in the cloth she'd tugged from the table in the room where the birthday party had been held. There had been a satisfying crash as dishes, glasses and food went flying when she yanked it off. She'd barely had time to cover her nakedness before the two men who'd escorted her there had come back to march her back to her room. They had been silent, but their leering expressions had spoken volumes. Cassie had never felt so cheap and used in her life.

She shivered and pulled the thin material tighter around herself. 'I'm going to escape,' she repeated defiantly. 'I'm going to get out of here before things get any worse.'

'Don't be so stupid,' said Tanisha bluntly. 'Think about it for a minute. If you stick it out, you'll be free and independent at the end of it – but if you run now, you'll finish up with zero. Zilch. Everything you've gone through already, you'll have gone through for nothing.' She paused and smiled bitterly. 'And there's one more thing. Exactly how do you think you're going to escape, anyway? What are you going to do? March up to his majesty and say, "excuse me, terribly sorry, but I've changed my mind after all. Call me a taxi, I'm leaving"?' She shook her head. 'I don't think so. This guy's shelled out serious money for our services, he's not going to give up his investment just like that.' She shivered. 'And I wouldn't fancy someone like our wheelchair-bound friend being pissed off with *me*. How do you think he's going to react if you break your contract?'

'I don't care any more,' muttered Cassie. 'I've had enough.' She stood up and flung off the stained cloth. 'Now, if you don't mind, I'm going for a shower–' her lips twisted in distaste at she felt the stickiness between her thighs '–to try and wash the last couple of hours off me.' Naked, she strode towards the shower room.

'What about the phantom peeper?' grinned Tanisha.

'Stuff him!' snarled Cassie, banging the door behind her.

Tanisha shook her head. Cassie would feel better after her shower, then she'd see sense and change her mind.

But after her shower, she didn't.

For the rest of the afternoon, Cassie paced the room like a caged tiger, trying to plan out how she would do it. Go for the housekeeper or the maid when they brought the food? No chance. You could bet your sweet life there was a couple of goons lurking in the background, waiting for just such an eventuality. She couldn't be the first one who'd tried to get away.

Under Tanisha's anxious gaze, she tested the bars on the windows and the lock on the door. She groaned. There wasn't even a millimetre of give. You'd need a crowbar to shift them – and the most lethal thing in the room was an emery board. She wouldn't get far with that. But she brightened; perhaps she could steal a knife, next time they were fed? Then her face fell again. The cutlery was that bloody plastic stuff – about as much use as a chocolate fireguard.

'Give it up,' advised Tanisha, from the comfort of the bed where she was lounging, playing patience with the obscene playing cards. 'There's only one way out of here, and that's to go through with the deal.'

Cassie's shoulders sagged and she stared hopelessly out of the window, and then her eyes widened at the sight of an enormous black car coming up the drive. 'There's someone coming,' she gasped. 'Maybe they'd help me get away.' As the car drew up, she thrust her hand between the bars and began banging on the window.

The chauffeur opened the door and a stocky man in a dark suit climbed out, shaking the creases out of his expensive suit. Once he was satisfied, he reached in and helped out an almost skeletally thin woman, dressed in a designer coat with a fur collar. Cassie's hopes soared. Surely another woman would take pity on her predicament? She redoubled her efforts.

Their faces turned upwards at the noise of her frantically beating hands, and Cassie quickly shrank back from the glass. Her heart sank as she recognised the man. He'd been at the auction. The last time she'd seen that fat, self-indulgent face, it had been wreathed in a prurient leer as he fumbled between the thighs of the sobbing girl he was leading away behind the stage. There was no help to be found there.

She turned her pleading gaze to the woman beside him, taking in the exaggerated make-up that failed to hide the raddled skin beneath. The scarlet lips were thin and twisted in a dissatisfied pout, the eyes that stared up into hers hard and knowing, gleaming with an almost febrile excitement. Cassie's spirits fell further. The man was bad enough, but there was an air of cruelty about the woman that made her stomach lurch.

The couple exchanged amused glances, then the woman stood on tiptoe and whispered something in the man's ear that made him roar with laughter. He smirked up at Cassie and made an obscene gesture – obviously a promise of things to come. Her hand dropped to her side and she turned away from the window, sickened, glad that she hadn't been able to hear what had been said.

'God, what a pair,' muttered Tanisha, who had come to stand beside her. 'She's got a face like a skull wearing lipstick. It looks as if she's been in a famine, and he looks as if he caused it!' She shuddered. 'Imagine them in bed. It must be like an elephant fucking a skeleton.'

'Don't,' protested Cassie, visualising it all too clearly. What was even worse was that she could also visualise herself trapped in the middle, his bloated belly rippling as he thrust between her reluctant thighs, while the woman suckled her breasts like a scrawny vampire. She shook her head to rid herself of the horrifying vision.

'Let's hope he's not bisexual,' said Tanisha dryly. Cassie stared at her. 'Poor Tom. Fatso there would squash him like a fly.'

Cassie shivered. 'Poor Tom' was right, but she'd been so wrapped up in her own plight she hadn't even spared him a thought.

'We should all try to get away,' she exclaimed. 'All three of us. Before it's too late.'

Tanisha stared at her in dismay. 'You're not still thinking about that, are you?' she demanded. 'Forget it. I told you already. There's only one way out of here. You shut off your mind and do what you're being paid to do. It's only for a few weeks, and after that you can go home and forget all about it. Come on,' she urged. 'Don't think about it. Think of the money. Think of the freedom that money can buy.'

'I can't,' said Cassie desperately. 'You could pay me the contents of Fort Knox and I'd still never be able to forget what's happened. I've got to get out of here.'

'Please yourself,' shrugged Tanisha. 'But I still think

you're making a big mistake. You'll never get away with it. Even if you did get out, you'd be looking over your shoulder for the rest of your life, waiting for someone from this weird set-up to catch up with you.' She patted Cassie's arm. 'Come on, pet. Give it up.'

Just then the door opened and they both jumped. But it was only the silent maid, with yet another meal. She wheeled the trolley in, then departed as quietly as she'd come. Cassie watched listlessly as Tanisha filled two plates and carried one over to her.

'Come on,' Tanisha ordered. 'Eat something.' Cassie pushed the plate away. Tanisha pushed it back. 'Look,' she said firmly, 'if you are going to try and escape, you won't get far if you keel over from lack of food, now will you?'

Cassie looked at her. She had a point. She was going to need all the strength she could get. She picked up her plastic fork and forced herself to eat.

That night, as Tanisha snored gently beside her, Cassie lay awake for hours, staring up at the ceiling. When she finally did sleep, it was only to doze fitfully, and it seemed only a matter of minutes before she was startled awake again.

She lay, staring into the darkness. What had woken her? She remembered the horrible night she'd been molested and she quivered, fearing there was going to bc a repetition, but the room was empty and silent, apart from Tanisha's regular breathing. She relaxed for a moment, then stiffened again as light washed over the ceiling. Her pricked ears picked up the sound of wheels on gravel. Car doors opened and closed and she could hear low-voiced conversation and quiet laughter.

Careful not to disturb Tanisha, she climbed out of bed,

tiptoed over to the window and peered out. Dim light spilled out from the front door, casting distorted shadows and silhouetting dark shapes. There was a rumble of male voices, interspersed with the higher tones of women.

Another dark car drove up and disgorged more people. A high-pitched shriek of maniacal female laughter made Cassie jump and wrap her arms round her shivering body. Light glinted off eyes and teeth, and glistened on sleek furs. There was something inhuman about the scene. She swallowed, her throat dry. The animals were gathering.

Shivering, she crept back to bed, even Tanisha's sleeping warmth failing to comfort her chilled body. Her mind raced. Now that these people had arrived, what was going to happen next? A wave of dread washed through her.

She definitely had to get out of there – and she had to get out soon.

Chapter Twelve

'Come on, sleepyhead, rise and shine,' grinned Tanisha, poking Cassie's recumbent body. 'You can't sleep all day. It's nearly time for lunch.'

Cassie sat bolt upright and groaned in dismay; the day was half gone already and she was still trapped. How could she have been such an idiot? 'Oh, my God!' she gasped. 'I can't have slept in. Not today.'

'Oh yes, you can,' said Tanisha. 'You've been snoring like a pig all morning.' She frowned. 'Anyway, what's so special about today?'

'You don't understand,' moaned Cassie. 'It's started properly now. There were people arriving all last night. I saw them.' Her eyes dilated with horror at the memory. 'God alone knows what they're going to do to us. We've got to get out today.'

'Speak for yourself,' muttered Tanisha. 'I'm not going anywhere. I've told you, I need the money. I knew what I was in for when I signed up.' She grinned. 'So I'll just close my eyes and think of England.'

'How can you joke at a time like this?' protested Cassie. 'It's not funny.' She shuddered, remembering the gathering crowd. 'You didn't see them.' She leaped out of bed and started hunting round for something to put on. All she could find was the Roman costume, still lying crumpled in the corner where she had flung it, and the skimpy white terry robe. She wriggled into both, tying the belt firmly round her waist.

'What do you look like?' chuckled Tanisha. Cassie

glanced at herself in the mirror and groaned. She was perfectly decent from the waist up, but both garments were so short that her long legs were completely uncovered and the least move revealed the lower curves of her buttocks at the back and – even worse – her shaven mound at the front. The effect was more obscene than if she'd been totally naked. She tugged at her clothes in a futile attempt to cover herself.

She stopped abruptly as the door opened and the food trolley was wheeled in. Despite her lack of appetite, she helped herself to an enormous plateful and made herself eat every last mouthful. She might have to make it last a long time. Once it was finished, she forced herself to take more. Tanisha looked at her in astonishment.

'Good grief, girl,' muttered Tanisha, as the maid wheeled the depleted trolley away again. 'What's got into you? I've never seen you eat so much.'

'Fuel,' explained Cassie. 'I'll need it, if I'm going to make a run for it.'

'You're mad.' Tanisha sighed with exasperation. 'You're never going to get out of here. Face it. There are bars on the window, locks on the door. How do you think you're going to manage it? Fly?' She shook her head. 'It's impossible.'

'Oh yeah? That's just where you're wrong. I'm going to walk through that door – and never look back.'

Tanisha shook her head at this display of stubbornness. 'How silly of me,' she muttered. 'Of course, now why didn't I think of that?' She raised an eyebrow. 'But aren't we forgetting one little detail here?' She leaned forward. 'It's *locked*. Remember?'

'It's not,' crowed Cassie triumphantly. 'Look!' She padded across to the door and demonstrated, moving it just enough to show Tanisha. 'The latch couldn't have clicked properly when the maid took the trolley out. Now, hand me one of those playing cards.'

A little puzzled, Tanisha did as she was told. Cassie slipped it between the tongue of the lock and the door frame, then closed the door firmly.

'There,' she said, feeling pleased with herself. 'From the outside it looks as if it's locked, but when I want to leave, all I have to do is pull out the card and the door's open again.'

Tanisha looked even more puzzled. 'You mean you're not just going to make a run for it now?' she asked.

'Of course not,' scoffed Cassie. 'I'm not stupid. Chances are those two bouncers are still hanging around somewhere in the corridors. I'll give it an hour. By that time they'll probably be having their own meal in the kitchens, while the guests–' she pulled a face '–are having theirs in the dining room. The place should be pretty much deserted.' She held up her crossed fingers. 'I'll go then.' She looked at Tanisha anxiously. 'Come on, come with me,' she pleaded urgently.

'No chance,' said Tanisha. 'I still think you're mad. What do you think they'll do to you if they catch you?' She cringed. 'It doesn't bear thinking about.'

'They won't catch me,' insisted Cassie, with a confidence she didn't really feel. 'And once I'm safely out of here, I think they'll still have to pay me my money.' She smiled slyly. 'Just to keep my mouth shut.' Her eyes sparkled with enthusiasm. 'I mean, what would the tabloids make of dear Mr Channing's strange sexual proclivities? And him such a pillar of the community, as well. Shock! Horror! Read all about it!' She shook her head. 'No, don't worry, I think I'll be safe enough.'

'Please yourself,' sighed Tanisha. 'Just be careful. I think these people are far more dangerous than you imagine. I wish you'd see a little sense and change your mind.'

'Well, I'm not going to,' muttered Cassie. 'Now, where's the rest of those cards? We can have a couple of games to pass the time.'

They played half-heartedly, Cassie's mind ticking off the slow minutes. She waited till she thought an hour had passed, then waited some more. With no clock in the room it was difficult to judge – and time had a nasty habit of dragging when your heart was in your mouth. You only had to spend five minutes in a dentist's waiting room to know that. Finally, she flung down the cards and looked at Tanisha.

'Last chance,' she said, hopefully. 'Are you sure you won't come with me?'

Tanisha shook her head. 'No thanks,' she muttered. 'And for God's sake, be careful.' She ran her eyes over Cassie's pathetically inadequate clothing. 'You're not exactly equipped for the great outdoors, are you?' She clicked her fingers. 'Hang on, I've got an idea.' She disappeared into the shower room and reappeared clutching a towel, which she deftly twisted, sarong-style, around Cassie's waist.

She stepped back and studied her with satisfaction. 'There, it's not perfect, but at least it's better than running around the countryside with your backside hanging out.'

'Thanks,' she said, and then her smile vanished as her conviction evaporated a little. 'Well, I'd better go now. You be careful, too.' The two girls hugged.

'Good luck,' whispered Tanisha. Cassie nodded uncertainly, and tiptoed to the door. For one horrible, heart-stopping moment, she thought her trick with the playing card hadn't worked, then the door creaked open. With a final wave to Tanisha, she peered into the corridor, then slipped out and pulled it closed behind her.

Heart pounding, she flattened herself against the wall and held her breath. No voices. No footsteps. Nothing. Cautiously, she crept along the corridor, poised to flee at the least sound. Still nothing. At the end of the corridor she racked her brains, trying to work out which direction to take. Finally, she gave a mental shrug and turned right, crossing her fingers that her luck would hold.

It did. At the end of the next corridor she came to the top of a shabby, uncarpeted staircase. She breathed a sigh of relief. She was obviously in the servants' quarters. That ruled out the chance of running into any of the guests. Now if only they were all eating, she'd be fine. Sending up a quick prayer, she began to descend the stairs.

At the foot, she froze. Voices! Hardly daring to breathe, she listened. They didn't seem to be coming any closer. A short lobby led directly to the back door, but before she could reach it, she had to pass the opening to what must be the kitchen or the servants' staff room. That was where the voices were coming from. Her theory about everyone having lunch seemed to be about right. Now, if she could just get to the back door, she would be free.

Scarcely daring to breathe, she tiptoed to the opening and cautiously peeked in, to see a dozen or so people sitting around a long wooden table. She ducked back as there was a sudden roar of laughter, then darted past the door while they were all occupied, expecting at any moment to hear shouts and the chairs scraping back and the pounding of feet as they came in pursuit. But nothing like that happened. She breathed a small sigh of relief, then turned her attention to the heavy door in front of her. At first, her heart sank at the barrage of locks and bolts that faced her. Then she managed a little smile; someone up there must love her. There was only one bolt pushed home. All the rest were already drawn back. She reached out and tested it. There was the faint scrape of metal on metal, and she froze and held her breath. What if they heard it?

Just at that moment there was another burst of laughter from the kitchen and she took her courage in both hands and hauled at the bolt. It resisted, and then with another metallic squeal of protest it drew back. She pulled the door and it inched open. She was free!

The chilly air struck through the thin terry robe and she shivered, aware of her bare feet on the cold flagstones. She pulled the material up around her throat and looked round. What now? She had to get as far away as possible as soon as possible, before they noticed she was missing. She took in the expanse of neatly cut lawn that fell away from the garden steps. It led down to a wood. If she could just get into that, they'd never find her. She scampered down the steps and ducked behind the bushes that surrounded the lawn, making her way towards the distant trees.

Twigs and stones hurt her feet as she hurried along, glancing nervously over her shoulder. She winced as a trailing bramble scratched her bare legs, but the trees were nearer now. Ignoring the pain in her feet, she hurried on.

Panting, she leaned against the rough bark of a tree and breathed a sigh of relief. She'd made it. She was safe. All she had to do now was work her way to a road and stop the first car that came along.

Then she froze, as a chilling, high-pitched, ululating sound echoed around the wood. What the hell was that? It came again and it dawned on her what she was hearing. It was a hunting-horn. Was there a local hunt round here? Surely Channing wouldn't allow that on his land; there was far too much he'd want to keep hidden. The sound came again and a wave of horrified realisation washed over her. They were hunting all right – and she was the prey!

As if to confirm her suspicions a gleeful shout of, 'Yoicks! Tally ho!' rang through the air. She heard the sound of galloping horses and, with one horrified glance behind her, she fled deeper into the woods.

Gasping to fill her rasping lungs, she staggered through the undergrowth, oblivious of the branches that tore at her, not even noticing when the towel around her waist snagged on a gorse bush and was ripped away. The sound of her laboured breathing filled her ears, her thudding heartbeat indistinguishable from the sound of the thudding hooves behind her. She stumbled and fell, and instinctively pulled herself to her feet and stumbled blindly on.

The wood was thinning now. In the distance she could see a road, running along beside it. If only she could reach it in time. She redoubled her efforts. Her hopes soared again. There was a car parked there! She sucked in great lungfuls of air and ran on. Her mouth was parched and her throat burned. As she drew nearer, she could make out the shape of someone standing beside the stationary vehicle, and her spirits soared as she realised her ordeal was almost over.

And then she stumbled to a halt and stared in disbelief and despair at the waiting man. It was one of the minders. He grinned into her horrified eyes and she whirled around and set off at an oblique angle back into the woods, the sound of breaking brush close on her left-hand side. Blindly, she crashed on.

A searing pain in her side brought her to a halt in a small clearing. Breasts heaving, she glanced round fearfully. Tears sprang to her eyes as she took in the ring of half-a-dozen grinning faces that looked down on her, the silence broken only by the snorting horses and the sound of her own panting. Her eyes darted round, looking for an escape route, then, like a cornered animal, she broke for a gap in the circle.

They reacted as if it was a signal. There was a triumphant yell and the nearest man swung from his horse and dived after her. For a moment she thought she'd made it, then his hand caught in the collar of her robe and she was jerked backwards as the material ripped away and she fell, naked, to the floor of the clearing.

She scrambled to cover herself, cowering away as he leered down at her. The tight-fitting riding breeches outlined his engorged genitals as his thick cock pushed against the close-fitting material. One hand held a short riding-crop. With taunting slowness he reached for his fly and began to unbutton himself.

'To the victor go the spoils,' he announced, as his prick sprang free, its swollen head shockingly dark against the cream material. There was encouraging laughter from his cronies as they watched avidly. Cassie whimpered and tried to crawl away. A scream of pain broke from her lips as the crop whistled through the air and landed on her exposed buttocks.

'Not so fast, my pretty,' gloated the hunter. 'I haven't had my reward yet.' He fell to his knees behind her and a strong arm slipped beneath her belly, pinning her tightly against his groin. She screamed again as she felt his prick piercing her mercilessly, forcing its way deep inside her. The hand holding her slipped down her belly till it was between the lips of her sex. He rubbed her clitoris roughly and gasped with pleasure, enjoying the feel of his cock as it slid in and out of her. She moaned as the other hand fumbled at her breasts, tugging and twisting at each of her nipples in turn. Her breasts bounced with each thrust, intensifying the feelings radiating through her body. He pounded harder, his balls slapping against the tops of her thighs, and she groaned in despair. It was happening again; the strange alchemy that transformed pain into pleasure. Her hips began to move and she pushed back to meet each thrust, forcing him deeper and deeper inside her, feeling every inch of him filling her to bursting. Her eyes closed to shut out the leering audience and concentrate on her burgeoning orgasm.

He groaned and she felt him pulsing as his jism spurted into her depths, and she shrieked with pleasure as the jerking triggered her own climax, and she sagged against him. A round of ironic applause brought her swiftly back to reality and her eyes widened in horror as the next man swung off his horse and strode across the clearing, his cock already in his hand. Surely they couldn't all be going to take their pleasure with her? She whimpered with trepidation.

The second stranger was already reaching for her when a cool voice interrupted them.

'That's enough! I have other plans for our Miss Grey.'

She looked up through tears to see Channing being wheeled carefully down the rough path into the clearing by two of his minders. He waved an imperious hand and, still grumbling, the hunters turned away and kicked their horse into a canter, leaving them alone.

Channing pulled the tartan rug from his knees and flung it at her. 'Cover yourself,' he ordered. Totally defeated and dishevelled, Cassie did as she was told. He signalled to the taller of the two men. 'Escort the young lady to her room, again.'

The man stepped forward and took Cassie's arm in a grip of iron.

Channing smiled, but his eyes were cold. 'And as for you, Miss Grey,' he said stiffly, 'I shall speak to you about this disgraceful behaviour tomorrow.' He snapped his fingers again and the second man obediently turned the wheelchair and began to push it back the way it had come. Cassie was dragged, stumbling, along behind it, her mind racing fearfully.

What the hell was going to happen to her now?

Chapter Thirteen

As the adrenaline from her frantic flight through the wood wore off, weariness overwhelmed Cassie. The muscles of her thighs trembled with reaction and when she stumbled for the third time and almost fell, Channing snorted with exasperation and snapped his fingers again. 'For God's sake, carry her,' he ordered. 'Otherwise we'll be here all day.' With a smirk, the larger of the two bodyguards obeyed and Cassie was forced to endure being slung unceremoniously over his shoulder like a sack of coal. She didn't even have the strength left to protest, and the rest of the journey back to the house was a miserable combination of discomfort and shame.

Her humiliation was complete when they reached the house again. As she raised her head weakly, she could see grinning faces leering from the windows, revelling in her distress. Channing wheeled himself towards the ramp at the front door, while she was carried round to the back. The servants' entrance, she thought bitterly. How appropriate! The door that she'd thought was her path to freedom opened, then closed behind her with a dull thud, sealing off all hope. She closed her eyes and sagged limply against the broad back of the thug who was carrying her. There was no escape, why bother even trying?

The muffled scream jerked her from her self-pity and lethargy. For a moment she thought she'd imagined it – just one more detail in the nightmare she was enduring – but then it came again. Higher this time, and with an edge of panic that set every nerve in her body jangling. She began to struggle.

It was useless. All that happened was that her captor's grip tightened. She gasped with discomfort as his fingers dug into the backs of her thighs, and he chuckled as their remorseless progress continued.

'Want to see what's happening, do you?' he asked. 'All right then.' He sniggered. 'Your wish is my command, milady.' The screams became louder as he padded along the corridor. Finally, he stopped in front of an open door and turned so that Cassie was facing it. 'Here you are,' he chuckled. 'Take a good look.'

She raised her head and stared in horror at the scene in front of her.

Her first impression, reinforced by the screams, was that the room was painted in blood. The late afternoon sun shone through the closed red curtains, bathing the flushed faces in a lurid glow. It glinted off the teeth and eyes of the grinning audience, making them look like feasting vampires – an impression enhanced by the way the wine in their glasses swirled almost viscously with each languid gesture. Smoke writhed up from cigarettes and expensive cigars and hung in layers on the heavy air, almost, but not quite, concealing the glimpses of exposed breasts and genitals, the busily working fingers. She shuddered. It was a scene from some anteroom to hell.

But it was the feral expression on the faces that frightened her most; as if all humanity had been leached away, leaving only animal lust behind. Reluctantly, she dragged her eyes away from the audience and followed their avid gaze to the raised platform at the far end of the room, to see what had riveted their attention.

For a moment she wasn't quite sure what she was looking at. It was simply a distorted tangle of naked limbs and torsos. Then the pieces began to fall into place.

An ornately carved chair stood in the centre of the stage, and sprawled in it, her legs over its arms so that her vulva gaped obscenely, was the most obese woman Cassie had ever seen. Her huge breasts were supported by the mound of her belly, and folds of sweaty flesh almost obscured her slack sex. Her flabby face was caked in gaudy make-up.

Between the massive thighs stood a familiar figure. Cassie gasped. Tom! It was Tom! He looked even smaller in comparison with the hulk in front of him. He was bent forward, his head trapped in what looked like a miniature version of the old-fashioned stocks that Cassie had seen in museums, his face forced forward into the yawning cunt in front of him. As Cassie watched, the woman writhed, pushing herself harder against him, almost suffocating him in her humid wetness.

Behind Tom stood a tall thin man, covered from head to toe in skin-tight leather. Even his face was covered in a close-fitting leather helmet, with a closed zip where the mouth should be. Only the eyes, glinting from two slits in the mask, showed that this nightmare figure was human – that and the swollen, plum-coloured penis, jutting from the strategically cut hole in the costume. Cassie's eyes widened as the figure raised the whip in its hand and brought it down viciously on Tom's quivering buttocks. He jerked and screamed again, his voice muffled by the woman's wobbling thighs.

She moaned and giggled as the vibrations triggered off another spasm of pleasure, her flesh rolling as she rubbed her obscenely swollen nipples. There was an appreciative spatter of applause from the audience. The leather-clad figure leaned forward and stroked Tom's shrinking buttocks, then turned his attention to his own cock, oiling it till it glistened, pulling and kneading at it until it swelled even further. Then, leaning over, he parted the cheeks of Tom's arse, to reveal the tightly puckered anus. Tom froze in horror as one oily, leather-gloved finger forced its way inside his body, and began to move slowly in and out. When the monster was satisfied Tom was fully lubricated, he hunched over, inserted the swollen head of his cock and pushed his hips forward. There was a heart-rending groan and Cassie watched in horror as, inch by slow inch, the rigid penis disappeared into Tom.

The bizarre figure began to move, faster and faster, his balls slapping against Tom's arse as he thrust. A hand snaked under Tom's belly to grasp his flaccid penis, stroking and tugging until it got a response. Cassie's eyes widened as it swelled, long and thick, its head bulging grotesquely from the leather fist that pumped it. Tom attempted to twist away, but that only forced him further onto his tormentor's prick. His whimpers became those of tortured pleasure and his tongue began to dart into the wet vulva in front of him. The obese woman's squeals and moans intensified under his attentions. Linked together in lust, the trio thrust and rocked like some demented seesaw.

Cassie closed her eyes against Tom's humiliation.

Luckily, her captor intervened. 'Seen enough, have you?' he demanded. 'I hope you enjoyed it.' He chuckled and slid his fingers up between her thighs. 'It'll be your turn next.' As he turned away, jouncing her carelessly on his shoulder, Cassie could hear one last muffled scream, which died away to whimpers and moans. She groaned inwardly. Poor Tom. Like her, he'd got a lot more than he bargained for.

Her pity was washed away by a wave of fear. 'Her turn next', the thug had said. Her all-too-vivid imagination immediately replayed the scene just witnessed, with herself in the starring role. It was *her* face thrust deeper and deeper into the swamp of the fat woman's cunt. *Her* poor cheeks that the lash cut down upon. *Her* trembling buttocks that were forced apart as the nightmarish leather creature rammed his rigid prick up her anus. She moaned at the very thought of it all.

'Turns you on, does it, you randy little slut?' sniggered the thug, misinterpreting her reaction. 'Well, don't worry. You won't have long to wait. The master's got something really special lined up for you – and your friends.' He deposited her roughly in front of the door of the room, and grinned down at her. 'Maybe he'll tell you about it when he sees you tomorrow.' Still smirking, he unlocked the door, pushed her in and banged it closed behind her.

For a moment she stood, staring at the blank face of the locked door, too tired even to think.

A hand on her shoulder made her jump and spin round. 'Are you all right?' asked Tanisha. 'You look awful.'

'I feel awful,' muttered Cassie, limping across to the bed and collapsing gratefully onto it. 'You were right. It was hopeless. I should never have tried to get away in the first place.'

'You were set up,' said Tanisha, grimly. 'I listened at the door after you left. The two bodyguards were laughing about it. Talking about "the hunt", who'd get "the brush", and wishing they'd been in at "the kill". You never stood a chance. They only allowed you to get as far as you did to make the chase more interesting.'

Cassie stared at her in despair. 'You mean, they knew about it all the time?'

'Of course they did,' said Tanisha. 'Why do you think the door was left open? It wasn't an accident at all. They left it like that on purpose so you'd try to get away. While you were running for your life, they were out there on the come again, bringing with it temporary freedom.

But it didn't. Instead, her mind started churning over the horrible events of the day, and, even worse, the possibilities the next would bring. What would Channing do to her for attempting to escape? She shook her head. She was probably worrying about nothing. It wouldn't be fair to punish her. He was the one who'd set it all up in the first place. If she thought about it logically, she'd done exactly what he'd wanted her to do. She could hardly be punished for that... could she?

The sheets tangled round her as she tossed and turned restlessly. Music and laughter and the tinkle of glasses disturbed her even more, making sleep impossible. Finally, she gave up and padded across to the window.

She must have dozed for longer than she'd thought. It was dark outside, the trees and bushes nothing but a black, shadowy mass, outlined against the sky. The only light came from the front windows of the house, which cast a yellow rectangle on the gravel of the drive and the edge of the lawn. Distorted silhouettes moved back and forth across it, like puppets in a shadow play.

Her curiosity piqued, Cassie craned her neck to see more. If she moved right to the edge of the window and flattened her face against the glass, she could see into a tiny corner of the room – see the people instead of the puppets. For a moment she couldn't believe her eyes. The *shadows* hadn't been distorted at all. It was the *people* themselves who were twisted and misshapen! As if their sadistic natures had finally manifested themselves physically. She shook her head. It was impossible; she must be imagining things. Either that or her recent experiences had affected her mind. She peered again, holding her hand to the window to cut out reflection, so that she could see more clearly. Nothing changed. Then it dawned on her what she was looking at and she breathed a sigh of relief, grateful that her sanity was still intact.

They were having some kind of fancy dress party. The distorted heads were simply grotesque masks. As she watched, a dog stood for a moment with its back against the window, its stubby tail wagging up and down. Cassie blushed and took a step back from the glass. It wasn't a tail at all! The man, whoever he was, was actually *facing* the window, his dog-mask on the back of his head. As she watched a hand, male or female, she didn't know and didn't care, reached round and grabbed the rigid cock, and pulled its owner back into the room and out of her sight.

The window remained empty for a few seconds, then a couple took the place of the dog-man. Like him, they were naked, except for their masks – one of a stag with branching antlers, the other of a cat. Both were female, their bodies writhing together as their hands ran over each other's breasts and explored the shadowy valleys between their thighs. As Cassie watched, they were joined by a third person, male this time, in a clown mask. He slid an arm round the women's shoulders, grabbing a breast in each hand, his thumbs stroking the swollen nipples. The masks remained impassive as the women returned the compliment, their hands meeting on his prick, moving up and down in unison with the fingers they were thrusting in and out of each other. There was a screech of drunken laughter as his skinny buttocks suddenly jerked and his seed spattered against the window-pane and ran down in viscous droplets. Cassie pulled a face of disgust as they, too, turned and vanished into the whirl of smoke and throbbing music.

A shark swam into view next, the blank black eyes and gaping jaws so realistic that the effect on top of a female body was one of some horrible mutation. An experiment gone terribly wrong.

The shark's companion obviously didn't feel the same. His lizard head was cocked at an expectant angle as he kneaded the shark's sagging breasts enthusiastically, then reared back in ecstasy as the shark slid its way downwards. Cassie watched in horror as his swollen penis disappeared inside the huge jaws, as they engulfed his lower body and began to bob up and down. Logically, she knew that the woman inside the costume was simply sucking him off, but, at this distance, his expression of pleasure could equally well have been a grimace of pain. It looked as if he was being eaten alive.

Suddenly the head stopped bobbing, the shark stood up and the couple stared into the room as if someone had just entered.

The silence, when it came, was almost as much of a shock as the scenes she'd just witnessed. The music and laughter shut off as abruptly as if a knife had come down and cut off all sound. For a moment there was nothing but an expectant hush – then it was broken by a familiar voice. Cassie stifled a nervous giggle. His master's voice! She couldn't make out the words, but whatever he said, it was greeted by a roar of approval, then silence fell again, broken only by the slow beating of a drum. There was a pause, which was followed by a chilling shriek that split the night.

Cassie's stomach knotted in dismay. That was Tanisha! As she listened, trembling, the shriek came again – and again. Suddenly feeling sick, Cassie covered her ears and fled to the bed, pulling the pillows over her head to shut out the whimpers of pain and distress.

She lay there for what seemed like forever, trying not to think about what was happening to her friend. Time stretched out endlessly in the darkness and fingers of light were beginning to pierce the night sky before the sounds of revelry finally faded away and she heard footsteps in the corridor.

The door swung open and Tanisha practically fell into the room. Cassie sat up in bed and her mouth fell open as she looked at her friend. Her eyes were puffy with crying, her buttocks were covered in fine weals and, worst of all, there was a perfect crescent of teeth marks in the soft flesh around one black nipple.

'What happened?' she gasped. 'What have they done to you?'

Tanisha tried to smile with bruised lips. 'Don't ask,' she whispered painfully. 'You really don't want to know.'

'Here, let me help you,' said Cassie, leaping out of bed. She slid an arm round Tanisha's waist. 'Can you walk?'

Tanisha nodded and Cassie helped her through to the shower room. She grabbed the bathroom stool and shoved it into the shower cabinet. If the water ruined it, tough sodding luck! 'Here, sit on this,' she ordered. Gratefully, Tanisha did as she was told and Cassie turned the spray on so that the water was barely dribbling out. Trying not to touch the worst weals, she gently soaped her friend's bruised body, then washed the bubbles away, patted her dry and helped her through to the bedroom again.

Tanisha lowered herself gingerly into bed and Cassie pulled the covers up over her shoulders. 'Try and get some sleep,' she advised. 'You'll feel better in the morning.'

'It already is morning,' mumbled Tanisha, then fell instantly into a sleep of total exhaustion. Cassie climbed in and lay beside her, watching through the window as dawn crept slowly across the sky.

She was right, it was morning… and today she had to face the master!

Chapter Fourteen

Cassie stayed in bed for as long as she could, huddled under the covers, putting off the evil moment when she would have to get up and face another day. She was beginning to lose track of time, one day blending into another, great tracts of boredom interspersed with moments of pain and terror.

Tanisha lay beside her, silent except for the occasional whimper in her sleep. Cautiously, Cassie pulled back the sheet and examined the marks on their bodies. She shivered. The teeth imprints around Tanisha's nipple had bloomed into one bruise, making it look as if one breast had an areola twice the size of the other. What kind of animal did that sort of thing? She closed her eyes and prayed she would never find out.

She was so lost in her thoughts that she didn't hear the door open again. A sharp slap and a harsh voice brought her bolt upright, one hand clutching the covers to her breasts, the other holding her stinging cheek. 'You... you frightened me,' she gasped, staring up into the stern face of the housekeeper.

'Serves you right,' the woman snapped, glaring at Cassie with contempt. Her right hand clenched and unclenched as if she was itching for an excuse to slap her again. 'Lying there at this time in the morning. You aren't being paid to lounge around doing nothing. Do you think this is some kind of holiday camp?' She flung an armful of clothes onto the bed. 'Get up!' she ordered.

Obediently, Cassie did as she was told, trying vainly to

hide her nakedness from the woman's probing gaze.

'Get yourself dressed and get something to eat,' she went on. 'The master wishes to speak with you. I shall be back to collect you in half an hour. No later.' She ran her eyes over Cassie's shrinking body. 'If you aren't ready by then, I shall call the men, have them dress you forcibly and drag you before the master.' She smiled cruelly. 'I am sure they would find that amusing.' With a final contemptuous sneer, she turned on her heel and stalked out again.

'Miss Congeniality nineteen-forty-nine,' muttered Tanisha from under the covers. Cassie jumped.

'I thought you were asleep,' she accused.

'I was,' groaned Tanisha, 'but Miss Sweetness and Light put a stop to that. I just kept my mouth shut in case she started on me as well.'

'Thanks,' said Cassie grimly. 'Nice to know your friends will back you up.' She remembered the marks on Tanisha's battered body and bit her lip. In a situation like this, they were *all* on their own. It would be better not to forget it. 'Sorry,' she apologised, 'you had a hard night. Go back to sleep.' She looked down and smiled ruefully. Tanisha already had.

Gingerly, she picked up the clothes the woman had left and examined them. To her relief, they were perfectly normal. She might even have picked them out herself if she'd been going out clubbing and fancied looking a bit tarty. Admittedly the tight black lycra skirt was short and the red top was low-cut, but there was nothing particularly kinky about them. She looked round for the underwear, and her lips tightened. How silly of her. That was too much to expect.

She slipped the clothes on and looked at herself in the mirror. The top hugged her breasts and her nipples stood out against the clingy material, while the skirt clung to her thighs like a second skin. With the stiletto shoes, the whole effect certainly was a bit tarty, but if she walked slowly and didn't bend over, she didn't look too bad. She stared at her reflection in satisfaction. If the thugs were expecting a free peepshow, they were in for a disappointment this time.

At that moment the door burst open again. The look of disappointment on the housekeeper's face revealed that she'd been hoping she'd find Cassie still cowering in bed and had been looking forward to dragging her out, begging pitifully for mercy. Deprived of the excuse to abuse her, she looked sourer than ever.

Pleased with her minor triumph, Cassie favoured her with a smile. 'All ready,' she said brightly. 'What kept you?'

'You'll be smiling on the other side of your face soon, missy,' hissed the old hag, and Cassie's brief moment of ascendancy immediately crumbled. The woman would make a really bad enemy, so it had probably been a really silly idea to antagonise her. She obviously despised the girls who came here. Cassie looked at the woman's scrawny figure and wondered how much of it was jealousy; envy of the money they made and the looks they were blessed with. Or – and an even more disconcerting thought – perhaps she wanted to be one of the bodies sacrificed on the altar of Channing's depravity.

Cassie shook her head to remove the unpleasant picture of the housekeeper stretched naked and splayed, shrieking her pleasure as she was whipped and abused.

'On your feet,' ordered the woman. Her face was blank again, carefully schooled into an emotionless mask. Cassie shuddered as she got up; somehow that was even more frightening than the brief flicker of disappointment she'd front lawn on their horses, all dressed up in red coats and jodhpurs, as if it was a proper fox-hunt. They even had one of those thingamajigs. You know, a big silver bowl with punch or something in it.'

'A stirrup cup,' said Cassie, bitterly. 'Oh yes, one must do these things properly, mustn't one?' She groaned inwardly. All that pain and humiliation for nothing. She'd never had a chance. Her so-called 'freedom' had been an illusion. It had all been a charade for the amusement of her tormentors, and like a complete idiot she'd fallen for it.

She longed for a hot bath, to soothe her aching body, but she had to settle for the inevitable shower. Running the water as hot as she could stand, she scrubbed the worst of the forest dirt from her body and rubbed her scratches and bruises with cream from the cabinet. Finally, she collapsed into bed and pulled the covers over her head. If they wanted her again, they'd have to drag her out kicking and screaming. Not that that would stop them, she thought miserably. They'd probably enjoy it.

She heard the maid come in with the food trolley, but was too exhausted to get up and eat. Then she must have dozed for a while, because the next thing she heard was the sound of harsh voices. She scrunched her eyes tight and huddled into a tight ball, tugging the bedclothes protectively around her, expecting every minute that they would be pulled off and hands would haul her out. She held her breath and waited, cringing.

Nothing happened. Instead, silence fell again. Cautiously she stuck her head out. 'Tanisha?' she called softly. There was no answer. The room was empty. Cassie shivered, caught between a mixture of pity for the other girl and relief that this time it was someone else who was going to suffer. She closed her eyes and willed sleep to seen earlier. At least that had made the woman seem human.

Despite Cassie's compliance, the woman took the opportunity to seize her and pull her towards the door, her bony fingers digging into and pinching the soft flesh of her underarm. Struggling to keep up with her in the awkward stiletto heels, Cassie stumbled along the corridors until the housekeeper stopped and tapped on yet another closed door.

'Come in,' ordered Channing's emotionless voice. The housekeeper opened the door and tugged Cassie in after her.

'The young lady to see you, sir,' announced the woman deferentially, though her flashing eyes suggested that, given the choice, 'young lady' were the last two words she would have used to describe Cassie.

'Thank you, Watkins, that will be all,' he said, dismissing her. With obvious reluctance she left, closing the door behind her, and Cassie gazed around in amazement.

The room was fitted out almost like an operating theatre, its white-painted walls gleaming under the overhead light. Against them stood a couple of theatre trolleys, laden with equipment. In the centre stood a waist-high couch, upon which Channing was lying, face down, naked, except for a towel covering his buttocks. A tall middle-aged woman in a white smock, grey-blonde hair pulled back in a tight bun, was bent over him, massaging his back and shoulders. The smell of aromatic oils filled the air.

'Enough,' he ordered, snapping his fingers. 'Miss Grey can take over from here.' The woman stopped massaging, wiped her hands and silently took her leave. Cassie stood waiting. He raised his head and glared at her. 'Don't just stand there, girl,' he snapped. 'Get on with it. I'm waiting.'

She stared at the array of oils on the nearest trolley.

What on earth was she supposed to do now? Seeing his look of impatience, she grabbed the nearest vial, poured some of its contents into the palm of her hand and gingerly began to rub.

'Oh, for God's sake,' he snarled. 'Can't you do anything right? Harder than that, I won't break.' Cassie took a deep breath and dug her fingers as firmly as she could into the muscles of his back, marvelling at the strength of his upper body in contrast to the thin, wasted legs. His skin felt warm and firm beneath her hands. Gaining confidence, she began to knead and pummel. He gave a groan of satisfaction and for a few moments there was a contented silence. Lulled by her own rhythmic movements, Cassie began to relax.

Too soon.

'So, you don't like staying with us,' he commented casually, as though the question was of little consequence. 'You've changed your mind about our little agreement.' He turned and smiled at her over his shoulder. 'Now, why didn't you just say so, you silly girl?' he chided. 'Instead of trying to run away like that?'

Cassie stared at him, fresh hope shining in her eyes. 'You... you mean, that's all I had to do?' she gasped. 'Just tell you I wanted to go home and that would have been it?' He continued to smile and she closed her eyes and groaned at her own stupidity. Everything she'd gone through could have been avoided. The pain, the humiliation, the shame of being screwed in front of a leering audience. What an idiot she'd been. 'So I can leave whenever I want, then?' She smiled, relief washing through her.

'Of course… you can't!' He grinned broadly, savouring the expression of stunned disappointment on Cassie's poor face. The grin turned into jeering laughter that echoed in her ears. 'You should see your face,' he spluttered. 'What a picture. Did you really think you would get away that easily?' He went off into another mocking peal of amusement.

She stared at him in horror, her heart sinking. How could he be so horrible – offering her hope like that, then snatching it away for his own perverted entertainment? The others might have abused her body, but he had abused her emotions, and that was infinitely more cruel.

'You bastard!' she hissed. Rage overwhelmed her and for a moment she could hardly think straight. She looked round desperately for something to strike back with and her eye fell on the other trolley. She took in its contents at a glance. Condoms, lubricants, a speculum that indicated someone obviously liked to play doctor, and a selection of vibrators. Her lips set grimly as she reached for the longest, thickest one – black and ribbed at the base of the bulbous knob. She had nothing left to lose, so she would see how he appreciated being on the receiving end for a change!

She grabbed it with oily hands and, with one swift movement, whipped off the towel, slid the brute up between his legs and pressed it as far as she could into his rectum, the end sticking out obscenely. Without considering the consequences, she switched it on. There was a low-pitched whine and it began to vibrate.

His body arched and stiffened and his mouth opened in a soundless 'O' of disbelief as he attempted to reach back and pull it out.

'So, you can feel that, can you?' she goaded, slapping his hand away. 'So how do *you* like it?'

His only answer was a strangled moan as he rolled over on his side, still trying to grasp the throbbing vibrator and remove it. She grinned viciously and a wave of cruel power surged through her as she stared down at his helplessly twitching body. The boot was on the other foot now and she could hardly believe how good it felt. Her nipples stiffened against the soft fabric of her top and warm moisture flooded her vulva – then her eyes widened as she caught sight of his groin.

Instead of the softness of impotence she'd expected, he had a raging erection, his cock swollen almost to bursting point. It speared out, the head tight and purple, a small bead of moisture gathering at its tip. He looked down at himself in astonishment and an uncertain smile crossed his face.

'Well, don't just stand there, girl,' he croaked, reaching out to grasp her. 'Do what you're paid to do.'

'No... no...' she whispered, shaking her head and backing away, hands behind her back. This wasn't supposed to happen. All she'd wanted to do was give him a taste of his own medicine, not turn him on. The thought of having to impale herself on his rampant prick was totally repulsive. Her one consolation was that, trapped by his wasted legs, he couldn't reach her to force her participation.

But it was a false consolation; if he couldn't reach her one way, he was clever enough to reach her by another.

'You wanted out, didn't you?' he gasped. She looked at him, hope rising again. 'Well, this is your chance to earn your freedom. What have you got to lose? Nothing.' He paused. 'I could ring for the guards, have them screw you in front of me and *then* fuck you myself. Or I could call Watkins back. I'm sure she'd be delighted to teach you a little lesson in obedience and respect.'

Cassie shuddered at the thought. Despite feeling like a moth being hopelessly drawn to a dangerous source of light, she made her decision. If she didn't obey voluntarily, he would have her forced – of that there was little doubt.

So, she gingerly approached his twisted body. His hands shot out and gripped her like steel, hauling her on top of him, his cock, trapped between their bodies, still pulsing in unison with the movement of the vibrator buried inside him.

Hauling her into a kneeling position, he tugged up her skirt to reveal her plump, shaven pudenda, her sex opening like some exotic man-eating flower, glistening pinkly as he pulled her astride his face. He gripped her hips, forcing her down so that her juicy sex hovered tantalisingly above his lips. She moaned and slipped one hand behind her to grasp his throbbing cock, gripping it tightly as she pumped it up and down, while the other stroked her clitoris. He moaned and his tongue flickered out, tasting her sweet juices. She lowered herself further and it was her turn to moan as his tongue pierced her, lapping at her, sucking the hard bud into his mouth and nibbling at it gently. He reached up and pulled down her top, her breasts tumbling free into his waiting hands, his thumbs kneading her swollen nipples.

Panting, she pulled herself away and wriggled down his body towards his eager cock. She groaned as she parted the lips of her sex with one hand and took him in the other, sliding his hot length slowly inside her as she began to rise and fall. He groaned and tried to pull her hips harder against himself, but she resisted him. He was hers to use, not the other way round. She moved slowly, withdrawing until the swollen head of his cock was almost out of her, then plunging back, feeling every inch of him filling her, savouring every quiver of the vibrator as it was transmitted through his prick, sending waves of sensation through her body. At last it was too much for her. Her movements became frantic as she rode him, faster and faster, ramming his prick as far into her as it would go. Her long blonde hair tossed wildly as she flung her head back, her mouth opening in a scream as he moaned in release, swelling and jerking inside her, triggering her own tumultuous orgasm. She juddered and collapsed against him, utterly spent.

It was at least five minutes before she recovered, climbed stiffly from the couch and adjusted her clothes. Averting her eyes, she pulled the vibrator from his rectum and covered his groin – his detumescent penis still gleaming wetly from her juices – with the towel. Throughout it all he gazed at her silently, his wolfish eyes glinting.

Finally, she could stand the silence no longer. 'Well?' she said meekly, 'hasn't the master got anything to say for himself?'

His face broke into a smug leer of satisfaction. 'That's the first time I've fucked–' one eyebrow quirked humorously '–or should I say, *been* fucked, since the accident,' he said. 'I'm very grateful to you.'

She looked at him hopefully. 'Does that mean you'll keep your promise? That I can leave now?' she asked.

He gave a harsh snort of laughter. 'Leave? And deprive me of such a jewel? Whatever gave you that idea?' His lips curled in a sneer. 'Promises are like pie crusts; made to be broken. Did you think *that*–' he indicated their recent activities with a cursory wave of the hand '–was going to make me fall madly in love with you and grant your every wish?' He shook his head at her naivety. 'Oh no, my dear.' His expression of smugness increased. 'Haven't you learned the simplest things by now? You disobeyed me by running away, and for that you must be punished. And punished severely.'

'But – but that's not fair,' protested Cassie. 'You set me up. You had the door left open. You made the guards stay away.' She glared at him. 'You *wanted* me to try and escape. How can you turn round now and blame me? It just isn't fair...' she complained again, hopelessly, on the verge of tears.

'But, young lady, life isn't fair,' he explained patiently – patronisingly. 'You should know that by now. You lost your job, while the man who fired you is living perfectly happily without even giving you a second thought. You were blackmailed into taking this job. You have been consistently abused since you got here.' He gazed at her in amused exasperation. 'And you still talk about "fair"?' He shook his head. 'It seems you still have a lot to learn.' His smile became unpleasant. 'And it seems that I must teach you.'

He pressed a button, concealed beneath the table, and the door swung open. The tall, white-smocked masseuse walked in. He smiled at her. 'Miss Grey has been kind enough to do me a favour and so she must be rewarded.' He looked Cassie up and down. 'You have a very pretty body, my dear, which I have every intention of putting to good use in the very near future. But everything can be improved.' He put a finger to his lips. 'Ah, yes. A little extra adornment for those luscious breasts, I think.' He clicked his fingers at the masseuse.

Cassie shrank away as she approached, backing away until she was trapped against the wall. She put her hands up to defend herself, but it was useless. With muscles developed by years of performing massages, the woman simply caught both Cassie's wrists and twisted her arms behind her, forcing her towards an upright chair in the corner. Before she knew what was happening, her arms were deftly tied to the back.

Without a word, the woman pulled down Cassie's top. Forced forward by the pressure on her arms, her breasts thrust proudly out, the nipples soft and vulnerable. Channing lay back, watching with avidity. Cassie gasped as the woman took her nipples between her fingers and twisted them sharply until they stiffened under her attentions.

Satisfied, she walked across to the trolley and returned with a small kidney-shaped basin in one hand. Cassie's eyes widened in horror as she saw the long sterilised needle. 'No,' she whimpered. 'Please, no.'

Ignoring her pleas, the woman took a small tube and sprayed the contents onto Cassie's nipples. Icy coldness was followed by blessed numbness as she took the needle and, with infinite care, slid it through Cassie's shrinking flesh. Finally, she fitted a tiny gold ring through each nipple, joined by a thin gold chain.

'Excellent,' said Channing, tipping his head sideways to admire the effect. He smiled into Cassie's tormented eyes. 'You see?' he said. 'I told you life was unfair. You gave me pleasure and I have rewarded you with pain.' He held up a finger. 'But that pain has, in turn, made you more beautiful. As the French say, "*Il faut suffrire pour Ítre belle*".'

His smile widened and she looked at him in dread.

'And you must look your best, my dear,' he purred. 'Once you have recovered, I have something rather special in mind for you and your two little friends.' He chuckled. 'There are other rewards to look forward to.' He clicked his fingers again and the door opened.

Sobbing and cradling her wounded breasts, Cassie stumbled from the room.

Chapter Fifteen

The next three days passed in a blur of pain and exhaustion. Cassie slept and woke, drifting from the nightmare world of sleep to the even worse one of reality. Even Tanisha's efforts to make her eat failed, as she escaped back into oblivion.

On the third day she was woken by a brisk slap. Her eyes snapped open, expecting to see the hated face of Watkins glaring down at her. But it wasn't. It was Tanisha.

She held her cheek and looked up at her friend's angry face with hurt eyes and a total lack of comprehension. 'What did you do that for?' she whimpered. 'I want to go to sleep.' She closed her eyes again. Another sharp slap followed the first.

'You ain't dead yet, girl,' snarled Tanisha. 'But you soon will be if you go on like this. Get your skinny white ass in gear and get out of that bed – before I drag you out.'

Still holding her face, Cassie scrambled out from under the covers and sat sulkily on the side of the bed. 'You didn't have to hit me,' she snapped.

Tanisha grinned. At least Cassie was showing a bit of spirit, instead of just lying there.

'Oh yes I did,' she snapped back. 'You turning into a zombie, girl.'

A cup of coffee and a steaming plate of food were thrust under Cassie's nose. 'Eat!' Tanisha ordered. 'You've got to get your strength back.' Her face became grim. '*He* wants to see you.'

There was no need to ask whom she was referring to.

'Why?' asked Cassie, her stomach shrivelling.

'I don't know, do I?' muttered Tanisha. 'That damned housekeeper was in with another kinky outfit this morning. It's over there on the chair.' She pointed. Cassie concentrated on her food, refusing to look in case it spoiled her already paltry appetite. 'He's coming along later this morning.' She looked at Cassie in awe. 'You must have made a big impression on him, if he's coming here, instead of having you hauled along to see him.'

Cassie winced and touched the rings in her aching nipples, from which the thin gold chain dangled. If she'd impressed him, he had a funny way of showing it. 'I don't care,' she muttered rebelliously. 'He might want to see me, but I don't want to see him.' Strengthened by her first decent meal in days, her spirit was coming back. She finished her last mouthful of coffee and rolled back into bed, turning her back and pulling the covers over her head. Her muffled voice came defiantly from beneath the duvet. 'He can go to hell! I'm on strike!'

Tanisha glanced fearfully over her shoulder. 'You can't do that,' she insisted.

'Just watch me,' muttered Cassie, pulling the covers tighter.

She was still in bed when the door opened and Channing wheeled himself in.

'Why aren't you ready?' he demanded. 'The car's waiting for you.'

'I'm not going anywhere,' Cassie said defiantly. 'I'm on strike.'

'Don't be ridiculous,' he said. 'We have a deal. If you refuse to abide by it, you will not be paid.'

She sat up, long hair tousled, and glared at him. '"We had a deal"? Well, what about you?' She blushed with indignity. 'You said I could "earn my freedom" if I did what you wanted. What about *that* deal?'

He smiled coldly. 'I said you had a *chance* to earn your freedom,' he corrected, and then shrugged. 'You also have a *chance* to win the lottery. Unfortunately these things seldom happen.' His smile vanished. 'Now get up and get dressed. You've got work to do.'

'Forget it!' she exclaimed. 'I'm not doing anything I don't want to. And you can't make me.'

Channing became very still, and when he spoke again, his voice sent shivers down her spine. 'Oh, I'm afraid you're wrong there,' he said softly. 'I can make you do anything I want.' He wheeled himself over to the bed and yanked off the covers. Cassie rolled away, turning her back on him.

It was a mistake. Her smooth, peach-shaped bottom presented an irresistible target. He leaned over and lashed out at it, his palm connecting with her tender flesh. Her buttocks quivered under the blow, the shape of his palm and fingers white against her skin, then flooding scarlet as the blood rushed back. She squealed with pain. His hand rose and fell again and again. She squirmed away and tumbled out of the other side of the bed, landing with a thud, arms and legs akimbo.

Before she could recover, he had spun himself round. The wheels of the chair stopped, bare inches from her splayed fingers. He smiled down at her as she lay there, breasts heaving, frightened to move. 'You're going to regret your rash behaviour,' he said quietly. 'No one disobeys me.' He clicked his fingers and the door opened. Miss Watkins stood there. 'Take Miss Grey to the Black Room,' he ordered. 'And teach her a little lesson in co-operation.'

Smiling grimly, the woman bent over, hauled Cassie to her feet and dragged her protesting from the room. She stumbled, naked, along the corridor until Watkins opened a door and pushed her through, following closely behind. Cassie whirled round and threw herself at the door as it banged shut, only to be hauled back by her hair and flung across the room.

She lost her balance and fell, hitting against a coarse wooden frame. Staggering, she pulled herself to her feet, ready to make another dash for the door – but Miss Watkins was too quick and too experienced. Seizing Cassie's arm, she pulled it up behind her back and forced her round, snapping a manacle round her free wrist, then twisting the other until she could trap that, too. As Cassie tugged futilely against her restraints, Watkins kicked her legs apart and manacled her ankles as well, so that she was spread-eagled against the rough wood, splinters digging into her already tender breasts.

She stopped struggling and took in her surroundings with a shudder. No wonder they called it the Black Room! Black walls, black drapery – even the wooden frame she was pinioned to was painted black. One wall was made of reflective black glass, in which she could see herself; her pale, naked body almost luminous in contrast. In the black glass another dim reflection moved towards her.

'Well, missy,' said Watkins, with satisfaction. 'Not so smart now, are we?

Cassie craned over her shoulder, frantically trying to see what the woman was doing. She froze as she caught sight of the thin leather whip dangling from a loop around her skinny wrist. Watkins rolled up her sleeves, took a firm grip of the handle, and raised her arm.

The noise came first: a thin, whistling sound as the lash flickered through the air, followed by a sharp snap as it landed on Cassie's clenched buttocks and curled round her hip. Then came the pain, so intense it seemed to Cassie as if an electric shock had shot through her. Her body arched against it, her breath rushing out in a soundless scream.

One blow followed another until Cassie lost count, reduced to a tremulous, exhausted wreck. 'No… no…' she sobbed. 'Please, no more… I'll do anything.'

Mercifully, the whipping ceased and Cassie sagged in relief.

'That's better,' smirked Watkins. She stepped forward and ran a professional hand over Cassie's shaking body, smiling in satisfaction. Despite the biting pain, the smooth skin was unbroken, the thin weals already fading into a general redness.

The hand lingered, tracing the warm curve of Cassie's back, drifting lower to explore the firm roundness of her buttocks. Cassie froze as the bony fingers slid between her thighs and parted the soft lips of her vulva, probing the warm wetness inside. The woman's breath began to come faster as her other hand snaked round to the front of Cassie's body, to squeeze the plump globes of her breasts.

'No,' whimpered Cassie, as the woman's hateful hands crawled all over her. Surely the beating was enough, without this added humiliation? She shivered with a mixture of shame and pleasure as Watkins' thumb expertly caressed the tight bud of her clitoris, eliciting an unwanted response. 'No... no…' she mumbled again as a pulse of heat radiated through her loins, mixing with the burning sensation from her beaten bottom. The attentions ceased and she breathed a sigh of relief – until she lifted her head weakly and glanced over her shoulder again.

The loathsome woman was stripping, her fingers fumbling eagerly at the buttons on her dull black dress. As Cassie watched with horrified fascination, she shed it like a lizard shedding its skin, to reveal scrawny shanks and pendulous breasts that contrasted horribly with the lacy black bra and panties she was wearing underneath. All too soon, those were shed as well and she stood there, like a pallid scarecrow, grinning as one hand stroked the swollen nipples on her dangling breasts while the other thrust between her own thighs. Her breath became heavier as she pleasured herself, then, as Cassie watched in horror, she turned to a small chest of drawers, pulled it open and reached in. Cassie gasped as she produced a black, double-headed dildo. Unable to drag her eyes away, she stared as the woman lowered herself and squatted slightly, parting the wiry bush of grey pubic hair to slide the horrible object deep into her cunt.

'Please... no,' she begged, as Watkins approached, licking her lips, the other half of the rigid plastic cock jutting from her body and bobbing with every step. Its head gleamed in the bright overhead lights as the woman advanced. Her pleading was useless. The woman's hands began their exploration again. Cassie could feel the heat radiating from Watkins' skinny body, the hard nipples boring against her back as the woman writhed against her, the dildo trapped between their closely pressed bodies. She flung her head back in torment as her nipples were teased and twisted, till they hardened, despite her abhorrence. The gold rings tugged against the swollen flesh, intensifying the sensation. She moaned in despair as the woman's fingers found her clitoris again, rubbing and stroking. Moisture began to seep between her thighs.

'You love it, don't you, you little slut?' gloated Watkins. 'You can't get enough of it.' Her fingers plunged deeper and Cassie moaned again, the muscles of her thighs beginning to quiver and loosen.

There was a fumbling behind her and she felt the plastic dildo jabbing and prodding at the entrance to her body.

She stiffened, clenching herself to try and prevent the horrible intrusion, but it was useless. Slick with her own juices, it slid easily upwards, piercing her. She whimpered as the cold plastic thrust its way deep inside her and began to move.

In the black glass, Cassie could see their reflection, the despicable woman's skinny hips jerking as she thrust at her helplessly bound body. She moaned as she watched the black dildo sliding in and out between the vulnerable lips of her vulva, her pale flesh shuddering under the onslaught. The thin gold chain jangled softly as her breasts bounced and wobbled with every vile movement. Her eyelids flickered shut as wave after wave of sensation radiated through her and she forgot everything as she savoured the tightening in her loins that preceded her orgasm. Balancing on the balls of her feet, she pushed her hips back to meet each thrust, revelling in the insatiable stiffness impaling her, moving quicker and quicker, her breath coming in short gasps – then she arched her back and screamed as her emotions exploded. Panting, she sagged against the wooden frame, exhausted and sated as the woman withdrew, the black plastic beaded with moisture. There was a disgusting sucking noise as she slid it out of her own body before cleaning it reverently and placing it back into its drawer, then began calmly dressing.

There was a ripple of sound, which grew louder and louder. Cassie's head jerked up as she tried to identify it. Horrified recognition dawned on her. It was applause! Frantically she looked around, searching for the source. Her eyes fell on the black reflective glass and a surge of intense shame rushed through her as she realised what she was looking at. It wasn't reflective glass at all. It was two-way glass, the kind that was used in expensive cars, so that the pampered occupants could look out, without being seen.

She groaned, her humiliation complete at the thought that an unseen audience had watched the whole sordid episode. The applause hung in the air, mocking her, and she leaned her forehead against the coarse wood as tears of shame and anger forced their way from beneath her closed eyelids.

Utterly cowed, she allowed Watkins to unfasten the manacles and pull her from the room, her head bowed and her hair hanging down over her face to mask her shame and humiliation.

After a quick shower, Cassie found Channing in the room waiting for her. Only an hour had passed, but to Cassie it felt like a lifetime.

'Well,' he smiled cruelly, 'have you learned your lesson yet, or should I have Watkins repeat it?'

Cassie caught the look of barely suppressed eagerness on the woman's face, and shuddered. 'No,' she whispered humbly, avoiding his eyes. 'I'll do whatever you want.'

'Good,' he said. 'Now get dressed.' He flung an armful of clothes at her. 'The car's still waiting.'

Conscious of his eyes on her naked body, she reluctantly picked the clothes off the floor and began to slip them on, her distaste growing with every garment.

There was a pair of tiny white panties, embroidered with rosebuds. These were followed by a short pink dress that barely covered the white panties. It had a white Peter Pan collar and a smock top. The rest of the outfit consisted of a pair of flat patent leather shoes with a strap-and-button fastening, and a pair of neat white ankle-socks.

'Excellent,' beamed Channing, as Cassie stood awkwardly in front of him in her new finery. He snapped his fingers at Tanisha, who was sitting in the corner, trying to look as small as possible. 'Now, do her hair.' He stared at Cassie, tapping his bottom lip, thoughtfully. 'Either bunches or pigtails, I think.'

Cassie sat in front of the mirror and stared as Tanisha's strong brown fingers deftly wielded the brush, transforming her. Her slightly damp hair was pulled into two tight plaits that hung down her back, tied off with pink ribbons that matched her dress. She gaped at herself in dismay. Apart from her generous breasts, pushing against the smocking, she looked like a girl about to go to a party.

'I... I...' she stuttered.

Channing chuckled. 'It's entirely appropriate, given that you're going to a tea party with your favourite uncle. Isn't that nice?'

Cassie barely heard his words, staring open-mouthed at herself in the mirror.

'Now come along,' he continued. 'You don't want to be late.' He spun the chair and wheeled himself towards the door. With a fearful glance at Watkins' disappointed face, Cassie reluctantly trailed after him.

The car was waiting at the front door, the chauffeur standing stiffly to attention as Channing wheeled up. 'Miss Grey is going to visit her Uncle Albert,' he smiled. 'You know where to go?' The chauffeur nodded obediently and opened the back door for Cassie, his eyes lingering on her thighs as the short dress rode up to reveal the white panties underneath.

The door closed and Cassie sank into the soft leather, recalling how she'd happily climbed into this same car not so very long ago. Now she'd give anything to go back in time and undo it all.

As the car drew away, leaving Channing sitting on the

gravel drive, she closed her eyes and tried not to think about what was ahead of her now.

All too soon, they arrived at their destination. 'Here we are,' the driver leered, staring at her avidly in the rear-view mirror.

He held open the door for her again and helped her out, his hand gripping her upper arm in case she decided to make a break for it.

They were standing in front of an antique shop, each of its two windows containing only a single item. In one, there was an ornate silver tea service. In the other, an exquisitely carved chair. There were no price tickets.

'If you have to ask the price, you can't afford it,' grunted the chauffeur, nodding towards them. He led her to a narrow door that flanked the shop, produced a key, opened it, ushered Cassie in, then closed it firmly behind her.

For a moment she stood looking around. She was standing in a small square entrance hall. Behind her stood the shuttered door and ahead of her was a narrow staircase, lined with framed photographs from bygone eras. Taking a deep breath, she began to mount the steps. So she was meeting a man who apparently had a fetish for women in pigtails and party dresses. After the events of the past few days, she was amazed it still had the capacity to surprise her.

The door at the top of the stairs opened and a beaming, elderly face looked out. So jolly was the expression that its owner could have got a job playing Santa Claus in any department store.

'Come in, my dear,' he smiled, taking her hand and leading her in. 'How's my favourite niece, eh? Uncle Albert's been waiting for you. I hope you're hungry.'

The heat hit her as soon as she entered and she stared

round in amazement. The shop windows might have been empty, but the flat above the shop was as cluttered as a Victorian drawing room. Every available surface held a cargo of bric-a-brac. She felt claustrophobic just looking at it all.

A roaring fire blazed in the grate, and on the hearthrug stood a small table, groaning with buttered crumpets, scones and assorted fancies. He led her to it. 'Sit down, my dear. Sit down.'

She did, and was almost swallowed by the oversized chair. Her legs dangled over the edge, barely reaching the floor.

'And how are you, my pet?' he asked, beaming at her.

'Er... fine, Uncle Albert,' she stammered.

'Good, good,' he said genially. He picked up a plate and began loading it with an assortment of cakes. 'Now eat up, there's a good girl.' He tapped the side of his nose and winked. 'I know how you young ones like sweet things.'

Cassie accepted the plate in bewilderment as he continued to chat on, treating her exactly as though she was his much-loved niece. He handed her a tall glass of lemonade to go with her plateful of food. Gingerly, she sipped it.

His next move was totally unexpected. Under the pretext of leaning over to offer her another cake, he jerked her arm so that the glass of lemonade spilt, soaking through her dress, splashing onto the tablecloth and dripping to the floor. She looked at him in dismay as his face flushed with temper, the jollity disappearing. Even more dismaying was the fact that a couple of buttons on the flies of his respectable tweed suit were open and his penis was peeking out, in an obvious state of excitement.

'You clumsy, ungrateful creature,' he snarled, his cock

nodding in agreement. 'Just look at the mess you've made. After all the trouble I've gone to! You're a very naughty girl.'

She cringed back from him. 'I – I'm so sorry... um... Uncle Albert. I didn't mean to—'

'That's just not good enough, young lady,' he snapped. 'Behaviour like that deserves a good spanking.'

Before she knew where she was, he had her over his knee. His face flushed with excitement and unaccustomed exertion, he flipped up her short pink skirt and pulled down her tiny white panties, to expose her rounded bottom, still pink from the attentions of Watkins and her whip. 'Bad girl!' he wheezed, gloating over her succulent flesh. 'Bad, bad girl!' She could feel his prick digging into her tummy as she wriggled on his lap, trying to free herself from his iron grasp.

Her struggles only served to excite him further. He was drooling as his hand rose and fell, smacking her bare bottom as it gleamed rosily in the firelight. She squealed as the stinging pain made her squirm and writhe, her feet, in their buttoned shoes, kicking the air. His eyes, fixed on the rippling globes of her bottom, sparkled in the firelight and his breath came in heaving gasps. As she wriggled she could feel him swelling even further, the heat of his excitement radiating through her pink dress. Suddenly she was unceremoniously shoved off his knees and dumped on the floor.

She sat there, legs sprawled, staring at him with wide-eyed dismay as he fumbled with the remaining buttons on his fly, his hands trembling. Eventually he succeeded in getting them open and his gnarled penis sprang into full view, as rigidly erect as that of a man half his age. She groaned with dread.

'That's a good girl,' he croaked throatily, saliva escaping

the corners of his mouth. 'Look what Uncle Albert's got for you. Why don't you come and give it a kiss, to show how much you love me and how sorry you are for spilling your drink?'

Shaking her head, she scrambled back, trying to get as far away from him as possible. But, surprisingly, he was too quick for her. Leaning forward, he grabbed her plaits. The pain was incredible, as if every hair on her head was being torn out by the root. She had no choice but to scramble forward again to relieve it. Whimpering, she edged towards him on her hands and knees. With a smile of satisfaction he pulled her head into his lap. The head of his prick bobbed and pushed against her tightly closed lips. Another warning tug on her plaits brought renewed pain and forced her, reluctantly, to acquiesce. He grunted and wheezed afresh as her pouting lips peeled apart, and then she almost gagged as he fed the bulbous helmet between them.

Head flung back, he gasped as the soft silk of her mouth closed over him. He thrust his hips upwards, easing himself deeper inside, stretching her jaw, the head of his cock sliding against the roof of her mouth and touching the back of her throat. His wizened hands clutched her head, pressing it deeper into his lap. The harsh material of his trousers agitated her cheeks as she choked and gasped for breath. 'Oooh, you dirty girl,' he moaned, as his movements became more urgent.

It was mercifully brief. Excited beyond endurance by her struggles and whimpers, he gave one last shuddering heave and ejaculated, collapsing back in his chair, the last few drops dribbling from his rapidly deflating penis as it plopped from her mouth. He gazed dreamily at her, tears meandering down her flushed cheeks, and smiled kindly over his glasses.

'Why don't you go and wash your hands and face, my dear,' he suggested, pointing to a door across the room. Tugging up her panties, she fled, sobbing, to do as she was told.

By the time she came back, his clothing had been adjusted and he was back to his original genial self. The rest of the 'tea party' passed quite without incident as he chatted politely and plied her with cakes and lemonade she didn't really want. She could hardly believe what had just happened.

When she left, he patted her on the head and pushed a coin into her hand. It was only when she was back in the car that she looked at it and discovered that he'd given her an old half-crown.

'Not bad,' said the driver, peering round intrusively to see what she'd been given. 'You must have pleased him; I've seen some of them coming out with only a threepenny bit.'

'What does it matter?' muttered Cassie, easing her aching bottom gingerly on the soft leather. 'None of them are worth anything. We went decimal nearly thirty years ago.'

The driver looked at her and winked. 'It's worth more than you think, my girl,' he grinned. 'That's your pocket money. It'll be added to your wages at the end of the contract. It means the old boy's just given you a tip of five hundred pounds.'

Cassie's mouth fell open. Five hundred pounds – for that? It hadn't been pleasant, but it had only lasted for five or six minutes at most. She sagged back in astonishment.

It was proof, if she had needed any, that the world had finally gone mad. Now she knew that whatever came next would no longer have the power to surprise her.

Chapter Sixteen

'Excellent,' decided Channing, turning the old coin over and over in his hand. He smiled at Cassie. 'You have done well.' He ran his eyes over her appraisingly, and nodded to himself. 'Yes, I made a good investment when I chose you. You seem to have a knack for this sort of thing.' He raised an eyebrow as he examined her. 'You have the innocent face of a frightened virgin – combined with the soul of a true whore.'

His words stung. Her breasts heaved beneath the ridiculous pink dress, their tender points chafing against the restrictive material. Her backside was still flushed and smarting from the attentions of the housekeeper and 'Uncle Albert' – but worse still was the element of truth in his insult. Stirrings of unfulfilled desire tormented her aching body and she had to resist the desire to squirm as heat from her chastised bottom sent tendrils of lust quivering through her. The pit of her stomach felt hot and heavy, and moisture seeped between her thighs. Ignoring her contradictory feelings, she raised her head defiantly.

Glaring back at him, she shook off the restraining hand of the chauffeur, who had escorted her to Channing's chambers. 'And you,' she sneered, 'have the soul of a true pimp.' Her gaze became scornful. 'And a paralysed one at that,' she taunted.

A flush stained his cheekbones and his eyes narrowed as her words hit home. For a moment she was elated at having hurt him so well with her cutting tongue, but then her elation disappeared as she watched his expression change. His anger was replaced by cold amusement, and a shiver ran through her. One should never pull a tiger's tail, even if he seemed to be sleeping.

'What a pleasant choice of words, my dear,' he said, with grudging admiration. 'A paralysed pimp. The phrase trips off the tongue, doesn't it? Almost poetically, in fact.' He leaned forward suddenly and she instinctively cringed away from the suppressed violence barely concealed beneath the civilised veneer. 'However, thanks to you, it isn't quite as apt as it might once have been.'

She watched in disbelief as, gritting his teeth, he put both hands on the arms of his wheelchair and struggled to push himself up. For a moment, he stood in front of her, swaying, then collapsed back again, breathing heavily. 'Not much, I admit,' he said, smiling wearily from hooded eyes. 'But as they say, "Great oaks from little acorns grow".' The smile became wider. 'And after all that effort I think I deserve a little treat, don't you?' He ran a hand over the front of his trousers and leered. 'Or shall we call it physiotherapy?'

Cassie's eyes widened in surprise and trepidation as they focused on the swelling bulge between his thighs. He wanted to fuck her again. Well, she wouldn't let him. She couldn't bear it. She turned to leave the room, but the chauffeur caught her arm.

'Going somewhere?' He leered down at her, his face so close to hers that she could smell the coffee and tobacco on his breath. She recoiled in disgust, her nose wrinkling. Anger flared in his eyes at her reaction and his grip tightened as he turned her back to face Channing. 'What shall I do now, sir?' he asked, his voice hopeful.

'Strip her,' Channing ordered.

'Certainly, sir,' he smirked, gleefully. Cassie flinched as his vicelike hand gripped the collar of her dress and yanked. For a moment the flimsy material cut into the side of her neck, then there was a long ripping noise as it gave, tearing in two from top to bottom. She grabbed frantically at the thin material, trying to tug the pieces together, to hide herself beneath the torn remnants.

It was useless. The chauffeur grasped both her arms and pulled them behind her back. The tattered folds of material fell uselessly to her waist, concealing nothing. Her breasts, thrust forward by her strained position, rose and fell as she tried to free herself, their rosy tips erect, the chain between them chinking gently as she struggled.

Her eye caught Channing's cold stare, and she froze. The bastard! He was enjoying this. The more she struggled, the better he liked it. Well, in that case, he was in for a big disappointment. Resistance was clearly futile, so why bother? She'd soon see how keen he was on fucking her when he didn't get any reaction. Avoiding his eyes, she focused on a point over his shoulder and forced herself to go limp in the chauffeur's arms. For a moment he staggered under the unexpected dead weight, then he recovered and hauled her upright again. She stood silent and motionless in front of Channing, her arms hanging by her sides, like a wooden marionette whose strings had been cut.

He looked at the limp figure before him. The torn dress; the tiny white panties; the long legs in their little white ankle socks and patent leather shoes. He smiled, understanding. 'Passive resistance,' he purred. 'How clever, my dear.' His lips tightened. 'But not clever enough. I very much doubt that you'll be able to keep it up for too long.' A hand lashed out in a stinging slap that caught her thigh, making the flesh tremble and redden. Her breasts jerked with the blow, but she bit back her squeal of pain and remained silent.

He stared at her thoughtfully for a moment, then his hands snaked out again, gripped the torn material of the dress hanging round her waist, and ripped it away in one easy movement, so that it fluttered to the floor. Then he seized the white panties and tugged them down her thighs, till they reached her knees and slid the rest of the way to join the remnants of the dress. Still she refused to move. His eyes travelled from her full breasts, down the curve of her hips and belly to the smooth mound of her shaven pudenda. She was like some glorious, living statue. The only sound in the room was his ragged panting and the excited breathing of the chauffeur, who stood watching avidly and awaiting his next orders.

They weren't long in coming.

'Oh dear, oh dear,' sighed Channing, shaking his head in mock dismay. 'Miss Grey still hasn't learned her lesson.' His smile was cruel. 'It seems we'll have to teach her – again.' He clicked his fingers and the chauffeur closed in eagerly.

Cassie found herself being flung unceremoniously over Channing's knee, her bottom exposed to the attention of both men. Their hands rose and fell, her full bottom quivering with each blow, the colour changing from rosy peach to angry red as the blood flooded into the soft globes. For several minutes the thwack of flesh on flesh and the sound of Cassie's suppressed gasps filled the room. She ached to scream and try to wriggle free, to escape the waves of heat and pain that washed through her lower body, but she was damned if she'd give either of them the satisfaction. Biting her lip, she screwed her eyes shut and, apart from clenching her buttocks involuntarily against the punishment, lay limp and unresponsive in his grip.

At last Channing gave up. 'Stubborn, aren't you,' he muttered, a hint of admiration in his tone. 'But I've never been beaten yet. You'll give in, my lovely. They always do.' He nodded to the chauffeur and Cassie found herself being manhandled to her feet again.

Muscled arms slid around her body and greedy hands cupped her breasts, mauling and kneading. A horrible wet tongue traced a slimy path down the side of her throat as the chauffeur pinched her nipples, sending jolts of fiery pain through her. His teeth grazed her skin and she could feel his erection, like an iron bar, pressing against her buttocks through the heavy serge of his uniform. She gritted her teeth and suppressed a moan as the treacherous heat returned.

'Enough!' snapped Channing, and the chauffeur reluctantly released her, leaving her swaying and confused. His employer ran an amused eye over her. She refused to look at him, continuing to stare impassively at the wall behind him.

'It would appear that our company isn't stimulating enough for Miss Grey,' he said genially. 'Perhaps this might help.' Reaching forward, he parted her thighs, sliding his fingers into the wetness of her vulva and moving them in and out, while his thumb caressed the tight bud of her clitoris. The long muscles of her thighs quivered and slackened – but still she refused to give in to the tormenting sensations violating her. Her eyelids fluttered, but she bit her lip and remained motionless.

'Still not enough?' he grinned, removing his hand. 'I must be losing my touch. Perhaps I need some more help here.' He nodded to the chauffeur again, and Cassie heard the unmistakable sound of a zip being lowered. Her stomach churned with apprehension.

This time there was no barrier of serge to protect her. As the chauffeur moved in again, she could feel the whole length of his turgid erection pressing against her. As his hands returned to her breasts, her control broke.

'No,' she begged, gazing pleadingly at Channing. 'Not both of you. I'll do anything you want. Please. Just send him away.'

'Too late now,' he gloated, staring into her glazed eyes. 'Perhaps next time you'll be a little more obedient.' He snapped his fingers and leaned back to watch. 'Carry on,' he said to the brute.

Cassie whimpered as the chauffeur's hands crawled all over her body. His tongue slithered round her ear as he squashed her breasts together with one huge paw, while the other slipped down her belly, delving between her thighs. His middle finger slid inside her as he clamped her even tighter against his groin. She moaned as he bent his knees and she felt the tip of his prick pushing insistently between the lips of her sex.

He grunted, thrust upwards, and she whimpered hopelessly as the full length of him slid slowly inside her, like a hot knife sliding through butter. For a moment he remained motionless and she could feel every inch of his cock, then he began to move. She sighed with loathing… and delight.

'Very nice,' purred Channing. He leaned forward and Cassie flushed with shame as his strong hands pulled her thighs apart and he avidly watched another man's prick sliding in and out of her, the thick shaft squelching noisily between her lips as it pistoned. His thumb traced tiny circles on her clitoris until it stiffened under his attentions and she moaned again.

'I believe I can take over now,' he said breathlessly. His fingers fumbled with his zip and then *his* cock was free as well, standing rigidly to attention.

'Noooo…' she implored, no longer sure if she was protesting against her abuse or the fact that the chauffeur was obediently withdrawing from her body, to allow his employer to take his place. He spun her round till she was facing him, then Channing's hands gripped her waist and pulled her down onto his lap, and the spearing organ that waited there. He slid smoothly up inside her, and her mouth fell open as, for the second time in as many minutes, she was pierced and violated. Then his hands began to stroke her breasts again and she forgot everything in the maelstrom of sensations that flooded her body, and she closed her eyes and writhed against the throbbing cock that seemed to fill her to bursting.

Something hot and hard touched her lips and she opened her eyes again. The chauffeur was standing before her, his hips thrust forward, the knob of his penis dark and demanding. 'Open your mouth, slut,' he panted. She parted her lips to protest, and almost gagged as he thrust himself in. His cock was tight and swollen, slick with her juices. She tried to pull away, but this only excited him further. He grabbed the back of her head and pulled her towards him, grunting as her tongue slithered over the sensitive head. Another wave of desire ran through her aching body and, gasping for breath, she gave in to it, her reluctance melting. Deliberately she ran her tongue over his swollen shaft, sucking gently, revelling in his helpless moaning. She clutched his thighs and her head bobbed up and down, matching the pumping of her hips as she raised and lowered herself on Channing's rigid cock, pushing herself – and them – to the verge of an orgasm, then pulling back at the last moment, driving him wild.

Finally, she could bear no more. With one final thrust she triggered Channing's explosion, feeling his seed boil over inside her. At that moment the chauffeur groaned and his hips jerked, his prick spasming as he flooded her mouth, his salty emissions thick at the back of her throat.

She felt triumphant as he withdrew, knees trembling. But it didn't last long. She staggered and almost fell as Channing pushed her roughly away from him. She grabbed her tattered clothes and held them protectively against her as a wave of shame washed over her. What had she done? What was she turning into?

Channing smiled at her cruelly and raised an ironic eyebrow. 'As I said, you have the soul of a true whore,' he stated brusquely. 'You enjoyed every moment of that, didn't you, you little slut?'

She threw her head back and glared at him, boldly. 'I've survived though, haven't I?' she answered. 'You've done your worst and you still haven't broken me!' Without waiting to be dismissed, she turned and made for the door with as much dignity as she could muster, the chauffeur scrambling to escort her back to her room. As she opened it, she turned and said defiantly, 'And you never will!'

Channing stared after her with grudging admiration. He had to admit, the girl had spirit.

'"Done my worst"?' he mused, stroking his chin thoughtfully. 'Oh no, my naïve little protégéé.' His smile widened, tightening the scar on his cheek. 'I think you'll find you're wrong there.'

Chapter Seventeen

'Bastard! Bastard! Bastard!' Cassie exploded, banging the door shut on her escort. For once the clicking of the lock behind her felt as if she was shutting her tormentors out, instead of being locked in. Glancing round, her eye fell on the pile of plates on the food trolley. Grabbing them up, she sent them flying, one after the other, to crash and splinter against the wall. Staring at the greasy scraps of food sliding down the immaculate wallpaper and the shards scattered across the carpet, she gave a thin smile.

'Feeling better?' drawled Tanisha, in amusement.

'Not really,' she muttered. 'I won't feel better till I've put a hundred miles between me and this hellhole – and the perverts in it!' She walked stiffly across the room and stared over her shoulder at herself in the mirror. Parting the remains of her tattered clothing, she gasped at the sight of the scarlet handprints on her bottom. Gingerly, she ran a finger over her flushed skin and winced at the dull, throbbing pain even the slightest touch produced. Delayed shock from her ordeal made her sway unsteadily on her feet.

'Here, come and lie down,' said Tanisha anxiously. She slipped an arm round Cassie's waist and helped her to the bed, where she collapsed gratefully. Tanisha stood back and looked at the inflamed flesh. 'Better put something on that,' she advised, carefully peeling off what was left of Cassie's clothing. 'I'll get some cream out of the bathroom.'

She disappeared and came back with a bottle of lotion.

'Roll on your stomach,' she ordered. With a whimper, Cassie did as she was told. Tanisha poured some of the liquid into the palm of her hand and began to apply it gently, her supple hands stroking and soothing Cassie's aching flesh. She groaned with relief as the liquid began to work, easing away the pain.

'Mmm… that feels good,' she sighed, as Tanisha continued, her fingers kneading the tense knots of muscle in her neck and shoulders, then returning to her tender bottom and sliding down the long sweep of her thighs. Her eyes closed languorously as she gave herself up to the sheer pleasure of being pampered.

'Turn over,' said Tanisha huskily. Obediently, Cassie did. She lay on her back, one arm flung protectively over her eyes to shut out the light, the other limp at her side, her thighs parting slightly as her muscles relaxed. The creamy globes of her breasts flattened softly, their tips soft. Tanisha licked her lips as she looked at her.

Pouring more lotion into her palm, she turned her attention to the tense muscles at the side of Cassie's neck, running her hands down them and over her shoulders to the tops of her arms, then back again. Gradually she strayed lower, to the upper slopes of Cassie's breasts, then lower still, smoothing the cream over them, gently kneading the soft flesh, feeling the gradual stiffening of Cassie's nipples against her cupping palms. A quiet sigh escaped Cassie's parted lips and she stirred as if she was about to sit up, her eyelids fluttering.

'Shhhh,' hushed Tanisha, pushing her gently back against the pillow. 'Relax. Enjoy.' Her hands continued to work their magic. Cassie's skin gleamed under the coating of lotion as Tanisha went on stroking, down over the gentle curve of her belly, over her hips and down the outside of her thighs to the delicate ankles.

Cassie groaned as she began the return journey, her fingers trailing up the inside of her legs this time, leaving little trickles of pleasure in their wake. Tanisha caressed the silky skin on the inside of her thighs and they parted even further, showing the soft lips beneath, which parted too, like the fragile petals of some exotic orchid, opening to revealing its moist, pink centre.

Tanisha's lips curved in a sensuous smile as she teased the rapidly swelling bud of Cassie's clitoris into full erection, before deftly slipping her fingers into the welcoming warmth of her sex. As she began to move them slowly, she leaned forward and took first one, then the other, of Cassie's nipples between her lips, her tongue flicking over their rigid tips.

Cassie groaned and lifted her hands to caress Tanisha's lush body in return, but Tanisha pushed them firmly back down again. 'No,' she whispered breathlessly. 'Let me.' Cassie's arms fell back, her long blonde curls a tangled mass on the pillow as she gave herself up to the delightful sensations running through her body.

She gasped as the subtle black fingers moved faster, gleaming with lotion and her own fragrant juices. Her head twisted on the pillow as Tanisha's tongue continued to tease her nipples, then bent her head to trace a slow path of fire down her stomach to the eager vulva below. Withdrawing her hand, she gently parted Cassie's labia. Her cunt fell open, glistening like a ripe fig, and Tanisha's tongue replaced her questing fingers, swirling over Cassie's straining clitoris before she sucked it between her lips, grazing it gently with her teeth. Cassie whimpered, her hips thrusting upwards as the clever tongue alternately lapped and entered her, sending waves of wet heat surging upwards to spread through her entire body.

Her head buried in Cassie's groin, Tanisha's fingers,

still coated with Cassie's juices, found her own body, sliding between the lips of her vulva, to pleasure herself as much as she was pleasuring Cassie. They moved in rhythm with her tongue, her orgasm building with Cassie's until, their bodies arching in unison, they gasped their way to a beautiful climax.

Panting, Tanisha collapsed on the bed beside Cassie, her hand stroking back the blonde hair from the perspiring forehead of her friend. Smiling, the two girls entwined affectionately together, gleaming black flesh and pearly white pressed close, in a glorious tangle of limbs. Within minutes they were asleep.

In another part of the house, Channing leaned forward and clicked off the closed circuit television. The screen went dark, cutting off the delicious image of the sleeping girls. He leaned back again, his smile as twisted as his scar. Let them sleep. They might as well enjoy their brief interlude in their fool's paradise while they could.

The smile became a sneer.

Besides, they would need all their strength and endurance for tomorrow night!

Chapter Eighteen

'Oh my God! What time is it?' demanded Cassie, leaping out of the tangle of bedclothes and pushing her arms into the sleeves of her short white terry robe. She looked out of the window in dismay. The sky, which had been dark when they fell asleep, was darkening again. They must have slept for ages!

'What does it matter?' murmured Tanisha, yawning and stretching her magnificent body. 'We ain't going nowhere.'

Cassie shivered. 'It's not that,' she muttered. 'It's just the thought that we've been out of it for so long.' She shuddered as she remembered the small, white room, and the nightmare of those anonymous, panting bodies dragging her from bed and taking her against her will. 'I mean, anyone could have come in here while we were sleeping.' She flushed as she thought of prurient eyes looking down on them while they lay entangled.

'Well, they didn't, did they?' said Tanisha sensibly. 'So why worry?'

'Someone's been in,' Cassie contradicted. 'Look.' The food trolley was parked neatly against one wall, as usual, the plates covered by the metal hoods. Cassie strode across and put her hand on one. 'It's still warm,' she said. 'It can't have been here long.'

'Good.' Tanisha grinned, hauling herself reluctantly out of bed. 'I'm starving.' Naked, her breasts bouncing as she walked, she moved across and uncovered the food. While she filled her plate, Cassie wrapped her arms around herself and walked across to the window. The garden was deserted and even the windows, normally bright with light at this time of day, were dark, staring out over the empty lawn like blind eyes. Cassie shivered again, a sensation of foreboding making her feel sick with apprehension.

'What's wrong?' asked Tanisha, through a mouthful of food.

'I don't know,' said Cassie. She forced a smile, trying to make light of it. 'It just reminds me of one of those old cowboy movies. You know. Where the hero spits out his cigarette, scans the horizon and says, "I don't like it. It's too quiet", and two minutes later the Apaches come over the hill and massacre the lot of them.' She wrapped her arms tighter, feeling cold despite the oppressive hothouse warmth of the central heating. 'There's something horrible in the air. I can practically taste it.'

'You know your trouble, don't you?' said Tanisha. 'Too much imagination.'

'I don't think so,' said Cassie quietly. 'I've just got this awful feeling in the pit of my stomach.'

'Eat something, you'll feel better,' advised Tanisha.

Reluctantly, Cassie accepted the plate thrust at her and managed a few tasteless mouthfuls. It didn't help. With a sigh she put the plate down and turned towards the window again.

Then the door opened suddenly, making them both jump. The housekeeper walked in and stood eyeing them both, with a mixture of lust and distaste. 'Ah, Miss Grey,' she sneered. 'You're finally up. Good. The master wishes you to join his guests for dinner.'

'But I've already eaten,' protested Cassie.

The housekeeper's lips tightened into a parody of a smile. 'Oh no, my dear,' she said, with twisted amusement. 'You haven't been invited to *eat*.' Her smile became vicious and she watched Cassie's face avidly to savour her reaction to her words. 'You're one of the courses!'

'What do you mean?' gasped Cassie.

'You'll soon find out,' smirked the woman. 'Now come along. We don't want to keep the guests waiting, do we?' She grabbed the collar of Cassie's robe and pulled viciously, ripping it from her shrinking body. 'And you won't be needing that, either.'

With the woman's hand gripping her upper arm, Cassie was hustled along the corridors, down the stairs to the kitchen. Pushing open the heavy double doors, she shoved Cassie roughly inside.

Wide-eyed, she stared around. It was like a scene from hell. Vast pots bubbled on a seemingly endless series of cookers, filling the kitchen with clouds of aromatic steam. Cursing kitchen staff pushed past each other, carrying bowls of hot sauce or baskets of vegetables. There was a constant racket as enormous mixers whirred, the noise mingling with the clatter of plates and pans.

She giggled hysterically, feeling her sanity teeter. What were they going to do? Kill her and dismember her, then cook her and serve her up in a nice mushroom sauce? It made 'eating her' take on an entirely new meaning!

Her giggles died away; a huge man in a dirty-white chef's uniform approached and suddenly it didn't seem even remotely funny any more. A shiny cleaver hung loosely from one large hand, its edge encrusted with something she didn't care to think about. Beads of sweat stood out on his greasy forehead and his piggy eyes ran over her flinching body as if she was nothing more than a carcass of meat he was considering buying. She began to shiver uncontrollably, her bladder almost giving way with terror.

'Good,' he grunted, satisfied with his inspection. He clicked his fingers and two of the kitchen staff hurried across. 'Bring her over here,' he ordered.

Cassie backed away, but strong arms gripped her and dragged her forward.

'Please,' she begged. 'Please, no...'

They ignored her pleas. Her feet slipped on the greasy floor, and her eyes widened even further as she saw what lay ahead.

A long table was beautifully laid with a white linen cloth. It wouldn't have looked out of place in a banqueting hall, apart from two tiny details: the manacles which dangled from each corner, making ugly bulges beneath the white linen, and the fact that it was on small wheels, like some bizarre operating table. She gawped at it, trying to work out what purpose these could serve. She didn't have long to wait. Still struggling, she was whisked off her feet and laid out on it, the linen coarse against her tender skin. Her arms were hauled roughly over her head and her wrists clipped into the manacles at the top of the table, while the impassive kitchen staff pulled her legs apart and did the same with her ankles. She lay there, spread-eagled and totally helpless, staring up at them with terrified eyes.

'Wh... what are you going to do?' she gasped, writhing as she struggled to break free from the chafing manacles. A stinging slap from the chef made her freeze.

'Lie still,' he ordered. Fear dried her mouth as he raised the cleaver – and laid it down on the worktop behind him. She closed her eyes and breathed a sigh of relief. Whatever he was going to do, it was better than her worst imaginings.

Turning with a grace that defied his bulk, he picked up a bottle of olive oil and poured a little into the palm of his hand. 'Extra virgin,' he commented, with sardonic humour. 'How appropriate.' He rubbed his hands together, then began to apply the oil to her, his hands delicately stroking their way over her body. He lingered over the proud breasts, chuckling to himself as he kneaded them, his fingers tweaking and pinching her nipples, then slipping lower, sliding over the gentle curve of her stomach, down the length of her slender legs, then back up to the silken skin of her inner thighs. When he reached her vulva, she shuddered as two oily fingers slipped inside her. He removed them, raised them to his nose and sniffed, as if savouring the bouquet of a fine wine. She blushed with humiliation.

When he had finished, her body glistened like a statue of burnished marble. She lay rigid, waiting for whatever was going to happen next.

She didn't have to wait long. Raising his head from the contemplation of her body, he clicked his fingers again and his minions came hurrying forward with huge platters. She lifted her head, straining to see, and was rewarded with another slap for her pains.

'I told you to lie still,' the chef growled. 'I won't tell you again.' His lips parted in a cruel smile, revealing yellow, nicotine-stained teeth. 'Lots of hot fat and sharp knives in a kitchen.' He leered ominously at her. 'We wouldn't want you to have an "accident" and spoil that pretty body, now would we?' Terrified, she lay back, desperately schooling herself into total immobility.

He turned away and picked up something she couldn't see. When he turned back, he laid it on her stomach and she shuddered at its cold clamminess. The aroma of smoked salmon reached her nostrils and she finally realised what was happening. Her belly quivered as she suppressed an hysterical giggle. Dinner would be served all right – and she was going to be the dish it was served from!

The slice of smoked salmon, unseated by the movement of her stomach, left a trail of slimy coldness as it slithered slowly onto the table, and an exclamation of annoyance brought her back to her senses. This time the slap was even harder and she whimpered with the pain.

'I'm sorry,' she gasped. 'I won't move again. I promise.'

He lowered his hand and glared at her. 'See that you don't,' he warned. 'Otherwise you'll regret it.'

Closing her eyes, she tried to relax as he went back to his task, laying slice after slice of smoked salmon over her body, moulding it to her breasts. Once he had done that, he added the finishing touches. Scooped-out tomatoes decorated the crests of her breasts, like enormous, engorged nipples. Crudités were laid out in an ornate pattern that radiated from her navel like a sunburst. Curved lettuce leaves cupped her shaven mound, like some organic chastity belt.

At last he stood back and admired his handiwork. A smile of satisfaction crossed his face. Perfect! She was a work of art. An *edible* work of art. There was just one thing left to do before she was delivered to the waiting guests.

Still smiling, he picked up a carrot that had been peeled and carved into the shape of a rampant penis. He oiled it lovingly, then waggled it under Cassie's horrified eyes. 'My little variation on the apple-in-the-mouth theme,' he said conversationally. 'I envy the man – or woman – who gets this little titbit.'

Lifting the lettuce leaves covering Cassie's pudenda, he parted the lips of her sex and pushed the obscenely carved vegetable into her most intimate flesh, grinning as he thrust it in and out a few times for his own twisted amusement. The door of the kitchen opened and a waiter stuck his head round. Reluctantly, the chef dragged himself away from his perverted entertainment.

He stood back, ran his eyes professionally over Cassie

then, satisfied, rapidly placed bowls of mayonnaise and dip, plates of neatly buttered brown bread triangles and platters of carefully arranged salad round her supine body. Finally, he clapped his hands. 'Right, take her away,' he ordered. 'She's ready to be served.'

The next few minutes were a nightmare. As the table was pushed along the corridors, its wheels clattering over the uneven floor, the ceiling flashing past her eyes, a memory came back from Cassie's childhood. The terror she'd felt then, as she'd been wheeled towards the operating theatre to have her tonsils out, resurfaced. At least then she'd known that any pain inflicted on her was for her own good. This time the pain would be for the sick pleasure of a group of debauched perverts, who relished the suffering of their fellow human beings. It was not a reassuring thought. Her stomach tightened and the aroma of smoked salmon, intensified by the heat of her body, nauseated her.

All too soon they arrived at the door of the dining room. The waiter knocked, waited for a few moments, then pushed it open. 'The buffet, sir,' he announced, manoeuvring the table into position. There were squeals of appreciation; by moving her eyes, Cassie could see the guests' avid faces turned towards her. Channing, his face impassive, sat at the head of the vast mahogany table.

'Darling, how delightful!' exclaimed the scrawny woman Cassie had seen the night the guests arrived. 'I absolutely adore smoked salmon.' Her wrinkled, over-painted lips creased as she simpered at him. 'And what an original method of serving.' She waved her knife in the air and Cassie shivered as a lustful gleam brightened the dull eyes. 'I can hardly wait to tuck in!'

Cassie recognised other faces as well; faces she'd seen from the platform at her 'auction'. The old woman was there, with another youth – dark-haired, this time. One of her hands was moving slowly beneath the table and he was smiling, his ripe mouth open slightly, his lips heavy with a corrupt, precocious sensuality.

'Oooh! Me, too!' squealed a girlish voice that contrasted strangely with the body it issued from. The masculinity of the speaker was undeniable, despite his satin dress and high-pitched tones.

'I prefer chicken myself,' grumbled the scrawny woman's companion. He jabbed his fork in the air. 'I like a nice tender bit of breast.' His jowls quivered as he guffawed at his own joke. He turned to Channing, his bloated face purple with suppressed amusement. 'Suppose that accounts for the serving dish, eh?' he grunted, raising his eyebrows to underline the excellence of his wit. 'That way we all get what we want.'

'Of course,' said Channing smoothly. He waved an indolent hand, indicating Cassie. 'Now, ladies and gentlemen, do, please, help yourselves.'

The sound of chairs being pulled back savaged Cassie's nerves, bringing her to a fever pitch of terrified anticipation. She gritted her teeth to hold back a scream as the guests ringed her, like hyenas closing in on their prey.

She winced as the first knife slid smoothly between her skin and the slice of salmon that covered it. The scrawny woman held it aloft like a trophy, then dropped it into her gaping maw, closing her eyes as she chewed it slowly, savouring the hint of Cassie's fear-tainted sweat that added subtle flavour to the feast. 'Delicious,' she crooned, her knife poised again.

The fat man's face loomed above Cassie like a bloated moon as he leaned forward and slurped up one of the tomatoes that covered her nipples, his tongue lingering on the flesh beneath. He licked his lips, grinning with satisfaction, and leaned over to reach the other. A gust of stale sweat, barely masked by expensive cologne, wafted over Cassie, making her want to retch with disgust. She shuddered as he nibbled at the tomato, his teeth grazing her nipple, his thick tongue rasping over her tender flesh.

She writhed in a futile attempt to escape the disgusting molestation, her eyes frantically searching the room, as if help was magically going to appear from nowhere. She caught sight of Channing, still sitting at the head of the table, watching the scene before him with a cynical smile on his lips. She closed her eyes and moaned in despair. There was no help there – merely a gloating enjoyment of her predicament.

Her moans seemed only to inflame them. Cutlery was discarded as fingers pinched and poked at her squirming body, peeling away the layers of food to reveal the cringing flesh beneath.

'Oh, my, just look what I've found,' crowed the dark-haired youth, parting the lettuce leaves over Cassie's groin. He plucked the improvised dildo from its hiding place and waved it aloft in triumph, then he slipped it between his own lips, his tongue playing over it as he mimed an exaggerated act of fellatio for the appreciation of his fellow diners, concluding it by biting off the head with a disgusting crunching sound. When he had finished chewing and swallowed his prize, he turned his attention back to Cassie, his long fingers parting the gleaming lips of her sex. Leaning forward, he thrust his tongue deep into her moist vulva, making obscene slurping noises as he lapped at her.

She moaned again as she tried to deny the tormenting wave of sick pleasure that washed through her, but it was no use. Her body defied her. As he continued to plunge his tongue in and out, the fat man renewed his attack on her breasts, sucking first one swollen nipple, then the other, into his slobbering mouth. Anonymous hands kneaded and stroked her flesh and, as her eyelids flickered, she saw the she-male raising his skirt to reveal a thick cock thrusting against the thin silk of lace-trimmed panties. She closed her eyes again to shut out the sight as he fumbled to free himself and it sprang out, purple and swollen.

Like pigs at a trough, they jostled for position around her. Wet tongues laved her, until she was a squirming mass of sensation. Semen arched onto her belly to mingle with the oil that coated her skin – and was licked away again. Her head tossed from side to side as the perverted pleasure mounted until she could stand it no more. With an agonised scream, she climaxed, arching her back to meet the intruding tongue, then collapsed in exhaustion as the sensation ebbed away.

It was over as soon as it had begun. Laughing and chattering, her tormentors sauntered back to the table, leaving Cassie lying, humiliated and discarded, amongst the remaining scraps of food, her body aching, despair making her feel cold. She was never going to beat Channing. He'd won again.

With a bored glance in her direction, he picked up a small bell and rang it. As if he'd been waiting outside the door, the waiter hurried in. Channing indicated Cassie with a detached wave of the hand. 'Take her away,' he ordered. 'We've finished now.'

With an obsequious bow, the waiter did as he was told. As he wheeled her out, Cassie caught sight of an identical one waiting to be wheeled in. Tanisha was spread-eagled on it, sticky with layers of mousse and exotic fruit, the crests of her exuberant breasts covered with whorls of whipped cream, topped with cherries. Cassie closed her eyes to shut out her friend's distraught expression. Poor Tanisha. It was her turn now.

Dessert was being served.

Back in the relative safety of their room, Cassie stretched the stiffness out of her limbs and rubbed her wrists and ankles where they'd been chafed by the manacles. Wincing, she inspected her aching body, caused by the attentions of Channing's guests. *Guests*? That wasn't the word she'd have chosen. They were the human equivalent of a pack of rabid wolves.

Still, at least it was over now. She'd take a long hot shower to remove their foul smell and the disgusting stickiness that coated her. Moving stiffly to the bathroom, she stood beneath the shower and turned on the water. Sighing with pleasure, she shampooed her tangled hair and scrubbed herself all over with the sweet-scented soap, then stood beneath the spray, feeling the heat wash away the remains of her ordeal.

Once she'd finished, she gingerly patted herself dry, and returned to the bedroom. She'd curl up, pull the bedclothes over her head and forget about everything. But that was all she ever seemed to do since she had come to this hellhole. Escape into sleep, only to wake again and find she was in a worse nightmare than anything her unconscious mind could conjure up.

She already had the sheet in her grasp when a harsh hand seized her wet curls and jerked her round. She screamed with fright and pain, her heart pounding with shock. The housekeeper, entering on silent feet, had crept up unnoticed behind her.

She pushed her face into Cassie's, her breath, stale with garlic, wafting over her with every word. 'Not so fast, young lady,' she snarled. 'What do you think you're doing?'

'G-going to bed,' Cassie stammered, trying to pull away. But the woman jerked her back, tugging Cassie's head to emphasise each word.

'Oh no, you're not. You've got work to do. I've told you before, you're not being paid to lie around sleeping all the time.' She released Cassie's hair and gave her a push. 'Now get dressed, you're coming with me.'

Reluctantly, Cassie bent over to pick up her robe, which was still lying on the floor where the woman had dropped it when she'd dragged it off her earlier. The housekeeper's foot lashed out, missing her by a fraction of an inch.

'Not that, you stupid girl,' she hissed. '*That*!' Cassie's eyes followed the bony, pointing finger and she stared in dismay. Neatly laid out on the chair was some kind of bizarre outfit made entirely of black leather. Even lying there empty, there was something ominous and threatening about it. It gleamed darkly, like the carapace of some monstrous beetle.

'I can't wear that,' she protested.

'And why not, may I ask?' demanded the woman. Her foot tapped impatiently and Cassie could feel the barely controlled violence radiating from her like a low-grade fever, waiting to erupt. She thought fast.

'Er... I'm all damp from my shower, it'll stick to my skin,' she muttered. 'I won't be able to get it on.'

The woman shrugged. 'Is that all?' she said, with a vicious smile. 'We'll soon sort that.' Her hand shot out and seized Cassie's hair again, and she dragged her towards the dressing table. 'Here we are,' she said, seizing a flask of talc with her free hand and shaking it liberally over Cassie. Clouds of sweet-smelling powder drifted up, making her cough. The woman laughed and let go of her hair.

But the relief of being free quickly evaporated. The housekeeper's face set in a grin of lascivious enjoyment as she proceeded to rub the talc over every inch of Cassie's body, using it as an excuse to satisfy her own desires. Her hands lingered on Cassie's breasts, kneading the flesh, then ranged lower, fingering and groping more than was necessary.

'That's better.' She picked up the leather outfit and threw it at Cassie. 'Now do as you're told and put that on.'

Cassie shook it out and, staring at the housekeeper all the time in case she crept up on her again, stepped into it. Her eyes never leaving the other woman, she pulled the black leather up over her long legs and shimmied into it. Finally, she slipped her arms in and tried to close it over her breasts. It wouldn't meet. She tugged at the dangling laces, then dragged her eyes reluctantly away from the housekeeper and looked at herself in the mirror. Her mouth opened in shocked amazement as she gaped at the reflection that stared back. The black leather clung to her like a second skin, revealing more than it concealed. Her breasts thrust out exaggeratedly, pushed up by the laces she'd tugged on so futilely in her attempts to cover herself. The outfit curved over her belly, only to taper to a V that seemed to point at her groin. She was virtually naked, apart from thin strips that held up the leggings in the same way a suspender belt held up stockings. The eye was drawn irresistibly to her shaven pudenda and the tops of the thighs that gleamed milk-white against the black. When she turned slightly, she could see her buttocks shamelessly revealed. She blushed scarlet. Every move she made drew attention to her sex.

But that wasn't the worst of it – not by a long way.

Jutting from the V at her groin was a long, thick leather prick that bobbed obscenely with every movement. She gasped and reached down, trying to hide it with her hands, but its touch was so revolting that she drew them quickly away. Her colour deepened.

'That's disgusting,' she whimpered. 'What *is* it for?'

'You'll soon find out,' smirked the housekeeper. She bent down, pulled out a pair of impossibly high-heeled boots from beneath the chair, and thrust them at Cassie. 'Now put those on. I haven't got all day.'

Cassie sat down and obeyed, feeling the cold surface of the chair against her naked bottom. Once she had them on, the housekeeper grabbed Cassie's arm and pulled her towards the door.

Stumbling in the stiletto-heeled boots, Cassie was dragged along the many corridors yet again, the housekeeper cursing her under her breath. At last they reached yet another door in the seemingly interminable maze. The woman pushed and it swung slowly open, a black mouth waiting to swallow Cassie. She gazed at the darkness, then back at the housekeeper, her eyes imploring. A glimpse of amused pity in the woman's expression frightened her more than ever.

'Well,' she said, pushing Cassie forward, 'don't just stand there. Your audience awaits!'

Chapter Nineteen

The door banged shut behind Cassie and she found herself in total darkness. She flung herself at it, pounding with her fists, hurting her hands on the impenetrable wood. 'Please,' she begged. 'Please, I'll do anything... just don't leave me here.' Her only answer was the noise of the housekeeper's heels clicking briskly as she walked away, the sound fading and finally dying into silence. Hopelessness washed over her. She leaned her head against the door and wept softly.

A few minutes later, pulling herself together, she turned slowly and, with her back against the door, stood stock still, straining her ears for any tiny noise that might give her a clue to where she was or what was going to happen next. But there was nothing – nothing but her heartbeat and the sound of her own panting. Forcing herself to be calm, she held her breath and tried again, staring blindly into the darkness. Still nothing. There was a strange, *muffled* quality to her surroundings, as if she was an insect, trapped in a box lined with black velvet. It was strangely unsettling. Gingerly, she stretched out her arms. Her left met nothing, but her right made contact with a wall. She explored its surface cautiously with her fingers, feeling a layer of padded material. It brought no comfort, merely reinforcing the idea of being enclosed in some cunningly designed trap. One that concealed its deadly purpose beneath a veneer of luxury. What were they going to do to her now?

A horrible thought struck her, materialising from a long-ago history lesson. What was it they had called them? *Oubliettes*, that was it. Tiny, hidden cells or dungeons where inconvenient people or those who were no longer useful could be put and, as the name suggested, simply forgotten. Condemned to die of thirst and hunger in the total blackness of despair.

Her busy mind peopled the darkness with the mouldering corpses of previous occupants and panic threatened to overwhelm her. She'd already seen how brutal and callous these people could be. They'd already taken their pleasure from her at will. It didn't take much of a stretch of the imagination to realise that she was as unimportant to them as an empty box once the chocolates had been eaten; throw it in the bin and buy a new one.

Claustrophobia pressed in on her and she found it difficult to breathe. She straightened her back. She could either give in to it and curl up in a quivering heap or take her courage in both hands and try and discover exactly where she was – and if there was a way out. She chose the latter. Keeping her right hand pressed firmly against the wall, she took a step forward, then another, expecting to come up against the opposite wall – or something unspeakable – at any moment.

But she didn't. Her optimism returning, she took another step. Wherever she was, it was larger than she had expected and singularly lacking in bodies, dead or otherwise. Her fear of being trapped in an oubliette began to evaporate and she began to notice other little details. The air was fresh, for a start, and warmer against her skin than she'd expected. Dungeons were cold and clammy, not centrally heated for the comfort of their guests. She began to move forward with a little more confidence.

A confidence that was misplaced.

Her next step brought her up sharply as her foot came

in sudden, painful contact with an obstacle and she pitched forward with a scream. She heard a faint titter, swiftly hushed, and froze like a frightened rabbit, listening. There was nothing more and she shook her head and dismissed it. Her imagination was playing tricks on her. Hardly surprising in the circumstances.

Still prone, she groped in front of her and discovered the reason for her fall. She was at the foot of a series of shallow steps. Fumbling in the darkness, she counted them. There were only three. Old houses often had uneven floor levels, compensated for by unexpected steps and stairs. That must be it. Shakily, she got to her feet and began to mount them, standing on one while her foot felt for the next. Reaching the top, she began her blind, halting progress again.

She'd barely taken another four steps when the world exploded from darkness into light and blood. Scarlet blood that dripped from every wall in a waking dream of death and terror. She gasped and raised an arm to shield her eyes, dazedly trying to take in her surroundings. Her other hand automatically went to cover herself and brushed the obscene leather phallus that jutted from the front of her costume. She jerked it away as if she'd been stung.

As her eyes adjusted, the blood-soaked walls metamorphosed from the stuff of nightmares into the ordinary, red velvet curtains that draped the walls from top to bottom – but there was no comfort or reassurance in the realisation. The bad dream hadn't dissipated, merely changed direction. Like a butterfly pierced by a needle, she was pinned in place by a spotlight and it dawned on her that she was standing on a stage. The steps she'd so carefully manoeuvred had led to a raised dais covered, like the walls, in red. It was like being in some monstrous womb.

She peered from her circle of light out into the auditorium. She could see nothing but darkness, but she knew they were there. Faceless and expectant. Waiting. The silence was unbroken, but it was the silence of predators waiting for the prey to break cover so the hunt could begin.

She jumped and whirled round as a whisper of sound came from behind her. There was no one there and she realised she was hearing a recording. Soft tendrils of music insinuated their way into the silence. Her frightened mind placed it automatically: Ravel's *Bolero*. Its slow, erotic pulse held both a promise and a threat.

There was a faint click and another spotlight flashed on, illuminating what appeared to be an altar covered in black silk that shimmered as the light caught it. Laid out on it, like some blasphemous sacrifice, was a naked body. A small naked body. She gasped as she recognised the broad shoulders, the muscular torso, and the stunted legs. It was Tom!

He half-stood, half-lay spread-eagled face down, across the table. His wrists were fastened to the top corners with short lengths of chain, while slightly longer ones pinioned his legs to those of the table, so that he was forced into a bending position. Even from where she was standing, she could see red weals where the chain cut cruelly into his flesh. A bolster had been placed directly beneath his stomach, forcing his buttocks up and pulling them apart to reveal the puckered circle of his anus. Cassie blushed with embarrassment at witnessing the humiliation of his exposure. She closed her eyes to shut it out. A sibilant whisper from the audience made her open them again. Her hypersensitive ears heard the faint sound of a zip being undone; the rasp of a hand sliding up a stocking-clad leg; the moist sound of flesh on flesh. A wave of nausea hit her. She might not be able to see them, but she could imagine what was going on in the darkness. The avid fumbling and groping of beasts on heat.

Their expectancy was growing. She could practically feel it radiating towards her. She took a slow step back – then another. If she could only reach the back of the stage, and the velvet curtains, she could conceal herself behind them. Surely there must be a door hidden there somewhere? One more step. Almost there...

A shriek of fear escaped her lips as the curtains billowed outwards and two faceless figures materialised beside her and their gloved hands seized her upper arms in a grip of steel.

They were creatures from a nightmare. If her costume was designed to reveal, theirs was designed to conceal. Made from black leather, like hers, it covered them from head to foot, so that only their eyes showed – the blank, impassive eyes of sharks. Their bodies gleamed with a dull, oily sheen like those of huge black cockroaches, but the heads were worse: they had the heads of carrion birds. The nosepieces jutted out into terrible beaks that looked capable of tearing out entrails. Beneath them, zips curved in cold, metal-toothed smiles. They were sexless as Barbie dolls. Inhuman as robots.

She twisted vainly in their grip as they dragged her towards the waiting altar, so that she was directly facing Tom's exposed buttocks, the bobbing head of the greased leather penis aimed like an arrow at the target of his anus. There was a gasp of anticipation from the invisible audience.

A hard push in the small of her back shoved her towards him, and the dildo's tip grazed the puckered orifice. He flinched and writhed as it nudged against his unwilling flesh, seeking entrance. Horrified, Cassie pulled her hips back, so the monstrosity withdrew again.

The audience muttered in disappointment and one of her guards gave a muffled curse. Still gripping her arm to hold her in place, he reached down to his waist, unhooked a short, lethal-looking whip and raised it. There was a thin whistling sound as the lashes cut through the air and landed on the plump cheeks of Cassie's naked bottom. She squealed, jerked forward to escape the pain – and the head of the thick leather cock thrust its way into Tom's anus. He groaned hoarsely as it penetrated him. Cassie moaned in dismay at the pain she was inflicting, and tried to draw back again.

But she didn't succeed. As quickly as she pulled away, the lash of the whip sent her hips jerking forward again. With each spasm of pain, the gross leather phallus was forced more deeply into Tom's body, until it was buried to the hilt.

The music was becoming louder now, as it built to its climax, drowning out her whimpers as the lash rose and fell, choreographing the pumping of her hips to the insistent pulse of the music, the leather dildo sliding in and out of Tom's anus in a parody of lovemaking. First one member of the audience, then another, began clapping in time to the beat. 'Fuck him! Fuck him! Fuck him!' hissed a voice, which was taken up by the rest until it became a chant, an unholy hymn to lust and domination, rising in volume as the music reached its climax.

Tears trickled down Cassie's face as the music reached its explosive finale. A last vicious slash across her bottom reduced her to total collapse and, the obscene black phallus still linking their sweaty bodies, she fell across Tom's supine form. Completely demoralised, she lay there sobbing, feeling him gasping and shuddering beneath her.

'I'm sorry… ' she whispered, her tears dripping on his

naked back.

Hands gripped her, pulling her off him. He groaned again as the leather phallus slid reluctantly from his body, then fell silent. Cassie didn't know if he'd passed out or whether he was simply beyond reaction.

She had no chance to find out. The spotlight illuminating him clicked off and he disappeared into darkness as if he had never been. The audience had savoured his pain and humiliation; he was of no more interest to them.

A third spotlight clicked on and she recoiled as the nightmare continued. Before her was Tanisha, her wrists and ankles pinioned to the X-shaped frame Cassie recognised from her own horrible experience with the housekeeper. She was decked out like a plantation slave from the Deep South, her hair bound up in a red cloth, her body in a torn housedress, the rags barely concealing her gleaming black torso.

As Cassie watched, one of the grotesque leather-clad creatures, with one swift movement, caught the neck of the skimpy garment and tore it from top to bottom. It fell around Tanisha's waist, revealing the smooth back and the full curves of the sides of her breasts as they pressed against the rough wooden frame.

Before Cassie could move, the creature had spun on its heel and was coming towards her. In his hand was the whip that had so recently been used on her, its lashes stained dark with the perspiration from her body. She cringed back, waiting for the next blow to fall.

Instead, he thrust the whip into her hand and pushed her towards Tanisha. 'Punish the slave!' he ordered, his voice muffled and inhuman. Holding the whip behind her back, Cassie edged away, shaking her head – only to back into the other one, who had circled round behind her. A high-pitched giggle came from beneath the leather hood and gloved hands clawed savagely at her breasts. She whimpered and pulled herself away, lashing out with the whip. The blow fell harmlessly on the thick leather and the creature giggled and advanced on her again.

Barring her escape, the other one spun her round, seized her shoulders and shook her. 'Punish her!' he ordered again. 'Or *be* punished. The choice is yours.'

'I won't do it,' said Cassie stubbornly. 'You can't make me.' As soon as the words had left her mouth, she cursed herself for her own stupidity. Of course they could make her do it. They could make her do whatever they wanted – but it was too late to call them back.

'How altruistic,' the creature sneered, wrenching the whip away from her and dropping it to the floor. '"Greater love hath no man than to lay down his life for a friend".' He chuckled. 'Only in this case, you're a woman and it's not your life, is it darling?'

Cassie shrieked as cold, leather-covered fingers prised her thighs apart from behind and a thick cock tore its way into her in one savage thrust, the force pushing her forward, her naked breasts grazing the leather figure in front of her.

He chuckled again, reached for the concealed zip at his groin and pulled it down, releasing his swollen penis. It jutted out, bobbing obscenely. Grabbing Cassie's curls, he forced her head down towards it, so she was bent at the waist, almost losing her balance. If it hadn't been for the hands holding her in place, she would have fallen. He pushed the head of his cock into her mouth and began to jerk his hips, matching his thrusts to his partner behind her, while, to Cassie's shame, the audience clapped and stamped in time. In unison they ravaged her with robotic precision, grunting as their pricks plunged in and out of her helpless body until they finally climaxed simultaneously. As the one behind spasmed inside her, the one in front withdrew and his come erupted over Cassie's face, mingling with her tears. They stepped back, and Cassie staggered.

Picking up the whip, the creature offered it to Cassie again. 'Punish her!' he hissed. His gloved hand teased his flaccid cock until it began to stir again. 'Or do we have to teach you another lesson?' The look in the hooded eyes was threat enough. Cassie's flesh crawled at the thought of the two monsters touching her repeatedly with their lewd, prying fingers, forcing themselves on her once more. She shuddered. Even for Tanisha she couldn't go through that again.

Reluctantly, she reached for the whip. There was a hiss of satisfaction from the audience as she raised it and brought it down on Tanisha's back. Tanisha jerked and screamed, long weals rising on her soft skin. Cassie swallowed as she remembered how gently Tanisha had tended her cuts and bruises, but she forced the thought away, raised her arm and brought the lash down on Tanisha's writhing body again. And again. And again, her own sobs mingling with Tanisha's screams.

Finally, she could lift her aching arm no more. Dropping the whip, she covered her face with her hands and collapsed to her knees, head bowed with shame and remorse. The spotlights clicked off, leaving her alone in the darkness.

The performance was over.

Chapter Twenty

Cassie had no recollection of how she got back to the room. Had she passed out and been carried? She had no idea. All she knew was that when she came to, she was lying naked in bed. There was no sign of the horrendous costume she'd been forced to wear, only a dull ache in her buttocks and a foul taste in her mouth to remind her of what she had just been through. She closed her eyes and shuddered at the memory, then opened them again as a thought struck her.

Tanisha!

She flinched as she remembered the sharp crack of the whip as she'd brought it down on Tanisha's naked flesh. The way the lash had curled round the shrinking body as she hung against the whipping rack. The memory seared her mind. How would Tanisha ever forgive her for that? What if she'd hurt her really badly?

A low groan confirmed her worst fears, then she sighed with relief as Tanisha's eyes flickered open and her lips curved in a weak smile.

'Are you all right?' asked Cassie anxiously.

'I'll live,' Tanisha joked feebly. She winced as she sat up. 'Just don't expect me to go dancing.'

'Oh, God, I'm so sorry,' said Cassie, tears of remorse springing to her eyes at the sight of the livid weals on the smooth, black skin. 'I didn't want to hurt you – or Tom. They made me.'

'Not your fault, girl,' said Tanisha, more strongly. 'It could just as easily have been the other way round. And I know you tried. I heard what they did to you when you refused.' She forced a smile. 'Anyway. It's over now. Forget about it.'

Cassie sighed. Forget about it? Easier said than done. She had enough foul memories to provide a lifetime of nightmares.

The sound of a car door slamming startled them both and they exchanged glances. What now? More perverts arriving to be 'amused'? Not even stopping to slip a covering over her nakedness, Cassie leaped from bed and peered through the window.

'What is it?' asked Tanisha apprehensively.

'I don't believe it,' gasped Cassie. She smiled in jubilation. 'They're leaving!'

'What?' Tanisha joined her at the window and both girls stared out at the cavalcade of expensive cars drawn up in front of the house. As they watched, cases and bags were carried out by the ubiquitous minders and packed into the waiting boots. Their owners followed, laughing and chatting as they made their polite goodbyes. Cassie shuddered as she recognised some of the faces, astonished at how different they seemed in the light of day.

'They look so ordinary,' she marvelled. 'You'd never believe what they were really like, would you?' The fat man who'd sucked her breasts while he tossed himself off looked like a respectable member of the Rotary Club – and might well have been, for all she knew – while his skinny partner looked as if she'd be more at home arranging the church flowers.

'Can't judge a book by its cover,' muttered Tanisha. 'Forget the outside. Inside they're nothing but dirt.' She watched as, one by one, they climbed into their vehicles and drove off. 'Good riddance to bad rubbish,' she growled, turning away.

'But what's going to happen to us now?' fretted Cassie. 'Do you think there are more coming?'

Her question was answered sooner than she expected. The door opened and the housekeeper entered, followed by Simpson, the chauffeur, carrying their cases. With a knowing wink at Cassie, he deposited them on the floor and left.

The housekeeper forced her features into the approximation of a smile. 'Perhaps the young ladies would care to get dressed?' she suggested. 'Breakfast will be served in half an hour.'

'What the hell's going on now?' Cassie demanded, as soon as the door had shut behind the woman. 'What are they up to?'

Tanisha grinned at her. 'Don't you know what this means?' she asked. Cassie stared at her blankly and shook her head. 'Our time must be up,' she crowed. 'Our contract's over!'

'It can't be!' gasped Cassie. 'It must be some sort of trick.'

'Oh, yes it can,' grinned Tanisha. 'We've either lost all track of time stuck in here, or they're terminating our contracts early. And don't time fly when you're having fun!'

Cassie picked up her case, laid it on the bed and opened it gingerly. She wouldn't have been the least surprised if a stream of cockroaches had poured out or it contained something even nastier – but it held nothing more threatening than her clothes, neatly washed and pressed. She pulled out the new grey trousers she'd worn so cockily when she first set off, and shuddered at the feel of the supple leather. She grimaced and stuffed them at the bottom of the case, underneath everything else. She'd give them to Lyn. There was no way she was ever going to wear leather again. Instead, she took out a pale green dress in soft cotton. At least that didn't have any unpleasant connotations.

Tanisha was happily hauling on a scarlet skirt and blouse, emblazoned with green and yellow parrots. When they were both dressed, a discreet knock at the door was followed by the entrance of the housekeeper with the food trolley. She pushed it across to the window, then turned politely.

'Mr Channing will see you in his office in an hour,' she informed them. 'To settle up your accounts.' Cassie and Tanisha exchanged glances. It *was* finally over. The nightmare had ended at last.

'Thank you, Watkins, that will be all,' Cassie said loftily, enjoying the way the woman's face twisted at her words.

'Yes, miss,' she grated. As she left the two girls looked at each other and burst into giggles.

'Did you see her face?' spluttered Tanisha. 'If looks could kill, there'd be nothing left of you but a little smoking heap on the carpet.'

'Who cares?' said Cassie airily. 'There's nothing she can do now.' She turned to the trolley. 'Now where's that breakfast? I'm starving.'

'What are you going to do with your money?' she asked Tanisha, through a mouthful of kedgeree.

Tanisha smiled. 'Set up my own nursing agency,' she said. 'I've already checked it all out. With what I've earned here, I can get a bank loan for the rest.' She chewed thoughtfully. 'And that's where the money is these days – nursing agencies. If I set up my own office, I reckon I can have everything paid off and be free and clear in less than two years.' She looked at Cassie. 'What about you? What are you going to do with yours?'

Cassie's face clouded. The thought of her revenge had

carried her through all this, but now that the end was in sight, she realised she hadn't a clue how to go about it. What was she supposed to do? Hire a hit man? How much would that cost? Even if she knew where to find one, she was still out of a job. The money wasn't going to last forever. Sighing, she poured out the whole story.

'Any suggestions?' she asked when she was finished, looking at Tanisha hopefully. 'I mean, you don't know anybody who breaks kneecaps for a living, do you?'

'Sorry,' grinned Tanisha. 'Can't help you there; I'm poor but I'm honest.'

'I didn't think you could,' said Cassie glumly. 'It looks like they're going to get away scot-free.' She scowled. 'At least this lot here were honest about it, in their own way – and I got paid for the abuse. Those two are the worst sort. Respectable on the surface and rotten at the core. My God, if only the parents knew what they were like, they'd be out of their jobs so fast it'd make their heads spin!'

'So why don't you blackmail them?'

'How? As they so kindly pointed out, who's going to believe a disgruntled ex-employee? I mean, it's not the sort of thing you've got witnesses for, is it?' She shook her head. 'No, they've got away with it – and there's not a damned thing I can do.'

Her unhappy thoughts were interrupted by the housekeeper again. 'Mr Channing will see you now,' she said, nodding at Tanisha. With a sympathetic smile at Cassie, she followed the housekeeper out.

Half an hour later, she returned, beaming – and it was Cassie's turn. Hardly daring to believe that it was all over, she accompanied the silent woman down the corridor. Stopping in front of a door, she tapped, then opened it.

Cassie walked through.

She recognised it immediately as the office where she'd been before, the day she'd returned from visiting 'Uncle Albert'. She would have fled, but Channing's voice stopped her.

'Do take a seat, Miss Grey,' he said politely. She turned to face him and reluctantly walked across the room and took a chair in front of his desk. He smiled at her as formally as if they'd just been introduced.

'Your fee,' he said, producing a cheque book. She watched as he wrote in it, tore out the cheque and held it in the air. She reached for it, but he snatched it away before she could take it. 'Not quite yet,' he smiled. Her stomach shrivelled. She might have known it was too good to be true. She stared at him apprehensively, waiting for whatever was coming next.

When it came, she was astonished. Before her amazed eyes, he levered himself from his wheelchair and, with the aid of a stick, limped round to her side of the desk. He manoeuvred himself so that he was sitting on the edge of it and smiled down at her.

'You're walking!' she gasped.

'I am,' he agreed. 'And that's largely thanks to you. I think that deserves some kind of reward. Don't you?'

Cassie reached to cover her breasts protectively. The thin gold chain that linked her pierced nipples chinked softly. She stared at him, wide-eyed with fear, remembering what had happened the last time he'd said those words.

He looked at her face and laughed. 'Don't worry, Miss Grey, there's nothing to be frightened of. Your contract is finished – and I'm a man of my word.' He held out the cheque and she took it, then gasped at the amount written on it. She looked up at him questioningly.

'A little bonus,' he explained. 'As I said once before; you have a talent for this – and talent should be encouraged.'

'Th – thank you,' she stammered.

'But you still haven't answered my question,' he continued. 'Your reward.' He looked at her closely. 'Now what would you consider suitable? Hmm? A wardrobe of designer clothes? A car? A portfolio of stocks and shares?' He raised an eyebrow. 'Or do you have something else in mind?'

Her hands clenched in her lap. 'Revenge…' she said quietly, almost to herself.

He stared at her with interest. 'A girl after my own heart,' he said with respect. 'Now tell me; revenge on whom – and, more importantly, for what?'

For the next ten minutes he listened intently as she spilled out her story.

'I think something might be arranged,' he said, when she had finally finished. His lips twisted in amusement. 'In fact, it might be rather entertaining. What did you have in mind?'

'I don't know,' sighed Cassie.

'Leave it to me then,' he said. He smiled thoughtfully. 'I rather think a punishment to fit the crime would be suitable, don't you?' He eased himself from the edge of the desk and limped back to his wheelchair, collapsing with relief. 'That's settled then,' he said briskly. 'I'll be in touch once something's been fixed up. Now, if you don't mind, I still have Mr Patterson, the... er... short gentleman to see. Is there anything else?'

Cassie shook her head, realising that she'd been dismissed. Clutching her cheque, she got to her feet and walked to the door. As her hand touched the handle his voice stopped her. 'I'll ring you once everything's been organised,' he confirmed.

Cassie looked at him, then smiled slowly. 'I'll look forward to it,' she said.

A little while later she was in the back of the limousine, heading for home. As the house disappeared behind her in the distance, she relaxed into the soft upholstery and smiled in anticipation. If she knew Channing, Armstrong and Carr were in for the shock of their lives!

Chapter Twenty-One

'What's got into you?' demanded Lyn in exasperation. 'You've been like this ever since you got back. Lying around doing nothing, with a face like a wet weekend. Missing the high life, is that it? Swanning around on some rich guy's arm, pretending to be Lady Muck?' She glared at her friend. 'Honestly, you've cleared all your debts, you've got money in the bank, and you still look miserable. What's wrong with you?'

'I don't know,' sighed Cassie. 'I just can't seem to put my mind to anything.' It was true. She'd done a little desultory shopping, watched television with half an eye and tried to read a book without managing to take in more than a few paragraphs. She felt restless, her body empty and aching. Worst of all, it had been a fortnight now and she still hadn't heard from Robert Channing. She suppressed a snort of derision; man of his word? So much for his promise to 'arrange something'. He'd probably forgotten all about her as soon as the car disappeared over the horizon.

'Here, drink this,' ordered Lyn, sticking a glass of white wine under her nose. 'And once you've got that down your neck, you can trot your backside through to your bedroom and dig out your sexiest little black dress. It's Friday night. If you think you're going to lie on that couch and stare into space, you've got another think coming. You're coming clubbing with me. Let's see if pulling a good-looking bloke can put a smile back on your face.'

Cassie smiled wryly. Pulling a bloke, good-looking or

not, was the last thing on her mind. Lyn didn't know the half of it. She'd had more kinky sex in the past month than most people saw in a lifetime. She drained her wine. Still, anything would be better than sitting here, staring at the four walls and waiting for a phone call that wasn't going to come.

'Okay,' she agreed, putting down her empty glass. 'Just give me time for a quick shower first.'

'What do you think of this one?' she asked, coming out of the bedroom holding up a skimpy black dress. Her voice trailed off as she looked at Lyn and shuddered. She was standing in front of the mirror, slicking on shocking pink lipstick. She was wearing a brief top – and the grey leather trousers.

'What's wrong?' said Lyn anxiously, staring at the expression on her friend's face. 'You look as if you've seen a ghost.' She looked down at herself. 'You don't mind me wearing these, do you? You did say I could have them.'

Cassie got a hold of herself, and smiled at Lyn. 'Of course not, they're yours now. You can wear them whenever you like. Anyway,' she said, holding up the dress again, 'what about this one?'

'Brilliant,' agreed Lyn. 'If that doesn't get them salivating, nothing will.'

By the time they got there, the club was packed with overheated bodies, writhing on the dance floor and crushed against the bar. They fought their way through, ordered drinks and sipped them as they scanned the crowd.

'He looks rather nice,' commented Lyn, raising her eyebrows in the direction of a dark-haired man propped against the opposite wall. His eyes met hers and she lowered her lashes and smiled demurely. Two minutes later he had whisked her onto the dance floor. Cassie stared after her, envying her carefree innocence.

A voice interrupted her thoughts. 'Hi. All alone?' Cassie jumped and turned to face the man who'd spoken. Guileless blue eyes looked into hers from beneath a fall of blond hair. She smiled back. Mmm… nice. When he offered her a drink, she accepted.

His name was Alan and by the end of the evening, she'd made up her mind. She'd take him home and make mad, passionate love to him. Nothing kinky, just two bodies sharing straightforward, wholesome pleasure. After the last month, making love with someone normal would be a bit like eating something sweet to take a nasty taste out of her mouth. If he knew what she was thinking, she doubted if he'd be flattered.

But since he didn't, he was. 'Your place?' he suggested, enthusiastically.

'I'll freshen up, then get my jacket and meet you at the door,' she said. 'Give me ten minutes.'

'Told you you'd pull,' said Lyn smugly, when they met in the ladies'. 'Now, isn't this better than sitting at home?' She carefully renewed her lipstick, tucked it away in her bag, then smiled at Cassie in the mirror. 'And you've got the whole flat to yourself, too,' she grinned. 'David's taking me on to a party – so don't wait up.' She winked. 'And don't do anything I wouldn't.'

Cassie giggled, and they left the toilet arm in arm.

'Ready?' she asked, coming up behind Alan, who was standing, gazing anxiously at every girl who passed.

'I've been ready for ages,' he said, with evident relief. 'I was beginning to think you'd changed your mind and slipped away.'

'Sorry,' Cassie apologised. 'I was talking to a friend.'

She grabbed his hand and tugged him outside into the cool night. 'Come on,' she urged, 'let's get back to my place–' she turned and smiled wickedly at him '–and I'll show you I was worth waiting for!'

Back at the flat, she poured him a drink and sat beside him on the couch, her thigh pressing insistently against his. He took the hint. Putting his glass on the coffee table, he turned and took her in his arms. His mouth crushed down on hers, his tongue probing eagerly between her parted lips. He moaned with pleasure, one hand caressing the soft swell of her breasts then sliding slowly down over the curve of her belly to find the parted thighs beneath the short skirt. He pulled aside the flimsy knickers and his fingers began exploring her hot wetness.

'Perhaps we should adjourn to the bedroom,' she suggested huskily. Smiling, he scooped her up and carried her through.

'Now, where were we?' he asked, slipping off her dress to expose her full breasts with their rampant nipples. He grinned down at her as his own clothes followed, then he joined her, his breath coming faster as his mouth and tongue teased her, while his fingers plunged in and out between her thighs. With a groan he pushed his knees between hers, slid himself inside her, and began to thrust, slowly at first, then faster. Within a few minutes it was over. He came with an inarticulate cry and moments later he was asleep.

Cassie lay there, staring into the darkness, her body still yearning for release, her mind churning. It had been a complete disaster, as bland and flavourless as a meal without salt or spice. She groaned inwardly, remembering her experiences over the last month. The fear. The pain. The slow, reluctant build-up that finally exploded in mind-blowing ecstasy.

She groaned again as realisation hit her. They'd turned her into an adrenaline junkie, craving pain and pleasure the way an addict craved his next fix. What was she going to do now?

Her body provided the answer – at least for the present. Careful not to disturb the sleeping body beside her, she pictured herself forced to kneel and serve Channing as he thrust his prick roughly into her mouth, while the chauffeur ravaged her from behind. Her breath came faster as she pinched her nipples until they stung, forcing the fingers of her other hand roughly into her wet vulva. She writhed with an exquisite mixture of pain and excitement, trying to control her whimpering as she shuddered in release.

Satisfied at last, she fell into an uneasy sleep.

'That's me off to work,' called Lyn on Monday morning. From beneath the bedcovers, pulled over her head, Cassie heard footsteps coming along the hall and her bedroom door opening. 'Did you hear me?' Lyn asked, sticking her head round it. 'I said, I'm off.' She stared anxiously down at Cassie. 'Will you be okay?' she demanded. 'You're still acting a bit funny. You didn't even take up that bloke on his invitation to take you out again.'

'I'll be fine,' Cassie snapped. 'There's nothing wrong with me. It's your imagination.' She softened her voice. 'I *am* okay, honestly. Tell you what. Forget about shopping after work. I'll get something special in for dinner. Make up for being such a pain in the backside recently. How's that?'

'Great!' said Lyn. 'I'll look forward to it.' Reassured, she closed the door behind her and headed off, leaving Cassie to doze restlessly, tormented by unhappy dreams.

For a moment, when the phone rang, she hadn't got a clue what it was. Realisation hit her with a groan. The last thing she wanted was to try and explain to Alan that, no, she was perfectly sure she didn't want to see him again. She pulled the pillows over her ears and waited for it to stop.

But it didn't stop. Grumpily, she hauled herself out of bed, padded through to the living room and picked it up. 'What is it now?' she snarled – then gasped as she recognised the voice.

'Be at the school tomorrow night,' said Robert Channing. 'Half-past seven. It'll be empty apart from Mr Armstrong and Miss Carr.' He chuckled. 'I'm afraid something's come up and they've got to work late.' He paused. 'You are still sure you want to go through with this, aren't you?'

'Oh yes,' said Cassie, 'I want to go through with this.'

'Good,' he said. 'I'll be sending a little something round with Simpson tomorrow morning. I'm sure you'll know how to use it when the time comes.' He hung up, leaving Cassie wondering what he meant.

'You're a hell of a lot more cheerful,' said Lyn suspiciously. 'What's got into you?'

'Nothing,' said Cassie airily. 'But you were right; my debts are clear and I've got money in the bank. I've finally got round to celebrating, that's all.' She carefully placed the overflowing plates on the table and poured them each a glass of expensive Chardonnay. 'Cheers,' she grinned, raising hers. 'Bottoms up.'

'Bottoms up,' repeated Lyn, and they began to eat.

Next morning Cassie was up and dressed even before Lyn. Ignoring her friend's expression of surprise, she cooked breakfast and poured fresh orange juice.

Lyn looked at her across her bacon and eggs. 'You're

up early,' she said. 'Got something planned?'

'Mmm,' confirmed Cassie, through a mouthful of toast. 'You could say that.'

'Good,' said Lyn in approval. 'It's about time you started thinking about job-hunting again. Your money won't last forever.'

Cassie nodded in agreement, not bothering to disabuse her. She smiled. 'Hunting'? Yes. 'Job-hunting'? No. She had quite another target in mind. Or two targets, to be precise. Still, there was no point in going into that with Lyn. Didn't they say that innocence was bliss? To confirm Lyn's assumptions, she went through to the living room and picked up the previous night's paper. When Lyn came through to say goodbye, she was busy scanning the *Situations Vacant* column, with ostentatious eagerness.

As soon as Lyn had gone, Cassie flung the paper back down and began to pace the room, glancing at the clock every five minutes, waiting for Simpson to arrive with the mysterious 'something'. She had gone through four cups of coffee and had begun to give up hope, before the doorbell finally rang. She hurried to answer it.

'Mr Channing sends his compliments, miss,' he said handing over a large parcel, wrapped in brown paper. As she took it, he clicked his heels and made a mock bow, before turning and walking away.

She carried it through to her bedroom, her fingers already fumbling with the wrapping. It felt heavy and... and... knobbly? What the hell could it be? The paper parted and she dropped the parcel on the bed, staring at in dismay. It was horribly familiar. The black leather gleamed ominously. It couldn't be – could it? She held it up and shook it out. As it unrolled, a short, heavy-handled whip fell out and landed with a thump, its lashes spreading in a fan shape, black with the promise of pain. She shuddered uncontrollably. She'd been right. It was the costume she'd worn on that last terrible night. A brief image of Tom's body, flinching as the leather prick was driven home, flashed through her mind... then she remembered Armstrong's face, flushed and gloating as he brought the cane down on her poor buttocks, and began to smile. She stroked the thick leather dildo that jutted from the costume and her smile hardened. Yes, Robert Channing had been right. When the time came, she'd know exactly how to use it!

'You don't want the loo, do you?' asked Lyn, that evening. 'Only I'm off to have a bath.'

Cassie looked up from the book she was reading – or rather, pretending to read – and stretched, yawning. 'No, thanks,' she replied casually. 'I'm going out anyway. I'll probably be gone before you're out.'

'Going anywhere nice? Did Alan ring again?'

'No,' said Cassie, ignoring Lyn's smug smile. 'He didn't. It's nothing important, really. I just fancied getting out of the house for a while. Go for a walk or something. Get a bit of fresh air.' She smiled back. 'Enjoy your bath. I'll see you when I get back.'

'Okay,' said Lyn. 'See you later.'

Cassie waited until the sounds of singing and splashing told her that Lyn was safely out of the way, then put down her book and went into her bedroom. The costume was tucked under her bed, bundled up in its brown wrapping paper. She bent down, pulled it out and laid it on the bed. For a few moments she stared at it, debating the wisdom of her plan, then shrugged. They had it coming.

She stripped naked, leaving her clothes in a neat pile on the bed, then slithered into the costume, smoothing the leather over her legs and pulling the leather thongs tight across her ribcage, so that her breasts thrust out provocatively. She looked at herself in the mirror and gasped. With her jutting breasts and the smooth curve of her naked bottom, she looked like the heroine of some kinky, underground sci-fi comic. A small smile curved her lips; she reached for her lipstick and outlined her pout in scarlet, then, with infinite care, rouged her nipples so that they stood out like cherries, topping the whiteness of her breasts.

She giggled at her reflection. She knew her laughter was caused by nerves, but seemed unable to control it. Another giggle escaped from her dry mouth. She could just imagine the chaos she'd create if she walked out the front door looking like this! Opening her wardrobe, she rummaged at the back until she found her black winter coat. It was calf-length and would cover a multitude of sins. She only had one little problem. What the hell was she going to do about her massive leather erection? It wouldn't do for that to pop out at an inopportune moment.

She noticed the silver chain round the waist of the costume, and it suddenly dawned on her what it was for. There was a clip fitted to the middle that matched a tiny ring on the tip of the dildo. By fitting one to the other, the horrible black thing was pulled up, tight and flat against her stomach. She fumbled it into position. There. Now she was ready.

She slid her feet into the high-heeled boots and pulled them up, then stood and slipped her coat on. With it buttoned to the neck, she looked perfectly respectable. No one would ever guess what she was wearing underneath. The heavy material rasped across her nipples and she squirmed as a quiver of excitement ran through her. The base of her stomach felt hot and heavy and a tiny trickle of moisture dampened the tops of her thighs.

Calling goodbye to Lyn, she let herself out of the flat, her heels clicking as she went down the stairs to the street. She shivered again as the cold night air pierced her coat, finding the warm naked flesh beneath. Why hadn't she thought to call a taxi? With relief, she saw one cruising past, the reassuring orange light of its sign glowing through the darkness. Hurrying forward as fast as she could on her stiletto heels, she raised an arm to hail it.

Once inside, she gave the address of the school and settled back, closing her eyes and trying to calm the butterflies in her stomach. The journey seemed to last forever, yet end too soon. Paying the driver, she climbed out. As he drove away, she stood for a moment looking at the dark shape of the school building, with the single light, indicating the window of Armstrong's office.

She could leave it right here; turn on her heel and walk away with no one any the wiser. If Robert Channing phoned, she could say it didn't matter, she'd changed her mind.

Then she made her decision. No way were they getting away with it. They were going to pay for what they'd done to her. The staccato click of her heels echoed around the empty playground as she stalked towards the school and pushed open the door.

It was strange walking the familiar corridors when they were empty. Doors stood open, leading into darkened classrooms, as if inviting the unwary in to learn something they'd rather not know. Ignoring them, she made her way towards Armstrong's office and pushed her way in without bothering to knock. He was seated at his desk, with Carr beside him, poring over a folder. As the door banged against the wall, they looked up with twin expressions of astonishment. Cassie stood, outlined against the darkness of the corridor, and glared at them.

Armstrong was the first to recover. He leaned back and leered at her. 'Ah, Miss Grey. What an unexpected surprise. Do come in. And what brings you here?'

She stared at him without answering. He shifted uneasily in his seat, then regained his composure. His smile widened as he folded his arms across his pot belly. 'Perhaps I can guess,' he went on. 'You enjoyed our last encounter so much that you fancied a repeat performance. Is that it?'

Cassie stared at him in total disbelief. Did he honestly think she would willingly submit to his gross attentions again? That she would ever let him and the disgusting Carr so much as touch her? She shuddered with revulsion at the very thought. Controlling herself with difficulty, she stared at him.

'Don't be ridiculous,' she spat. 'I'm here because—'

'You made a big mistake,' he interrupted smoothly.

She stared at him in dismay. 'Wh-what do you mean?' she stammered.

'What do I mean?' he repeated, with a smug smile. 'Look around you, my dear. Miss Carr and I are working late on perfectly legitimate school business, and what happens? We hear a noise – and when we investigate, we find an intruder.' He grinned. 'And not just any intruder, but a disgruntled former employee bent on who knows what mischief.'

He leaned forward, propped his chin on his hands, and smiled at her. 'I rather think I should call the police, don't you?' Cassie stared at him in horror. 'But then, I'm not a vindictive man. Why would I want to spoil the life of an attractive young woman for a silly mistake? I'm sure we can sort this out without recourse to the law.' He shook his head. 'But it does look as if you're going to have a repeat performance after all.' His lips twisted cruelly.

'Whether you like it or not.'

He was on his feet and round the desk almost before Cassie had a chance to move. Carr stood, smirking, between her and the door, so she backed away from him, until she bumped into the wall behind her. She looked round wildly, but he was too quick for her. One hand fumbled at his flies, unzipping himself and allowing his thick penis to spring out, while the other grabbed the neck of her coat and ripped it away.

For a moment he was taken aback as her breasts, with their scarlet nipples, were revealed to his hungry eyes. Then he leered at her. 'Nice,' he chuckled appreciatively. 'Very nice. I see you're all ready for me.' His fingers twisted her nipples until she squealed and he forced her hand down to his cock. 'And I'm ready for you, too,' he said, his thick tongue licking over his lips.

His mouth latched on to her nipple, sucking and slobbering over her, while he moved her hand up and down the length of his shaft. Carr watched, then began to unbutton her blouse to reveal her shrivelled breasts, and Cassie groaned out loud. It was all a trick! Channing had set her up. She wasn't here to take her revenge – she was here to be hurt and humiliated. To go through the whole horrible experience again. How could she have been such a fool?

Armstrong lifted his head from her breasts, his mouth smeared with scarlet, like a feeding animal. 'The door, Miss Carr,' he ordered. Grinning, his crony went to do as she was told.

But she squealed and stepped back in dismay as Robert Channing limped into the room.

'What are you waiting for?' mumbled Armstrong, his nose buried in Cassie's deep and perfumed cleavage. 'I thought I told you to lock that door—!'

There was a blinding flash of light and he raised his head again – then blenched and let go of Cassie as if she was red hot, his penis shrivelling. He attempted to smile as he fumbled frantically, trying to hide himself. 'Er... Mr Channing, how nice,' he blustered. 'We weren't expecting a visit from one of the governors. Miss Carr and I were just... er... just...' His voice trailed off as it dawned on him that there was no way out of this situation.

Robert Channing smiled grimly. 'Oh, I know exactly what you were "er... just", Mr Armstrong.' He raised the camera in his hand. 'And so will everyone else, once this film's developed.' Carr whimpered and pulled her blouse tightly over her chest. 'I rather think your days at this school are numbered, don't you?' He raked his eyes over them scathingly. 'And at your age, I can't see anyone beating a path to your doorway to offer you anything else.'

'Wha... what do you want?' quavered Miss Carr.

Robert Channing smiled at her charmingly. 'What do I want?' he repeated. 'Why, I want exactly the same as you. I want to inflict pain and humiliation. I want to enjoy someone else's distress. I want to see someone brought to their knees and humbled.' His smile widened. 'It amuses me.'

Armstrong smiled with relief as he saw his way out. 'You can join in,' he offered eagerly. 'You can have her, too. She won't be able to complain. She shouldn't have been here in the first place.' He smiled slyly. 'We can all take turns.'

Robert Channing shook his head. 'Sorry,' he said, with mock regret. 'But that's not quite what I had in mind.' His expression became grim as he said, 'Take your clothes off. Both of you.'

Armstrong gazed at him in disbelief. 'Me?' he demanded in outrage. 'I'm the headmaster. You can't do this!'

Channing smiled. 'Oh, I think you'll find I can.' He clicked his fingers and it was Cassie's turn to gasp as two familiar figures walked through the door. Tanisha and Tom! What were they doing here?

She soon found out.

'Miss Carr and Mr Armstrong seem to be having a little difficulty complying with my request,' said Channing, politely. 'Perhaps you could help them?' Tom and Tanisha began walking towards the miserable pair, and they backed away.

'No need for that,' protested Armstrong. 'I'm doing it. See?'

Cassie stared in fascination as they stripped reluctantly. Finally, they stood there, stark naked. Armstrong held his shaking hands in front of his drooping prick and balls, while Carr tried to conceal her breasts and bush of greying pubic hair. They looked pathetic.

'Very good,' said Channing. 'Now, if you'll just bend over that couch, my assistants will see that you're comfortable.'

Armstrong bolted for the door, his plump buttocks wobbling, but it was no use. Between them, Tom and Tanisha dragged him back and strapped him face down over the arm of the couch, exactly as he'd done to Cassie so many weeks ago. Carr was seized and tied over the other arm.

'What are you going to do now?' whimpered the feeble Armstrong.

In answer, Tanisha peeled off her coat to reveal an outfit similar to Cassie's. Her huge breasts swayed as she positioned herself behind Carr, unclipped the whip from her belt and raised her arm, while Tom did the same behind Armstrong. For a moment there was silence, except for the frightened whimpering that escaped the victims – then the whips whistled through the air in unison and the whimpers turned to anguished shrieks as leather smacked on flesh.

When Tom and Tanisha had finished, Armstrong's and Carr's backsides were as scarlet as their faces and they were sobbing pathetically. Channing nodded at Cassie. 'Over to you now, I think,' he said.

She stepped forward, unclipping the tip of the leather dildo. It sprang free, huge and threatening. Armstrong looked over his shoulder and his eyes widened in shock. 'No,' he whispered. 'Please… no!'

But his shock was nothing compared to Miss Carr's as Tom unzipped himself to reveal his enormous erection. His prick was swollen with excitement and a tiny bead of liquid leaked from its smooth tip. As he approached, she recoiled in disgust. 'Suck it,' ordered Tom, harshly. She shook her head, dumb with horror, and he smiled. 'Please yourself,' he shrugged, grinning wickedly, 'but, if you don't, it's going to be a lot more painful at the other end.'

Her eyes widened even further. 'You... you can't,' she howled. 'I'm still a virgin. I don't like men. I've never had sex with one.'

'I'd never had sex with a woman,' said Cassie dryly. 'But that didn't stop you, did it?' She nodded at Tom. 'Go ahead… make her day.'

He thrust his prick into Miss Carr's face and her tongue poked gingerly out and licked the end. He pushed forward and she gagged as it slid fully into her mouth. After a short while he withdrew, walked behind her, and flipped her over so that she was lying on her back. He carefully placed himself between her thighs and ran the tip of his wet cock up and down her gaping cleft, then, with one thrust of his hips, sank into her. She shrieked. He jerked again and the rest of his prick sank home, reducing her to a low moaning. Tanisha walked over and straddled the woman, positioning herself so that her vulva was directly over her face. She lowered herself and the moaning became muffled.

Cassie smiled. 'Your turn now,' she whispered, smiling into Armstrong's horrified eyes. 'I hope you enjoy it as much as I did.' With one hand she parted his buttocks, while the other gripped the shaft of the leather dildo and aimed it at the puckered anus. She bucked her hips gently, enjoying the way he flinched each time the tip prodded against him. Then, tiring of teasing him, she rammed it home. The sound of his agonised howl was music to her ears.

'Not quite so much fun when you're on the receiving end, is it?' she said breathlessly as she pumped her hips, the dildo sliding in and out of his arse with every thrust. Its base pressed against her groin with every move, sending waves of heat through her body. She was soaking wet herself now, trickles of moisture beading the tops of her thighs.

She groaned with relief as she felt Channing move behind her. His arms snaked round her body and his hands seized her breasts, kneading and twisting her nipples until they stood out rigidly. She could feel his cock pressing against her from behind. Gasping, she parted her thighs to allow him entrance and groaned again, this time with pleasure, as his prick slid smoothly home. Each thrust from behind buried the leather dildo deeper in Armstrong's backside, but Cassie no longer cared. Head flung back, she revelled in sensation as Channing moved faster and faster, bringing her closer to a climax. Her final scream of pleasure mingled with the moans of her victims and she sagged with exhausted satisfaction, the dildo sliding free as she did so. Tom and Tanisha disengaged themselves too, and at a nod from Channing, dressed quickly and left to wait in the limousine outside.

'Feeling better?' he asked, raising a sardonic eyebrow as Cassie pulled up the collar of her coat in preparation for leaving.

'Much,' Cassie confirmed with a smile, as he held the door open for her.

'But what about us?' whimpered Armstrong. 'You can't just leave us like this.'

Mr Channing smiled cruelly at the two ugly, naked bodies sprawled over the couch. 'Oh, I'm sure you'll find some way of working yourselves free,' he said callously. 'Otherwise the cleaners are in for a bit of a shock tomorrow morning.'

He turned back to Cassie. 'What are you going to do now?' he asked. 'I'm sure Mr Armstrong would be delighted to give you your job back, if I suggested it.'

Armstrong nodded eagerly. 'Anything you say,' he agreed slavishly. 'Anything at all.'

Cassie shook her head; she had tasted the kiss of the lash – and found it sweet. There was no going back now.

She sighed, 'I don't think so. I've changed too much. I don't know what I intend to do next. I haven't got anything lined up yet.'

He offered her his arm, smiling. 'In that case, I have a proposition that might interest you.'

Cassie smiled back. With a last, indifferent glance at the snivelling wretches who'd finally had their punishment exercise, she took the proffered arm, walked through the door – and into the future.

Exciting titles available from Chimera

1-901388-20-4	The Instruction of Olivia	*Allen*
1-901388-15-8	Captivation	*Fisher*
1-901388-01-8	Olivia and the Dulcinites	*Allen*
1-901388-02-6	Belinda: Cruel Passage West	*Caine*
1-901388-09-3	Net Asset	*Pope*
1-901388-12-3	Sold into Service	*Tanner*
1-901388-13-1	All for Her Master	*O'Connor*
1-901388-14-X	Stranger in Venice	*Beaufort*
1-901388-16-6	Innocent Corinna	*Eden*
1-901388-17-4	Out of Control	*Miller*
1-901388-18-2	Hall of Infamy	*Virosa*
1-901388-23-9	Latin Submission	*Barton*
1-901388-19-0	Destroying Angel	*Hastings*
1-901388-21-2	Dr Casswell's Student	*Fisher*
1-901388-22-0	Annabelle	*Aire*
1-901388-24-7	Total Abandon	*Anderssen*
1-901388-26-3	Selina's Submission	*Lewis*
1-901388-27-1	A Strict Seduction	*Del Rey*
1-901388-28-X	Assignment for Alison	*Pope*
1-901388-29-8	Betty Serves the Master	*Tanner*
1-901388-30-1	Perfect Slave	*Bell*
1-901388-31-X	A Kept Woman	*Grayson*
1-901388-32-8	Milady's Quest	*Beaufort*
1-901388-33-6	Slave Hunt	*Shannon*
1-901388-34-4*	Shadows of Torment	*McLachlan*
1-901388-35-2*	Star Slave	*Dere*
1-901388-38-7*	The CP Sex Files	*Asquith*

All **Chimera** titles are/will be available from your local bookshop or newsagent, or direct from our mail order department. Please send your order with a cheque or postal order (made payable to *Chimera Publishing Ltd*) to: Chimera Publishing Ltd., PO Box 152, Waterlooville, Hants, PO8 9FS. If you would prefer to pay by credit card, please call our **24 hour telephone/fax credit card hotline: +44 (0)23 92 783037**.

To order, send: Title, author, ISBN number and price for each book ordered, your full name and address, cheque or postal order payable to B.B.C.S. for the total amount, and allow the following for postage and packing:
UK and BFPO: £1.00 for the first book, and 50p for each additional book to a maximum of £3.50.
Overseas and Eire: £2.00 for the first book, £1.00 for the second and 50p for each additional book.

*Titles £5.99 (US$9.95). All others £4.99 (US$7.95)

For further details of all our titles send for our free catalogue:

Chimera Publishing Ltd
Readers' Services
PO Box 152
Waterlooville
Hants
PO8 9FS

Or visit our WebShop at: **www.chimerabooks.co.uk**